DARK RIVERS

A WITCHBANE NOVEL

MORGAN BRICE

CONTENTS

DARK RIVERS

A WITCHBANE NOVEL

By Morgan Brice

Darkwind Press is an imprint of DreamSpinner Communications, LLC

Dedicated to my family, for their support and encouragement. And to readers, who are always looking for a good story, and thereby make it possible for writers to keep writing.

1

SETH

"This doesn't look like Pittsburgh." Seth frowned as he pulled into the RV park, following the directions Evan had pulled up from the app on his phone.

"It's not," Evan replied, flashing him a grin. "Welcome to Plum Township, next to Monroeville, in the eastern suburbs of Pittsburgh, Pennsylvania. We're here because it was the closest place to the city that I could find where we could still hook up the trailer."

Seth maneuvered the black Silverado pickup truck and the fifth-wheel trailer it hauled through the archway entrance of the Plum Fine RV Campgrounds. Over the last month, since they left Richmond, he and Evan had gotten the process of moving into a new park down to a science. Seth waited with the truck and trailer while Evan went in to pay a deposit—in cash—and get a lot assignment. Evan came back to rejoin Seth and help get the trailer hooked up to utilities, unhitch it from the truck, and bring the black Hayabusa motorcycle down off the lift in back of the RV.

"I think that's the slickest we've done this yet," Evan said, a note of pride in his voice as he handled the unhitching himself, under Seth's watchful gaze.

"Definitely goes faster with two," Seth agreed. "And you did that all just fine," he added, praise that made Evan smile.

"I'm not ready to back the trailer into a spot yet," Evan admitted, "but I like driving the truck." He glared at the motorcycle. "It's going to take a little longer to get used to the bike."

Seth slung an arm around Evan's shoulders and pulled him in for a kiss. "I think you're doing great." Evan tasted like coffee and cheeseburger from their most recent fast-food stop. He leaned against Seth, a brief acknowledgment of trust and intimacy that made Seth's heart beat a little faster. He'd never imagined that anyone could rock his world and claim his heart so thoroughly in just a few short weeks, but Evan had done just that.

"Where to first?" Evan's question jolted Seth out of his thoughts. Evan slipped up beside him and twined their fingers together, a reminder that wherever they were going, it would be as a team.

"I figured we'd eat lunch and then start running down some of the contacts Toby and Milo gave us," Seth replied. "Mark Wojcik left me a message, but I didn't want to try calling him back while we were on the road. And Simon Kincaide sent me a text, but again—not something I could look at while I was driving."

"Thanks for that," Evan quipped. "I'm fine with not turning into roadkill to answer a text."

They headed into the comfortable fifth-wheel trailer that had belonged to Seth's parents and now was home to Seth and Evan.

Seth flicked on the lights and used an app on his phone to turn on background music. The trailer had seemed a little too roomy when he was on his own, but now the ample living/dining area, galley kitchen, bathroom, and master bedroom fit the two of them just right.

"How about I fix us something for lunch, and you make phone calls?" Evan suggested, heading for the fridge. "Put it on speakerphone, and you won't get grumpy about having to relay everything."

"When do I get grumpy about that?" Seth asked with mock indignation.

"Every friggin' time," Evan replied without turning around as he dug through the leftovers in the refrigerator. Seth paused, taking in the view as Evan bent over to reach for the sandwich fixings. Evan wiggled his ass, swaying his hips enticingly.

"Is that an invitation?" Seth's voice was husky, and he palmed himself as his jeans got tighter.

"Sure thing—after we eat," Evan said with a coy wink over his shoulder. "Breakfast was a long time ago, and if I ever pass out during sex, I want it to be from a mind-blowing orgasm, not low blood sugar."

"Spoilsport," Seth grumbled, but his retort lacked heat since the look in Evan's eyes definitely promised good times later on.

As Evan set out a sandwich assembly line on the counter, Seth plopped down at the table and hit redial. "Hey, Mark. Sorry I missed your call. We were dodging Turnpike traffic. Got something or me?"

"No, I just thought we'd compare notes on Netflix shows." Mark Wojcik, another hunter, often traded intel with Seth on creatures, and they often called each other for advice on difficult hunts. His voice sounded more gravelly than usual.

"You got a head cold?" Seth asked.

"Damn ghoul caught me by the throat last night and squeezed hard enough to leave fingerprints before I got him with my knife," Mark replied. "So excuse me if I'm not Suzy Sunshine."

"Are you ever?" Seth's tone tempered the snark. "You okay?"

"I've had worse," Mark said. "Thanks for asking. Anyhow, you two make it to Pittsburgh?"

"Just outside. Gonna eat and then go chase down some leads I might have found. Whatcha got for me?"

"I've found a couple of names for you. Neither of them is the current ID of the witch-disciple you're chasing—"

"Noson Thane," Seth supplied. "That's his original name."

"But these date from the early 1900s and 1930s, and they might be your guy," Mark continued. "They fit all the markers—seemed to show up from nowhere, didn't have family in the area, stuck around for a dozen years or so, then turned up 'dead' or just vanished," Mark replied. "The 1900s name is Ewing Carmody, and the 1930s name is Andrew Wiegand. Carmody might have been in the McKeesport area, and Wiegand looks to have been around New Castle. That would fit because if this guy wants to keep being immortal a secret, he's got to move around, but he'd be staying in the area near Pittsburgh so he could keep an eye on his next victim."

Seth made notes as he listened. "Thanks, Mark. That helps. And if we can help you out, since we're almost in your neck of the woods—"

"I'll let you know if I could use extra hands," Mark promised. "I'm heading up toward Kane to handle a vengeful spirit problem. I should have decent cell phone reception, so call if you need me."

Seth promised to do so and ended the call. He looked up to see Evan plating two scrumptious-looking sandwiches and adding a heap of chips and fresh pickle wedges to both. Seth got up to carry his plate and a can of soda to the table, while Evan brought his food to join him.

"You heard all that?"

Evan nodded. "Yeah. I just hope we can figure out soon who Thane's passing himself off as now, before things come down to the wire."

"We should have time on our side," Seth said, snapping open his soda and waiting for the fizz to settle. "It's December. The next murder shouldn't be until Halloween."

Back in 1900, dark warlock Rhyfel Gremory was hanged by a sheriff and his deputies intent on putting a stop to his bloody rituals. Gremory died, but not without imparting his power and virtual immortality to his disciples, who fled from the sheriff's posse and vowed revenge. Each disciple chose a member of the posse for their vengeance. Every year, one of the disciples would kill the oldest adult male from the descendants of his chosen deputy.

Twelve years, twelve murders until the cycle came around again. Seth's brother, Jesse, had been the victim from their family, although the witch-disciple made a mistake—it should have been Seth. Jesse's death set Seth on a quest for vengeance to destroy his brother's killer and make sure the ritual murders stopped for good. Evan was supposed to be the next disciple's victim. Seth had saved his life, destroyed that witch-disciple, and in the process, he and Evan had fallen in love.

"But I don't want to count on the Halloween angle," Seth continued and took a bite from the sandwich. His full mouth muffled a groan.

"I thought you only made that noise with something else in your mouth," Evan said with a grin.

In reply, Seth slid his sock-clad foot up the inside of Evan's leg and flexed his toes gently over Evan's package. He'd gained a surprising amount of dexterity with practice and felt Evan's cock harden as he stroked the length of it with his foot.

"Eat first, fuck later," Evan teased, shifting a bit in his seat. Seth waggled his eyebrows in a playful response and took another bite of his sandwich.

Seth set down his half-eaten sub and crunched a potato chip. "Milo and Toby got us the name, Noson Thane, and if that's what the witch-disciple used before Gremory's death, then the Carmody identity must have been his first alias. Milo dug up a pile of stuff on the next name—Brunrichter—and now we've got the 1930s ID. Damn, I just wish we had something more current to go on."

Evan replied with his mouth full, his words garbled by his sandwich, but Seth thought it sounded like, "Be patient." He snorted in reply. "Yeah, right. Because if the disciple doesn't already know we got rid of Corson Valac back in Richmond, he'll figure out we're trouble when he finds out we're sniffing around his own trail. So, I want to be able to go after him before he comes after us."

Corson Valac had been the true name of the witch-disciple who had tried to kill Evan. Seth had stopped him, but only just in time. In his nightmares, Seth relived that night, arriving moments too late. From the times Evan had woken shouting and in a cold sweat, Seth knew that the warlock haunted his lover's dreams as well.

Hunting supernatural killers was new to both Seth and Evan. Two years ago, Seth had just returned from his time in the Army, happy to spend time with his parents and his younger brother, Jesse, who had just graduated from college. A night of ghost hunting and myth-busting went tragically wrong, and when it was over, Jesse was dead, Seth's sanity was under suspicion, and the killer had vanished. His parents' suspicious death in a car wreck while Seth was in the hospital left Seth with little except the RV, truck, and motorcycle —and a burning need for vengeance.

"And we will," Evan assured him. "We'll figure it out—together.

That means we already have an advantage over the last time." It had taken a lot for Seth to win Evan's trust back in Richmond since, at the time, Evan knew nothing about supernatural threats or dark magic and doubted their existence. Now, Evan was working hard to prove himself a full partner in everything, including researching their newest target.

Seth's phone buzzed, and he saw another text from Simon. "I've got to answer this," he said with a sigh, trying to ignore the fact that Evan's foot was now sliding inappropriately close to his own groin in delicious payback.

"Hi, Simon. What's up?" Seth greeted the caller. Simon Kincaide, a gifted psychic medium, was a resource to the tight-knit hunter community, with a specialty in legends, myth, and lore.

"Well, for one thing, I lay my bets that my weather's a lot better than yours." A slight Southern drawl colored Simon's voice.

"Myrtle Beach versus Pittsburgh? Yeah, that's a sucker's bet, unless there's a hurricane blowin'," Seth replied with a laugh. "No contest. It's cold enough to freeze your balls here, and it's only December."

"You and Evan are welcome any time," Simon said. "Some of your witch-disciples had to have gone south."

"No doubt," Seth said and mouthed "stop it" to Evan, who was grinning broadly as his toes groped Seth's groin. Seth wiggled a bit to free his stiffening cock.

"I just wanted you to know I looked into the local Pittsburgh legends involving witches and murders, like we talked about, and turned up some hits you'll want to look at. Added some older folklore stuff, too, where I thought it might be helpful. I sent it to your email about an hour ago. Let me know if you need something else."

Simon Kincaide had been a folklore professor before a very conservative donor to the college got him fired for teaching students about the supernatural. Now, he owned a shop in Myrtle Beach where he could put his gifts as a psychic medium to use giving private readings, leading ghost tours, and writing books about hauntings on the Grand Strand. On the side, Simon researched lore for hunters like Mark and Seth.

"Thanks, Simon. Send me the bill," Seth said. Seth squirmed as

Evan's foot pursued him. Normally, he wouldn't try to get away, but he wasn't sure he could keep his voice steady with the distraction.

"Already did," Simon replied. "Tell Evan I said hello." With that, the call ended.

Evan had managed to finish his sandwich while Simon was on the phone. Now, as Seth took a bite, Evan slipped from his seat, turned Simon to face him, and dropped to his knees between Seth's legs.

"Don't. I'll choke," Seth warned as he hurried to swallow.

"I don't care if you spit or swallow," Evan replied with a wink. He worked Seth's belt loose and undid his button-fly jeans, grinning when he saw the wet mark where leaking pre-come had darkened the cotton of Seth's boxer briefs. Evan freed Seth's stiff cock and licked a stripe from balls to head. Seth slid forward, offering himself up, sandwich forgotten.

Sometimes, Evan enjoyed teasing Seth, edging him until Seth begged for release. Now, Evan went for fast-and-dirty, working Seth's prick at a pace designed to get him off quickly. Seth tangled his fingers in Evan's dark hair, which was just long enough for him to get a good grip. Evan gave him a knowing look up through sinfully long eyelashes, a glint of lust and amusement in his eyes.

"Not gonna last," Seth warned. Evan hummed a response, lips still tight around Seth's shaft, and that was all it took. Seth bucked, Evan held his hips with both hands and swallowed down every drop of his lover's spend. When Seth's breathing finally slowed, Evan pulled off and looked up with a grin, letting his tongue slip along his lips for good measure.

"Come here," Seth growled. Evan rose on his knees to kiss him, letting Seth taste himself on Evan's lips. Seth pulled him to stand, then had Evan's fly unzipped and both his jeans and briefs down on his thighs in a heartbeat, returning the favor. Evan slipped his hands through Seth's short, dark blond hair. Seth gripped Evan's ass, keeping him right where he wanted him, as Evan began to pant and his whole body stiffened.

"Shit, Seth. Christ. So good. Oh, God. So close. Please, Seth—" Evan spilled down the back of Seth's throat, and Seth kept licking and sucking until every drop was gone. When he leaned back, they looked at each other with equally dopey and sated grins.

"Never underestimate the power of lunch and a quickie to wake you up after a long drive," Seth said as he shimmied into his clothing.

"I'm all for being a nomad if that's how we officially greet each new camping spot," Evan said, still a little breathless as he pulled his underwear and jeans back up.

Seth dropped a kiss on his cheek and stood. "Don't touch my chips and sandwich," he ordered. "I'm gonna brush my teeth and finish my lunch. I'm not full yet."

Evan waggled his eyebrows. "I'll give you full."

"Rain check," Seth called from the RV's bathroom. "Hold that thought. Work to do." He came back out and wrapped his arms around Evan. "God, I love you," he said, brushing a kiss over Evan's lips. He dropped back into his seat and made short work of the remains of his sandwich, as Evan sat across from him, finishing a soda.

"I think you should finish digging into the Brandon Clarke info," Seth said after he finished the last of his chips.

"Why me?" Evan asked, toying with the empty can. "You already got it started."

"Because you were a little uncomfortable about me gathering intel about you, back in Richmond," Seth said gently.

"I know better now," Evan countered. "I was just afraid—" He didn't have to finish his sentence. Seth knew Evan's fears had root in his stalker ex-boyfriend, Mike Bradshaw. Evan hadn't opened up completely about everything that had happened with Mike, years before, but Seth knew enough to know Evan's ex had been controlling and abusive—both physically and emotionally. Little by little, Evan shared more of that painful story, usually prompted by nightmares that left him trembling in Seth's arms while Seth coaxed him back to sleep, silently vowing to thrash Mike to a pulp if he ever crossed paths with the asshole.

"That's why I want you to see how the process works, first-hand," Seth coaxed. "We're trying to save Brandon's life, but we have to know everything we can about him to do that."

8

Evan nodded. "I get it, now. And I can do that. I've gotten really good at research."

Seth drew him close and stretched up to kiss his forehead. They were close to the same height, though Seth was a fraction of an inch taller and had twenty or so pounds of muscle on Evan. Seth's muscular frame had been built by high school athletics and his time in the military. Evan's lean muscle came from running, parkour, and their daily workouts and sparring. He might have a more slender build than Seth, but Seth loved Evan's defined muscles, and the flexibility earned through years of yoga paid off handsomely in the bedroom.

"You're good at lots of things," Seth said, stepping back before his twitching cock could make them go for round two. "And I mean it on that rain check. But right now, what do you say we go take a look at one of the places on the list Milo sent me?"

"Haunts or urban legends?" Evan asked, looking for his boots as Seth cleared away the dishes and tossed their empty cans in the garbage.

"Both," Seth replied, lacing up his own Timberlands. "Witches, murder, and restless ghosts—so the stories say."

They locked up the trailer and walked through a dusting of new snow to get to the truck. The RV park was almost deserted this time of year. Come summer, the pool and mini golf would be full of kids and families on vacation, and the activities room would echo with shouts from the air hockey and Foosball tables, or the bells and sound effects from the pinball machines and retro arcade games, vying for attention over the sports scores on the big screen TV. But now, with the bare trees and a sprinkle of unbroken snow, the empty park looked almost post-apocalyptic.

"Kinda looks like there should be zombies," Evan said, rousing Seth from his thoughts and proving their minds had run in the same direction. "I always wonder who the other folks are who are camped out at this time of year."

Seth shrugged. "Retirees. Loners. People who don't have anywhere else to go." The two years he had spent after Jesse's death, learning from Toby and Milo, seeking out hunts to hone his skills, had taken him far from his Indiana home, to plenty of places like this campground. Before, he'd kept the loneliness at bay by throwing himself into research or workouts, or dulling the edge of dreams and memories with whiskey.

Having Evan with him changed everything. Evan wasn't just his lover, he was his partner on the hunt, a companion on the road, the best friend he hadn't realized he'd needed. Seth couldn't imagine going back to the way things were, which just made him all the more intent on assuring that Evan stayed happy, safe, and with him.

Evan took his hand and gave it a tug with a look that told Seth his lover had guessed his thoughts. "Not going anywhere without you," he reassured. "Now come on. Let's go see this place Milo thinks we need to check out. Don't forget, it gets dark early this time of year."

NORTH PARK WAS about a half hour drive from their campground, and Seth found Irwin Road easily enough. The Silverado had snow tires, and Seth had plenty of salt, tire chains, and other cold-weather supplies—as well as a selection of weapons—in the locked steel box in the back.

"Doesn't look that scary to me," Evan observed, staring out the passenger window as his breath created a wreath of condensation on the glass.

"We aren't to the haunted part yet," Seth replied. They drove on until the asphalt road ended and the tires crunched on gravel. A "road closed" sign stood off to one side, but no barricades enforced the warning.

"Now what?" Evan asked, turning to look out the windshield.

Seth pulled off to one side, grabbed a duffel bag of gear from the back seat, and got out, as Evan did the same. The truck locked with a beep, and the two men stood shoulder to shoulder in the undisturbed snow.

"Welcome to Blue Mist Road," Seth said. "There's supposed to be a hanging tree, a haunted cemetery, a murder house, and a witch's lair."

"All on one street?"

Seth shrugged. "So they say. And a blue mist that rises every night."

"Gonna be hard to raise mist at this temperature," Evan said, rubbing his gloved hands together. Despite his heavy parka, woolen scarf, and knit hat, he looked cold. Seth had grown up with Indiana winters, but even he minded the chill.

"We'll be warmer walking," Seth said, heading off at a brisk pace. Both men carried their Glocks in holsters at the small of their backs, but the iron knives sheathed on their belts would be far more useful against restless spirits, as would the salt and iron filings in their pockets.

Evan kept pace with Seth as they headed down the gravel road. Closer to the park entrance, they had passed dedicated joggers and a few bird watchers who were out despite the snow. Now, the snow was unmarred by anyone else's passage, and only the crunch of their boots on the stones broke the silence. Trees lined both sides of the road, their branches forming a canopy overhead so that the farther Seth and Evan walked, the darker it grew although they were still a few hours from sunset. Seth felt a shiver down his back that had nothing to do with the temperature.

"There's no one here, but I feel like we're being watched," Evan murmured, and his breath made puffs of steam in the cold air.

"Yeah, me too." Seth was on high alert, and from the tension in Evan's clenched jaw, he knew his partner was ready to react, should their instincts prove right.

They had walked far enough that they could no longer see the truck. On the left, Seth saw a depression in the ground wide enough to have once been a driveway, though the house it went with was long gone. "The stories say that a family lived there," he said with a nod, trying to make out more about the land through the gloom. "One day, the father snapped and killed his wife and kids, hid the bodies in the septic tank. Years later, someone dug up the tank and found bones inside."

"Unpleasant," Evan said, wrinkling his nose where it peeked out above his scarf. "Are they the ghosts?"

"No one seems to know for sure." They walked for a while, stopping when a large, old tree with a thick trunk and sturdy, high branches came into view. In the dying light, it formed a dark silhouette against the gray sky. "Want to bet that's the hanging tree?" Seth asked.

"Who got hanged, and who did the hanging?"

"Depends on the person telling the story. Vigilantes. Thieves. Or the witch who used to live in that house, over there," Seth said, pointing to the snow-covered cement and brick rubble on the opposite side of the road that had once been the foundations of a long-gone house.

"Did she eat children?" Evan's humor didn't quite cover the uneasiness in his voice.

"Not that I've heard, although she supposedly opened portals to another realm."

"Shit," Evan said, his eyes widening. "Sounds like a witch-disciple working the ritual to summon Gremory's spirit. Maybe there's something to the legends, after all."

"That's why I wanted to come take a look," Seth said, staying close, although he'd drawn his iron knife with his right hand and his left gripped a container of salt in his pocket.

A path led off from one side of the road, toward a clearing where Seth could see rows of old tombstones, some of them leaning and askew. "And there's the cemetery. I didn't see anything particularly nefarious in the stories about it, other than people think it's creepy as fuck out here in the middle of nowhere."

"If the sun hasn't set yet, and there's no moon, where's that blue glow coming from?"

Clouds covered the sky, blotting out the dull, late-afternoon sun, and the overhead branches dimmed the light even more. Yet beneath the trees, the snow reflected a twilight indigo, and the shadows all around beneath the trees seemed to have grown darker.

Seth wasn't a medium, and he had no talent for seeing or hearing the dead. But his experiences hunting supernatural creatures attuned him to the presence of things that went bump in the night, and now he was certain that they weren't alone.

"We mean you no harm," Seth said to the blue glow and the empty forest around them. "We're just looking for information about the witch. Can you help us?"

A sparkling haze gradually filled in between the leafless trees, and as it shifted on the wind, Seth thought he saw forms and faces. Evan was already laying down a salt circle around where they stood, reinforcing it with iron filings. Both substances interfered with ghosts' ability to manifest and sapped their strength to cause harm.

"Seth, look." Evan pointed toward the hanging tree. Where only moments ago, it had been nothing but bare branches, now, a shadowed form swung slowly, suspended by a rope around its neck, the head tilted at an unnatural angle.

"We're here to end the killing," Seth said, forcing himself to look away from the hanged man, pushing back the memories of Jesse's body, suspended like that, soaked with blood. As if he could guess Seth's thoughts, Evan placed a hand on Seth's forearm, grounding him to the here and now. "We want to stop the witch that caused your pain, keep him from hurting anyone else."

Overhead, a cold wind stirred the branches, and the trees creaked and rattled. Seth shivered as the temperature dropped. Figures now stood amid the headstones in the old cemetery, and their stance suggested that they were ready for a fight.

"Give me something I can use to stop the witch," Seth begged the ghosts. "He went by many names—Thane. Carmody. Brunrichter. Wiegand. Whatever he called himself—we want to make him stop."

The wind carried the whispers of spectral voices, and the blue mist roiled with internal energy. Evan yanked off his gloves, then withdrew a small slate writing board and a piece of chalk from the pocket of his parka. As Seth continued to talk to the ghosts, he saw out of the corner of his eye as Evan carefully drew one of the sigils he'd been practicing, a bit of rote magic that was likely to come in handy.

Seth feared they might need to fight their way clear since the ghosts seemed more interested in intimidation than supplying information.

Seth's eyes widened as he saw movement. An invisible hand traced shaky block letters on a snow-covered embankment beside the road. W-A-T-C-H.

"Watch?" Seth repeated aloud. "Watch out? Watch for something?"

He could feel the press of spirits all around them, and Seth remembered that the ghosts of Blue Mist Road had a reputation for being unfriendly to intruders. Whatever their cryptic message meant, Seth had the feeling they had worn out their welcome.

The mist grew thick around them. Seth realized that the ominous figures from the cemetery had moved closer and that the hanged man was no longer suspended from his noose. He and Evan were safe for the moment within the salt circle, but they were also trapped inside their sanctuary.

"Ready?" Evan asked. He'd been practicing the small magicks that involved drawing arcane symbols and activating them with concentration; those had come more easily to him than the spoken spells Seth had learned. Seth recognized the drawing Evan made on the slate and hoped to hell the banishment sigil worked.

"Go for it," he said, crossing his fingers.

Evan closed the last line on the sigil and placed his fingertips on the magical symbol, imbuing it with his will and life energy. The drawing flared gold and then white, so bright Seth and Evan had to avert their eyes as a blast wave of light radiated all around them.

When they opened their eyes, the blue mist and the spirits it harbored were gone, as was the writing in the snow.

"Come on," Seth said, grabbing Evan by the arm and pulling him toward the truck. "Let's get out of here before they decide to come back."

2

EVAN

"It worked!" Evan practically bounced in his seat from the adrenaline as Seth steered the truck away from Blue Mist Road and headed back toward the campground. "I can't believe it really worked!"

Seth rolled his eyes. "When you phrase it that way, I don't feel nearly as safe as I did a minute ago. *I* believed in you."

"Yeah, but that was the first time under fire, so to speak," Evan said, unable to keep the smile off his face. "I've gotten the sigils to work lots of times when we practice, but I hadn't needed to do it when there was real danger. Score!" He couldn't resist pumping his fist in triumph, and Seth shook his head and chuckled.

"You saved us a whole hell of a lot of work fighting them off," Seth replied. "I was ready to try my banishing spell, but odds would have been good that if yours didn't work, mine wouldn't either. And I don't know if you noticed, but there were a bunch of pissed-off ghosts out there."

Evan settled back into his seat as the rush faded. "Yeah," he agreed. "Do you think they'll be dangerous to other people? Did we create a problem?"

Seth frowned, then shook his head. "I don't think we changed anything. People already know the area is haunted—enter at your own risk. The difference is, we actually knew something about the witch who killed those spirits, and we got the brunt of their anger."

"What do you think it meant, 'watch'?" Evan asked, glancing in the side mirror every few minutes as if he expected the spirits to follow them.

"No idea, but we'll figure it out," Seth replied.

Evan forced himself to take several deep breaths to release his tension. He reminded himself that Seth had more years to get used to the whole idea of supernatural threats, magic, and ghosts, a reality Evan was still doing his best to wrap his mind around.

"You okay?" Seth's voice had softened to a concerned rumble that gave Evan a warm feeling in his chest. Evan slipped his hand along the seat as Seth met him halfway and tangled their fingers together.

"Yeah. It's just a lot to take in. Training and learning all the lore and the sigils is like being back in class—all academic. Then you go out and have to actually use what you've learned, and it all gets a lot more real, fast."

"You're doing great," Seth encouraged, and Evan wasn't ashamed to admit that Seth's approval meant a lot to him. Seth had pushed him hard, spending hours when they weren't on the road teaching Evan to fight and shoot or quizzing him on the myths and legends that provided insight into the kinds of supernatural threats they faced.

"I have a good teacher," Evan replied.

Seth shrugged. "Not really, but I'm trying to give you everything I know. You need to be prepared, need to be able to defend yourself. I couldn't handle it if—" Seth didn't finish his sentence, but he didn't have to. Evan had already seen how far Seth would go to protect him, and the knowledge was both humbling and daunting.

"We take care of each other," Evan replied, realizing Seth was uncomfortable with his admission. "Watch each other's backs. That's what partners are for."

Seth smiled a little at that, which Evan took as a win. Their relationship was just a little over a month old, already forged in fire and blood. Regular people, one month into a new romance, might still be figuring out what restaurants and movies to go to as a couple, taking silly getting-to-know-you quizzes or exploring their partner's intimate likes and dislikes.

He and Seth had dodged bullets and dark magic, broken more than a few laws in the process of getting rid of one of the witch-disciples, fallen in love, and moved in together—on the run—after the first four days. Seth had supported Evan's independence by replacing his computer—and buying him a Glock. Evan had proven his commitment by shooting a ghoul that was going for Seth's throat and promising that he wasn't going to leave, though sanity might have argued otherwise.

"Get any new clients?" Seth asked, and Evan read the change of subject for the diversion it was.

"Some nibbles. I think it makes a difference being able to post real work in my online portfolio instead of demonstration pieces," Evan replied. "And my first customers were willing to give me testimonial quotes. Plus, a few of them have made referrals."

After the Richmond witch-disciple caused an explosion at the bar where Evan used to work, he'd needed to find a new job regardless of whether or not he went on the road with Seth. With a good computer and camera—and Wi-Fi—Evan could finally realize his dream of starting a graphic design firm, work he could do from anywhere.

"Lucky you—your customers will admit to using your services. Mine are all strictly non-disclosure," Seth said. During his Army days, Seth had been a computer ops specialist. Now, he used his hacking skills to ferret out information on the witch-disciples, breaking into databases and password-protected sites. To pay the bills, Seth ran a "white hat" computer security firm where he put those same skills to use stopping cybercriminals. Together, they usually more than covered their minimal expenses.

It beat having to hustle pool for gas money.

"Did that big job ever come in?" Evan asked. Seth said little about his customers, even to his lover, but Evan didn't mind. He appreciated Seth's computer abilities, but the intricacies made Evan's eyes glaze over. Then again, Seth grew equally restless after listening to Evan talk excitedly about camera angles, lighting, and apertures.

"Still tied up in red tape. Couple of smaller clients did, so we should be good for grocery money," Seth answered. Evan knew that their circumstances weren't hand-to-mouth, between what they earned and the nest egg Seth had stashed away from his inheritance. Their expenses were minimal, except for ammunition and the specialized items needed to fight the kinds of creatures they encountered.

Evan never knew he could feel so satisfied making do with so little. Then again, he'd never expected love to be quite so exciting.

"What do you want to do about Christmas?" Evan asked. The question popped out before he had a chance to think about it, and from Seth's startled look, he guessed the season hadn't really crossed his lover's mind.

"Shit. I guess it's December, isn't it?" Seth replied. "Sorry—it's just, we've kinda had a lot going on. I sort of forgot."

Seth was too used to being on his own, Evan thought. It pained him to think of Seth spending the last three Christmases without his family. Had he visited Milo and Toby, the older hunters who had taught him the ropes of hunting supernatural creatures? Or, more likely, did he bury himself in his quest and pretend not to notice?

"I figured we could get a nice meal at least," Evan ventured. For Thanksgiving, he had surprised Seth by getting a take-out dinner with all the trimmings from a local grocery store. "We can probably find a place that does a good ham, maybe some scalloped potatoes—whatever you like."

Normal people who were dating for a month swapped stories about growing up, family vacations, holidays, and funny misadventures. He and Seth had spent a lot of the last month talking about things that went bump in the night that most people didn't believe were real. Or gingerly trying to explain what lay behind their nightmares and PTSD-induced breakdowns.

"Ham would be good," Seth said after a too-long pause. "Mom used to get the kind with a sugar glaze and put some cloves with it. Smelled great when she baked it. I wish I could have saved her recipes, but they went up in smoke with the house." With his parents and Jesse dead and the house a victim of a still-unsolved arson, Seth hadn't had any reason to stay in his hometown.

"I didn't mean to bring up bad memories," Evan said, realizing that he might have ventured into difficult territory.

Seth shook his head and gave Evan's hand a squeeze. "No, they're not bad. Really good memories, which makes it harder, maybe." He took a breath. "It's okay. We should talk about this stuff."

He drummed his fingers on the steering wheel, and Evan waited for him to continue. "Jesse loved Christmas more than anything. He was the one who insisted everyone get matching sweaters, or flannel shirts, or one awful year, onesie pajamas," Seth recalled with a chuckle. "You know those old-fashioned 'Union suits' with the panel on the ass that buttons shut? In red, of course. Something different every year, and we had to take pictures."

Seth looked pensive, so Evan picked up the conversation. "We always had church stuff around Christmas. Mom was in the choir, Dad always put up the big manger scene they did out in the parking lot, and from the time I was little, the three of us ended up getting roped into being angels or shepherds or wise men in whatever pageant was going on. One year, I had to be a cow."

"We weren't real religious," Seth put in, "but Mom always wanted a candlelight service on Christmas Eve, so we'd find a different one each year to go to. They were pretty. The music was nice. Then we'd get to open one small present that night. Everything else would be Christmas morning, and we'd have a big breakfast."

"It was pretty much all church, all the time around our place," Evan said. "For a long time, I didn't mind, until I figured out I was gay and that I'd be in trouble if they found out. Even so, around Christmas, I could forget a little that I didn't belong and get caught up in the spirit."

Evan's secret high school boyfriend had been pressured into outing them, and Evan had run away when he realized his parents intended to ship him off for "conversion therapy." He'd been on his own ever since—until Seth.

"What do you get for Milo and Toby?" Evan asked.

"I usually send them a bottle of scotch," Seth replied. "One size fits all, and you can never have too much."

"Sounds like a fit," Evan agreed.

"What did you have in mind for Christmas, besides food?"

Seth asked.

Evan shrugged, feeling the old melancholy set in that usually came from thinking about his family. "I don't know—anything's good as long as we're together. Bake a ham. Or maybe order Chinese food and go to a movie?"

"I thought watching *Die Hard* was part of the holiday tradition," Seth said. "I've got it on Blu-ray."

"Only if we can have popcorn and a fuzzy blanket," Evan said, making an effort to pull himself out of his sudden funk. "It's important to do these things the right way."

THE NEXT DAY, Evan stayed home to research while Seth went into Pittsburgh to meet with a private investigator he'd hired to find information that wasn't online and needed a "local touch." Outside, the snow came down in big flakes, not enough to pile up, but plenty to cover the nearly empty campground and make it look clean and fresh.

As much as Evan enjoyed being with Seth, they spent so much time together that he cherished the few hours he got by himself. Evan found a holiday music playlist and turned it up, filling the trailer with familiar tunes. The first few years after he'd left home, any reminders about the season sent him into depression. But one year, sitting alone in the dark in an empty apartment, Evan had vowed he would take back the holidays and start enjoying them on his own terms. He had the feeling Seth hadn't gotten that far and promised himself that he'd find a way to make the season special for both of them, now that they were a couple.

A couple. Evan dawdled with his coffee for a moment, letting the reality of that phrase set in. At twenty-four, he'd only had a few real relationships before, none of them good. Between Trey, who'd outed him, and Mike, who turned out to be abusive, Evan had wondered whether he'd ever find the right guy. He'd figured out quickly that he wasn't into the club scene, and one-night stands scratched an itch but left him feeling empty.

And then Seth showed up, dangerous and protective, stubborn and tender, and Evan's heart had made the decision for him before his head ever had a chance. Evan's fingers absently traced the mark Seth had left on his neck from their lovemaking the night before, feeling his cock stiffen at the memory. He tried to remind himself that although circumstances hadn't given them the chance to go slow, they still needed to build a foundation, get to know each other, do all the things that built a solid base. Still, they'd both jumped into this relationship feet first, guns blazing, and Evan hoped with all his heart that this time would be for good.

With a sigh, Evan gathered his thoughts and sat down at the table where his laptop waited. They had a potential victim to rescue.

Right now, he didn't have much more than a name—Brandon Clarke—a photo, and a family tree that proved Brandon was a descendant of one of the unlucky deputies who hanged Rhyfel Gremory all those years ago. That was more than they knew about Noson Thane, the witch-disciple who was gunning for Brandon, but hunting down Thane fell more into Seth's expertise since it would take hacking to unravel the many aliases and erasures.

Brandon Clarke, on the other hand, was an open book once Evan started digging. He didn't feel obliged to hide, something Evan envied, having been forced to practically disappear online to avoid his stalker-ex.

"Penn State grad, twenty-eight years old, likes football and snowboarding, and he's 'in a relationship,'" Evan mused. He looked through Brandon's social media sites but couldn't find a photo of Brandon and his partner together.

"That's odd," Evan said aloud, sitting back and sipping his coffee as he considered the possibilities. "Maybe it's new, and they aren't to the 'couple selfie' stage yet."

Then again, I'm "in a relationship" too, but I haven't plastered pictures of Seth and me all over the internet. Evan knew his situation was a little different. Not only were they trying to fly under the radar when it came to law enforcement—since offing dark warlocks tended to raise messy questions—but there was no need advertising what they looked like or where they were to the witch-disciples who might want to know.

"Okay, so maybe he's dating a cop. Or someone in the military. Or a celebrity." All of those situations might be reasons for not having significant other pictures on Brandon's sites. Evan made a note about prying further into Brandon's love affair later and went back to finding out whatever he could that might help them save the man's life.

Evan's phone chirped, and he reached for it without glancing at the number, since only Seth, Mark, Milo, and a few others had his number. "Hello?" he answered, expecting to hear Seth tell him why he'd be late heading back.

"Need to re-establish your credit rating? We can help. Credit Services can rescue your good name and help you rebuild your financial future—"

"Fuck you," Evan muttered to the robocall and hung up. *How did they get my number?* he wondered, then remembered something he'd read about cell phone numbers being recycled. *I guess the last person who had my number was a deadbeat.* Evan finished his now-cold cup of coffee, went to the kitchen for a refill, and settled back down at the table.

Another hour of digging turned up articles about Brandon's high school football team, pictures from family vacations and spring break road trips, and more recently, a nice write-up about the emergency medical technicians of the Emsworth Volunteer Fire Department.

"Huh. So he's an EMT," Evan said. He studied Brandon's photo. Assuming the shot was recent, Brandon looked like he was in good shape, but not nearly as bulked up as the firemen in the calendars that had been jack off material back when Evan was single. Brandon's reddish hair, green eyes, and pale skin looked like he might have Irish in his ancestry and gave him a bookish appearance, despite a smile that said he knew how to enjoy himself.

Now that Evan knew what he was looking for, the posts Brandon made about "the crew" made more sense, probably referring to the gang at the fire station. Brandon wasn't an obsessive social media user and often went days between posting. Even then, it was more likely to be a funny picture or amusing video than a personal photo. Still, there were enough personal posts that Evan felt like he had a little insight into Brandon's sense of humor, taste in music, and favorite foods.

It's taken me a month to find out that much about Seth, and we're living together, Evan thought, though he had to admit his own circumstances were beyond unusual.

He also quickly discovered that Brandon loved coffee. At least, he certainly talked quite a bit about being at Kona Café, an independent coffee shop near the fire station. It took a bit more research to figure out that Brandon worked days at the Kona Café and nights as an EMT.

"When the hell does he sleep?" Evan muttered. A comment caught his eye, and he found himself engrossed in an online discussion between Brandon and another man debating the pros and cons of whether Brandon should jump from working part-time at the fire station or trying for a full-time EMT job with a local hospital.

If he's thinking of making a step up in his career, he's ambitious, or at least wants to make more money, Evan thought. *Wonder what his S.O. does for a living? Is he straight or gay? And is the mysterious "better half" local or long-distance?*

A ping alerted Evan to new email. Two messages were follow-ups from inquiries, telling Evan he had new projects. The third drew a frown at the subject line: *"Richmond Renter—Need Help with Fire or Water Damage?"*

The email was a standard pitch from a company that did disaster clean-up, but that didn't stop Evan's heart from beating just a little too fast, as if someone somewhere knew too much about him.

"Calm down," he told himself. "Probably came from a public records search after the fire. My name had to be on the rental agreement and the insurance papers. Just a business prospecting for new customers."

Evan wasn't a computer geek like Seth, but he knew that websites tracked users and compiled information, which was something Seth had shown him how to avoid as soon as they started working together. Evan also had no illusion about how private any data might be related to his old apartment, his job at Treddy's, or his life before stalker-Mike forced him into self-imposed lockdown.

Still, it rattled Evan a little to get two contacts that seemed so on target out of the blue. *Should I mention it to Seth? It's probably nothing. I can explain it away pretty easily, so it's got to be data mining in action. If it keeps happening, I'll definitely tell him, but until then, we've both got more on our plates than we have time to deal with.*

With that resolved, Evan went back to digging and got so caught up in the cyber scavenger hunt that he didn't look up until Seth gave their knock-signal at the door. He sat back and rubbed his eyes, shivering as a blast of cold air accompanied Seth inside.

"I hope you didn't freeze off anything I was looking forward to playing with tonight," Evan said as Seth stomped snow from his boots and started to strip off his winter gear, layer by layer. He took a moment to admire the way Seth's gray Henley shirt pulled just right across his muscled chest, the outline of firm thighs beneath denim, and the sparkle of snow in Seth's dark blond hair. Damn, the man was totally fuckable.

Evan stood and walked over to where Seth stood in front of the electric fireplace, warming himself in front of its heat vents.

"Don't—I'm like ice. You'll get cold," Seth said, taking a half step back as Evan moved toward him.

"You'll get warm. Come here." Evan wrapped his arms around Seth, repressing a shiver when Seth's fingertips brushed against him.

"Told you," Seth chided, although he pulled Evan closer in the embrace. Evan leaned in to kiss Seth's cool skin, starting with his nose and both cheeks, and ending with his lips. Seth grabbed his ass and tugged them together, so Evan ground against him, rubbing their cocks together.

"You really don't want me to give you a hand," Seth breathed. "My fingers are so cold, we'd shrivel and die."

"I've got you," Evan assured him, walking Seth backward until he leaned against the wall, then loosening first Seth's jeans and then his own before he pushed their briefs down far enough to wrap his warm hand around them both. He leaned in, nipping and licking at Seth's collarbone, seeing a flush spread across his lover's face as warmth chased away the cold.

Seth pivoted, flipping them, and pinning Evan against the wall with a move that surprised him and sent a thrill of excitement through him from head to toe. Seth let Evan keep jacking them, but his hands kneaded Evan's ass through his briefs, sliding up and down his crease, teasing at the waistband with a chill that made Evan shiver.

"More," Seth rumbled, taking control of the kiss. Evan let his head fall back against the wall, baring his throat, and Seth moved in to make the most of it, marking him on the spot between neck and shoulder, running his tongue up the side of Evan's neck, and then kissing his way down from ear to lips until Evan was breathless.

Nights were for endurance, seeing how long their lovemaking could last. Quickies were for connection and release, and Evan poured everything he felt into his reaction to Seth's body pressing him into the wall, his warm breath on Evan's skin, his lips claiming him. Evan's hips bucked forward into the circle of his hand, sliding against the velvet skin of Seth's cock in exquisite friction, as his palm slid up their shafts and over the heads. He made sure his thumb caught that sensitive spot just below the ridge and ghosted across the slit, and Seth came hard, thrusting against him and spending over his fingers, and Evan was only a breath behind him.

They were both trembling and sweating, breathing hard. Seth dropped his forehead to Evan's shoulder, and for a few moments, they just stood together, recovering from bliss.

The reality of quickly-cooling come had Seth stepping back as Evan went to wash up and bring out a wet cloth to clean them both up.

"Welcome home," Evan said with a grin. "I missed you."

"Missed you, too. I could get used to saying 'hello' like this," Seth said, tucking them both back in now that his hands had lost their chill. "Excellent way to warm up, too."

"I'll keep that in mind," Evan replied. He glanced at the clock on the microwave. "Pizza okay? I got a little lost in what I was doing and forgot the time."

"Pizza's fine, and I didn't expect you to have dinner ready, although I won't turn it down if you feel like cooking." Seth walked the cloth back to the bathroom and washed his hands while Evan cleaned up in the kitchen and turned on the oven.

"We have a frozen pizza, and there's enough bagged salad for another meal," Evan said after checking the fridge.

"Works for me. I used to get by on cereal or cold sandwiches most nights," Seth admitted.

"Yeah, well. That was then," Evan said, his chest tightening at the loneliness implied in Seth's statement.

"Believe me, I'm not complaining." Seth planted a kiss on Evan's cheek as he stepped around him to get them both a beer from the fridge. They bumped hips and slid against each other, maneuvering in the tight space as Evan chopped up vegetables for the salad, and Seth cut the plastic wrapper away from the frozen pizza.

Once the salad was made and dinner was in the oven, they brought their beers back to the table and settled in to wait.

"So what was your private eye like?" Evan asked, and took a long pull from the beer. He knew when he angled his neck just so that Seth couldn't look away, that he'd be watching Evan's Adam's apple bob as he swallowed, thinking of other uses for his throat. God, it was a wonderful thing to have a steady partner, to get the chance to find out what turned him on and have it matter for more than a night or two. Evan didn't think he'd ever get tired of the exploration, the discovery.

Seth cleared his throat and shifted a bit, so obviously, Evan's little show had its intended effect. "His name is Alex Wilson. Former U-Pitt linebacker. Couple of years older than I am. Works part-time for another P.I. named Lawson. Seems like an okay guy, I guess."

"Did he find what you had him looking for?" Evan stretched out, leaning back and crossing his legs at the ankle.

"Yeah—at least, he's working on it," Seth replied, taking a swig of his own beer. "I've got him going through stuff that hasn't been digitized in some of the local historical society archives, about places where I'm pretty sure Thane lived for a while. I gave him the new names we got from Mark, so he's looking into those men as well. Photos, articles, anything he can find."

"Has he turned up anything yet?" Evan asked.

Seth slid a folder across the table. Evan had gotten used to everything being on computers, and it surprised him how much of the hunter world was still on paper—old manuscripts, lore books, grimoires—things that were probably better off not being on the internet.

The pictures in the folder were grainy—poor initial resolution not made any better by multiple photocopy generations. Some were group photos of railroad workers in clothing from what Evan guessed was the 1930s. A few were obituaries, and more than one were police mug shots or autopsy pictures. Despite the limitations of the era's equipment, faces were still recognizable in most of the images. "What am I looking at?" Evan asked.

"Some of the victims of the New Castle 'murder swamp,'" Seth replied. "Also known as Hell's Half Acre."

"Murder swamp?"

Seth nodded and took another swallow as if he needed it to tell the awful story. "The swamp is just outside of New Castle, in a section called West Pittsburg—no final 'h' like the city has—along the Beaver River," he said. "It's where police found decapitated, sometimes dismembered and partly burned bodies from around 1925 through the late 1930s. Mind you, those dates are just when they found the bodies that turned up—doesn't mean they discovered all of them, so the dates could go earlier or later."

Evan felt a chill that had nothing to do with the snow outside. "Any pattern to the victims?"

Seth met his gaze with a somber expression. "Young men, usually naked. At least fifteen of them, maybe more. Many of the victims were never identified."

"Fuck," Evan said, feeling his stomach drop. The details fit what they'd seen the Richmond witch-disciple do with the vagrants and hired muscle he'd sacrificed when he needed to boost his magic. *What he would have done to me if Seth hadn't gotten there in time—*

"Hey." Seth's voice pulled Evan from his dark thoughts. Seth reached over to lay his hand on Evan's, gently stroking a finger over his skin. "You're safe. We're going to keep you that way—and figure out how to save Brandon, too. This whole thing is like a puzzle. We just have to put the pieces together."

"Was it like this, finding me?" He had been so afraid that Seth was another stalker, like Mike, when he found out that Seth had come to Richmond looking for "Jackson Malone."

"Well, you made it a challenge," Seth said, fondness tempering his words. "No photos online. Three different names."

"Friends and family have always called me Evan," he interrupted. "I hate 'Jackson,' and 'Sonny' made it easier to keep the drunks at the bar from finding me."

"All good reasons, but it made you hard to find," Seth said.

"Hard for you," Evan noted with a slightly bitter edge. "Corson Valac already had me in his sights." Evan's aliases might have kept his ex from finding him and made it tough for Seth, but the witch-disciple hell-bent on his murder had been right under Evan's nose the whole time.

Seth squeezed his hand. "You did what you had to do to protect yourself," he said, meeting Evan's gaze. "You were dodging your sleazy ex. Having an immortal warlock out to kill you isn't exactly a normal kind of thing."

"It is for us." Evan managed a wan smile. He let out a long breath. "Anyhow, I'm really, really glad you found me."

Seth slipped his fingers around so that they were holding hands. "So am I."

Evan knew he needed to get his head out of the past and into the case before Brandon ended up dead. He reluctantly pulled his hand back and paged through the rest of the folder. The victims who had been matched to the photos looked unremarkable, men whose faces spoke of hard work and tough conditions. They probably worked on the railroad or in menial jobs nearby, nobody who would be noticed. Some of the others could have been boxcar hobos, looking for work or leaving the Dust Bowl. Thane would have had plenty of victims for the taking. The thought of Thane getting away with his crimes for so long tightened Evan's gut with a surge of anger.

"What does Alex know about the real situation?" Evan asked, pulling himself back to the here and now.

"Nothing," Seth replied. "I plan to keep it that way. I told him I was working on a book about the Cleveland Torso Murderer—"

"Who?" Evan's voice rose a note or two.

"There was a guy in Cleveland—a doctor from a wealthy family—who confessed to Elliott Ness—"

"The federal agent from the Untouchables who chased gangsters during Prohibition?" Evan asked, remembering an old movie.

"Yeah. Him. Anyhow, the guy died in an asylum, but they think he might have killed at least forty people."

"Doesn't sound like he could be one of the witch-disciples then. Just ordinary, garden-variety batshit crazy."

Seth nodded. "The Cleveland thing is just the cover story. For a while, some people thought the doctor might have been behind the bodies in the murder swamp, but that got disproved later."

"It just gives you a reason to be looking into the swamp near New Castle without coming off like a possible serial killer," Evan filled in.

"It sounds worse when you put it that way," Seth said with a grimace. He finished off his beer as the timer sounded, and they both went out to the kitchen to load up their plates and snag a second round of drinks.

"You think Alex believes you?" Evan asked as they settled into their seats again.

"Maybe. He might figure I'm a journalist instead of a novelist, but the cases are long cold, and everyone associated with them has been dead for decades. Shouldn't really make much difference why I'm interested," Seth said, and took a big bite of the pizza, pulling away with strings of melted cheese attached.

Evan dug into his salad, waiting for the pizza to cool. "So, what are you hoping to find?"

Seth took a moment to answer until he had finished his bite. "Don't know. Maybe nothing. But if I'm right and Thane was Andrew Wiegand in the 1930s near New Castle, then maybe there's a link. Maybe something that didn't matter to people at the time will stand out to us—and help us figure out who he became after that."

"Corson Valac kept the same initials every time he changed names," Evan recalled.

"That might have been his kink, but it doesn't seem to hold true for Thane. Maybe Valac was more of a cocky bastard, and Thane is cautious, meticulous. Which sucks because it's gonna make it harder to catch him."

Seth listened while Evan caught him up on everything he had learned about Brandon from his day's work.

"I figure you've got a file on his ancestors that led you this far, right?" Evan asked. Seth nodded. "I promise not to freak out if you let me read it," he added with a grin. "Fresh eyes, you know?"

Valac had changed identities and professions every twelve years, like clockwork. But from what Seth had uncovered so far, Thane seemed inclined to linger in his personas, and Evan desperately hoped that might prove to be the warlock's undoing.

"It's on a flash drive," Seth replied. "I'll give it to you. Brandon's older cousin, Sprague, was the most recent death—twelve years ago on Halloween. The official cause was listed as a homicide—police said it looked like he'd been in a knife fight. The family contested it, argued that Sprague kept his nose clean, wasn't into gangs or drugs, but from the record, it looks like the cops found evidence on the body to the contrary."

"You think Thane planted it for a cover-up?"

"Yeah," Seth said. "Maybe he had the cops in his pocket. Or like in Richmond, he was one."

Evan's heart sped up at the memory, and he forced himself to take a deep breath. Thankfully, Seth didn't say anything, although Evan was sure he noticed. "And before that?" he asked, glad his voice stayed steady. He needed to show Seth that he could handle the job, no matter how gory the details.

"Brandon's Uncle Peter, Sprague's father, vanished twenty-four years ago in the fall. Peter was the eldest son, and Sprague was the oldest of his generation. Brandon's father died from a heart attack. So that moves his eldest son up to the next in line to die."

Evan thought about the man he'd spent all day getting to know via the internet. From everything Evan could find, Brandon Clarke seemed to be a nice guy working two jobs and living a normal, reasonably happy life. The idea that some sick fuck could snatch him and murder him, snuff out that spark, made Evan furious. He realized some of his anger came from how much Brandon's situation paralleled his own, back in Richmond.

"So what's next?" Evan asked. They polished off the pizza in record time, as well as their salads.

"Nothing tonight," Seth said, helping to clear away the plates and empty bottles. "I vote for watching a movie, curling up with some popcorn, and cashing in that rain check," he added with a lascivious grin. "And then going out to the murder swamp in the morning."

Evan made a face. "You had me happy about everything until the last bit, about the swamp." He scraped the plates and put them in the sink. "But I guess it can't be helped. At least we're not going out there at night."

"From what Alex told me, it's not the kind of place to go tramping around in the dark," Seth replied, heading to the couch where he grabbed the remote and held out a soft throw blanket to entice Evan to join him.

"Popcorn—remember?" Evan said, sticking a bag in the microwave. In minutes, the smell of buttery goodness filled the RV. He dumped the contents into a bowl and squirmed into a comfortable position between Seth's legs, leaning on his chest. Evan kept the popcorn bowl on his own lap where they could both reach it, and Seth drew the blanket over their legs before flicking on the TV.

The action movie was splashy but predictable, and Evan found himself nodding off, warm against Seth and wrapped in the throw. He drifted off, but his dreams melded with the sound effects from the movie, gunfire, and explosions, and the smack of fists on flesh as someone took a brutal beating.

Mike stood in the doorway of their apartment back in St. Louis. "You didn't take out the garbage." His voice held the promise of violence, as did the tension in his body, ready to attack.

"I was going to, right after dinner." Evan's tone was conciliatory, hoping to avoid another fight.

"You forgot."

"I—"

"Can't fuckin' do anything right, can you?" Mike snapped. "Lose your fuckin' head if it weren't attached. Why do I put up with your shit?" He kicked a kitchen chair and sent it spinning across the tile floor, forcing Evan to jump out of the way and flinch from the crack of the wood against the counter.

"Mike, please don't—"

"Don't tell me what to do!" Mike's voice thundered in the small room, and Evan couldn't help cringing back against the cabinets, trying to make himself small, trying to avert the storm he knew was coming.

"I wasn't, honest — "

"And now you're lying to me. I pay more than my share for this apartment so you can pay off the student debt on your worthless degree. I got a friend to hire you at the bar, or you'd still be begging for a job. And you can't even tell me the fuckin' truth?"

With every sentence, Mike strode closer, like a lion stalking his prey. Evan was trapped in the corner, heart thudding so hard he thought it would break through his ribs. He knew the look in Mike's eye, smelled the gin on his breath, and he braced himself, knowing the blow would fall before Mike even telegraphed his punch —

The kitchen vanished, but Evan felt the beating in every bruised muscle of his body. A burly enforcer pushed Evan deeper into the abandoned railway tunnel, heedless of the mud and stinking water that pooled around their feet. At the end of the tunnel, lit by a circle of candles, was a large stone slab. An altar, where Corson Valac intended to make a sacrifice that would renew his immortality and strengthen his power.

And that sacrifice would be Evan —

"Evan! Baby, you're all right." Seth's pleading voice sounded far away, but Evan clung to it like a lifeline.

"Please, Evan. Wake up. You're safe. I've got you. Not gonna let anything or anyone hurt you, I swear. You're safe, baby. Please, wake up."

Evan thrashed awake, trying to free himself from the bonds that held him. He lashed out, landing a solid punch when someone tried to grab him, still too disoriented in the darkness to know which of his nightmares was his reality.

The bright light blinded him for a moment. Then Evan saw the throw blanket he had kicked free, popcorn all over the floor, and Seth, pressing a tissue to his bloody nose.

"Oh my God. Seth—did I do that? Fuck, I'm so sorry." Evan could feel himself beginning to hyperventilate as the adrenaline from the nightmares converged with his guilt over hurting Seth as he fought his way to consciousness.

"I'm okay," Seth assured him. "Won't even need to stick a tampon up my nostril," he added.

"Eww."

Seth's smile told Evan the obnoxious image was meant to distract him. He moved slowly as if Evan were a skittish horse. "Is it okay if I come closer?"

Evan nodded, trying to sort out the mix of feelings that overwhelmed him. Fear. Guilt. Shame. Self-loathing. And anxiety—when would Seth decide enough was enough?

Seth sat down close enough for their legs to touch from hip to knee. "Is it okay to hug you?" he asked, taking his cue from Evan. Evan nodded again, tearing up, afraid to try to speak.

Seth wrapped his arms around Evan and drew him close. Evan stayed rigid for a moment, then collapsed against Seth, and they fell backward, tangled up together, with Seth curled around him, sheltering and protecting. "I'm here," Seth murmured, pressing his lips against Evan's temple. "I'm here. I've got you. That's it. Just…let go."

They sat in silence for a long while, with Seth's strong arms wrapped around Evan. *Oh, God. I hope he never lets me go.*

"Not going anywhere," Seth said as if he could read Evan's mind. "Shh. You're safe."

Evan breathed in the smell of sweat and soap and aftershave that was so *Seth*, taking comfort in the way the other man held him close, shielding him with his body. Evan made himself focus on Seth's heartbeat and the rise and fall of his muscular chest. Only then did he realize his face was wet with tears.

"I'm sorry," Evan said in a muffled voice.

"Nothing to be sorry about," Seth said quietly, his cheek resting against the top of Evan's head. "You've been there enough nights when my dreams got out of control. Just returning the favor."

Evan wanted to say it wasn't the same at all because those other times it was *Seth* waking in a cold sweat, wide-eyed and shaking. And this was *him*, falling apart and washing out as a badass sidekick.

"This doesn't change anything," Seth said, running a hand up and down Evan's back. "Just another kind of scar. We'll get past it."

Evan nodded and drew a shaky breath. "I don't know why I dream about him sometimes. If I knew, I'd fix it."

"Sometimes your brain just serves up random shit, especially if you haven't finished sorting through it," Seth replied. "At least, that's what the therapist they gave me in the hospital said." He chuckled. "Maybe not those exact words, but close enough."

"I never knew what would set him off," Evan confided in a voice just above a whisper. He blinked away tears, and Seth tucked a tissue into Evan's hand so he could dab his eyes and nose. "Most of the time, it wasn't anything at all that was wrong—just an excuse to throw a few punches, knock me around. God, I was so scared back then because I had nowhere else to go. Couldn't go home—they didn't want me. Wasn't making enough to be on my own. I guess Mike saw an easy mark when he picked me."

"Abusers know how to pick their victims when they're vulnerable," Seth said, stroking Evan's dark hair. "That's on him, not you." He paused. "How did you get away?"

"One night, Mike overdid it. Made a mess of me. Black eye, finger-prints on my neck. I couldn't afford not to show up for work, but I couldn't hide that I'd been in a fight. My boss, the bar owner—big guy, former boxer—took one look and knew what had happened. He took three hundred dollars out of the safe, drove me to the bus station, and made me give him my phone so I couldn't be tracked. Told me to go as far as I could and never come back. Then he slipped me a .22 pistol and watched me get on the bus."

"And Mike?"

"Pretty sure my boss mopped the floor with him if he was dumb enough to come looking for me," Evan said with a bitter chuckle. "I ran, and I kept running. Moved every few months for a while, then once a year—different cities and states. Worked under the table when I could and couch surfed, so I didn't show up on anything official. If I could have pulled off a whole 'witness protection' new ID, I would have. Kinda jealous of how good Valac and Thane are at that kind of thing."

Seth's grip tightened a bit. "They've had over a century of practice, and they're the predators. They're not used to having to look over their shoulders."

"There were a couple of times I thought I saw Mike," Evan went on. "Usually, it was just someone who looked like him. It always pretty much ruined me for the whole day, feeling like I needed to pick up and run. When I got to Richmond, I leveled with Liam about what happened, and he promised to go to the police with me if Mike ever showed up. Then it turns out, one of the cops was the guy who really did want to kill me."

Seth wrapped one large hand around the back of Evan's head, pulling him safely against his neck and shoulder, while the other hand continued to rub comforting circles on his back. "I'll do more than go to the police if that fucker ever shows up," Seth vowed in a quiet voice. "I'll kill the bastard."

"Seth—"

"I love you, Evan. And I'm going to do everything in my power to keep you safe—against crazy dark warlocks and rabid werewolves and batshit assholes," Seth promised. Evan thought it was possibly the most romantic thing he'd ever heard.

A little while later, Evan pushed away, calm but still a bit embarrassed despite Seth's assurances. He knew he was a mess, hair askew, eyes red and puffy. Seth just looked at him fondly, though he saw a hint of worry in his lover's eyes. "Come on. Let's wash up and go to sleep," Seth urged. "I'll be right beside you."

THE NEXT MORNING, Evan woke feeling worn out and hollow. His sleep had been dreamless, but not restful. Seth stayed close, reassuring with a touch or a kiss or a murmured word whenever Evan stirred. On one hand, he felt relieved at having finally told Seth more about what happened with Mike. On the other, the discussion made the memories more vivid.

"Hey." Seth nudged him gently and kissed his shoulder. Usually, they'd take advantage of morning wood to have a quick tumble before their shower, but Evan guessed that neither of them were in the mood today. "You up for going out today?"

What did it say that visiting a "murder swamp" was an improvement over marinating in his own thoughts?

"Yeah," Evan said, his voice rougher than usual. "Just let me get cleaned up, and I'll be good to go."

By the time Evan was out of the shower, Seth had fixed breakfast—bacon, scrambled eggs, toast, coffee, and orange juice. "Come eat before it gets cold," Seth said, and Evan was glad his boyfriend didn't make a big deal about giving him the once-over to assure he was all right. He'd be okay if he could just stay busy and keep his mind occupied.

"This looks wonderful," Evan replied, touched that Seth had gone to so much effort. They usually saved real cooking for weekend breakfasts. "Thank you."

"My pleasure," Seth said, his voice warm. "I already ate, so you go ahead while I duck in the shower and then we can go. I set out two travel mugs, so we can bring the rest of the coffee with us. It's damn cold out there."

The drive took about an hour. Evan watched the snow while Seth kept his attention on traffic. "You'd think people who live where it snows would know how to drive in it," he grumbled, swerving to avoid a sports car fishtailing all over its lane.

"It's kinda like being in a video game," Evan replied. Despite everything, he couldn't help thinking how pretty the trees were outlined in white.

"Yeah—Frogger," Seth answered. He'd turned on a classic vinyl channel, and the silence between them was comfortable, despite the turmoil of the night before.

By the time they reached West Pittsburg, Evan had managed to wrest his mood into a reasonable facsimile of "good," considering that they were heading to a place used by a serial killer for a mass grave.

"Not much to see, is there?" Seth said as they left the truck parked on the side of a road down near the river and walked along the berm. Bare trees and brown cattails stretched from the storm ditch to the river. Around the bend in front of them lay the remains of a railroad yard that had once been a thriving depot and now lay in disuse. The road had taken them out of sight of buildings or farms, and Evan felt exposed and vulnerable.

"The ground doesn't look very solid," Evan observed. Snow covered the spaces between the tree trunks, but bare spots showed where the wet marsh had melted the snow or turned it to ice.

"That's what Alex warned me about. Apparently there are firm places, but even the locals step wrong if they're not careful. Swamps and marshes are great places to stash bodies—the water speeds decomp, and odds are against having a lot of passers-by who might find something."

"Do you think a medium could talk to the ghosts? Someone like your friend, Simon?"

Seth shrugged. "Simon's all the way down in Myrtle Beach, and I doubt he can séance by Skype. So we're on our own."

"What are we looking for?"

Seth turned slowly to take in the stretch of swamp. "I'm not sure. Maybe…just to see it for ourselves. If the rail yard was over there," he said, pointing, "this wouldn't be far to come to dispose of a body."

"If Thane alternates between posing as a nobody and then turning himself into someone rich and powerful, that might account for why the bodies stopped showing up."

"Or did he keep using the swamp until he thought someone might have noticed?"

They both wore silver medallions for protection and carried salt and iron. Even so, Evan felt the temperature drop and the hair on the back of his neck rose. Branches began to sway without wind, clacking like dry bones. This time, no blue mist rose, and no ghosts stepped from the marshland. But Evan was certain they were no longer alone.

Once again, Seth called out to the spirits of the swamp, asking for their help. None of them chose to show themselves, but then again, they didn't attack, which Evan counted as a win.

It was cold enough that Evan shivered, despite his parka. He turned to glance at the truck and saw that the windows were covered with frost.

"Seth. Look." He pointed to the driver's window. An invisible hand scrawled five letters one by one in the frost in shaky letters.

"Matt E," Seth read aloud. He turned back to the swamp. "Thank you," he told the empty marsh. "Come on," he added, looked to Evan. "Let's get out of here. We got what we wanted. Now we've just got to figure out what the hell it means."

3

SETH

Seth left Evan with a kiss and a reminder to lock the door behind him. Despite Evan's assurances that he would be completely fine, Seth had to force himself to leave the campground. Evan wasn't the vulnerable young man he had been when Mike took advantage of him. He could hold his own in a fight against supernatural creatures, spar with Seth and win his share of rounds. And he was well-armed.

The events of the night before left Seth restless and worried, far more than he had let on. While he hadn't lived Evan's circumstances, he could relate far too well from his own PTSD over Jesse's death. The witch-disciple that had killed Jesse had thrown Seth around like he was a toy, beaten him unconscious, and when he woke, it was to find Jesse's mutilated body hanging from the tree where the deputies once executed Rhyfel Gremory. So Seth understood, and that just made the knot in his gut tighter.

Still, they had a would-be victim to save, and nothing would be accomplished by Seth hovering over Evan except to spark an argument. So Seth forced himself to head out to do more legwork, knowing that he needed to trust Evan to be able to take care of himself.

He was so deep in thought as he drove that he jumped when the radio dropped out and his phone rang. "Hi Mark," he said after a glance at the caller ID and hit the hands-free button. "What's up? How's your hunt in the Big Woods?"

"Cold. Look, I heard some intel and thought I'd pass it along," Mark Wojcik replied. "There are a couple of hunters down in the Pittsburgh area you might want to know about. They're pretty specialized; I hear they focus mostly on demons, but that might not be the whole story. Ex-priest and a former FBI guy. Travis Dominick and Brent Lawson."

"Are they legit?"

"I know Brent through Simon," Mark replied. "Helped him out with some lore on a big hunt in the middle of the state. Simon knew him first, mentioned him to me, thinking we might cross paths."

Seth chewed his lip as he thought. "So, do I bring them in or keep my distance?"

"If it were me, I'd keep my distance, for now at least," Mark said. "If you need reinforcements, decide then. The only reason I hesitate is that I'm pretty sure the ex-priest was part of the Sinistram."

"Isn't that the secret Vatican group you report to?"

"I work for the Occulatum. If we're the supernatural version of a SWAT team, the Sinistram is Vatican black ops. Ruthless bastards."

"You said he 'was' part of them. He's out?"

"Out of the Sinistram and out of the priesthood, so I hear. Runs a halfway house now, hunts demons in his spare time. You might not run into them at all since dark warlocks probably aren't their kind of thing. But I figured you might want to know they were out there, in case you need them—or need to steer clear of them."

"Thanks," Seth said. "I think we'll fly solo for now. Find out anything else about Noson Thane?"

"Yeah. My research person thinks he might have passed for a doctor at the old Dixmont Hospital—it was an insane asylum and haunted as fuck after it closed. Name was Roy Moser. Fits the profile— no previous history, credentials don't hold water, disappeared after twenty-four years and was never seen again, but there's no report about a death."

"Got it," Seth said. "Thank you."

"Any time. Take care—and watch your back."

"Will do. Stay safe—and warm," Seth advised. "I'll let you know what I find."

"Don't get chomped by anything," Mark retorted. "I'll talk to you later."

Seth navigated the Parkway and crossed the bridge over the Allegheny River to the North Side. Two famous sports parks caught his eye—Heinz Field to one side, and PNC Park to the other. Seth wasn't big into sports, but he'd seen enough games on TV to be a grudging fan of both the Steelers and the Pirates, and he admired the loyalty of their supporters.

His route took him past Heinz Field to Ridge Avenue, and the former site of the most notorious home in Pittsburgh—the Congelier house.

Although Seth knew the Congelier/Brunrichter house had been blown to smithereens by a suspicious gas line explosion in the late 1920s, he felt a stab of disappointment to track the address and find himself staring at one of the classroom buildings for the local community college.

He didn't know what he had been expecting, but certainly something more...interesting. Seth walked around the block, but any traces of the old home were long gone. Frustrated, he walked across the street to a diner and settled in at a table by the window, where he could still stare out at the vexing building.

"If I had to guess, I'd say you came for a look at the Congelier house." The server's voice startled Seth, and he castigated himself for letting down his guard.

"Do you know about it?" Seth asked as the server poured a cup of coffee.

"Hard not to, if you work around here," the young man replied. He wore a white t-shirt with the diner logo emblazoned in the center and a name badge that said "*Jimmy.*" The server was probably in his early twenties, with a purple Mohawk and skinny jeans that accentuated his thin build. Jimmy had medium gages in both earlobes and a well-inked sleeve on his right arm that looked like an aquarium of vivid fish.

"Fill me in. I'm from out of town," Seth replied.

Jimmy took Seth's order—a Reuben sandwich with chips—and walked it back to the kitchen before returning. The diner was still quiet, and everyone else had their food, although Jimmy stopped several times on his way back to top off cups of coffee and trade comments with patrons Seth assumed were regulars.

"Okay, you want to know about the house," Jimmy said, giving Seth a refill without needing to be asked. "They say that Congelier was some super-rich robber baron guy. When his wife caught him having an affair with a maid, she knifed both of them, cut off their heads, and then went crazy herself."

"Nice."

"It gets better," Jimmy said. "People said the place was haunted, so it sat empty for a long time. Then this new guy from out of town—Dr. Brunrichter—comes in and buys it. All well and good until the neighbors start hearing weird noises and people go missing. One night, there are screams and flashes of light, and someone calls the cops."

Jimmy paused dramatically, looking like he was enjoying his tale. "When the police broke in, they found a laboratory—like something out of *Frankenstein*, you know? And on the tables were dead bodies that were missing their heads." He grinned wide. "Then later, the whole place goes boom! Gas leak—or so they say," Jimmy added with a conspiratorial whisper. "I guess we'll never know for sure."

Jimmy headed back to the kitchen and came back a few minutes later with Seth's sandwich and a glass of water, then left him to eat in peace. He mulled over the grisly story, trying to make the various versions he'd heard align. Jimmy hadn't told Seth anything new, but he corroborated what he'd found elsewhere.

A local historian had debunked the entire sordid tale and claimed Brunrichter never existed. Yet the story persisted, with different embellishments depending on the website posting the information. As far as Seth was concerned, the part about the philandering husband and his murderous wife was the least important. The mysterious, disappearing Dr. Brunrichter with his penchant for dismemberment was much more interesting—and likely to be one of Thane's previous identities.

He had hoped that coming down to the location might spark some new revelation, but so far, Seth had more questions than answers. Thane was ahead of them, and unless Seth caught up quickly, Brandon —and maybe Evan—would be in danger.

Seth figured Evan might want some time to himself after the events of the previous night, so he had brought his laptop with him. He set up shop as he pushed his empty plate aside and decided to see what he could find about "Matt E."

For a moment, Seth stared at his screen, at a loss for where to begin. He knew that ghosts had limited ability to affect the real world and that any manifestation drained them of their energy. If the ghosts of the murder swamp went to the effort of providing the name, it had to be important, just like the mysterious "watch" clue from Blue Mist Road.

Seth went with his gut and looked up the known victims whose bodies had been pulled from the swamp. Many of the bodies went unidentified, since forensics was in its infancy, and without a head, making a definite ID was difficult. To his chagrin, none of the names came close to matching "Matt E."

He sat back and reached for his coffee. Jimmy kept his cup hot and full, earning himself a great tip when Seth was ready to leave. Seth drummed his fingers on the table, thinking. On impulse, he pulled up one of the files Alex had compiled, which Seth had downloaded. The list of names and dates was sobering—each one someone who had gone missing and remained unaccounted for from 1900-1980 around Pittsburgh and New Castle. After that, Seth had been able to compile his own list from online sources. But the old rosters hadn't been digitized—no use, since by now, the people named there were probably long dead.

Seth had planned to use the lists to help find possible victims of the warlock and clusters of disappearances might point him toward the witch-disciple's activities. Now, he scanned down, looking for anyone named Matthew.

"Okay," he breathed, as he found "Matthew Easton." He was a clerk in the First Bank and Trust in Livermore and went missing in 1940.

"Forty?" Seth mused under his breath. Official records said that the last victim of the murder swamp killer was found in 1939. According to the information Mark had dug up, Andrew Wiegand—Thane's 1930s persona—had vanished in 1940.

Was "Matt E" a clue that led to Thane's next alias—in Livermore?

Seth typed up the information in his notes, along with a reminder to go looking for more information on both Matthew Easton and Livermore. He was just about to start doing another online search when he noticed the time.

"Fuck," he muttered. Alex had asked to get together so he could pass on a few more documents that hadn't been ready yesterday, and Seth had agreed to meet him at a coffee shop over on the east side of town. He didn't want to leave Evan alone too long and wondered how much time was enough to give his lover time to put himself back together without making him feel lonely.

When in doubt, bribery worked wonders. Seth decided to raid the coffee shop and its next-door deli for dinner and dessert. He paid his bill, leaving a tip that had Jimmy waving goodbye with a big smile.

"SORRY TO RUN you back into town." Alex Wilson slid a folder and a flash drive across the coffee shop table. "These were supposed to have been here yesterday, but they didn't arrive until after you left. When it comes to getting old microfiche prints, sometimes I'm at the mercy of the archive volunteers."

Seth opened the folder, but as he scanned the photocopies, he was also sizing up the man across from him. Alex had played college football and still looked like a linebacker—broad-shouldered and solid. Since he looked like he was close to thirty and hadn't gone soft, Seth figured the man kept up a serious workout routine. He'd looked into the man's background before he hired him—former Pittsburgh cop who got his badge pulled because he lost his cool on a guy who beat up kids. Started working as a part-time PI for another former cop. With Alex's Black Irish good looks—dark hair and blue eyes—Seth was surprised that there wasn't a ring on his finger.

Maybe he's married to the job, he thought. That had certainly been true for Seth until he'd lost his heart to a certain former bartender.

"What do you know about Livermore?" Seth asked.

Alex frowned. "Mostly that it doesn't exist anymore. Why?"

Seth had found that much out himself with a quick online search. Livermore, Pennsylvania, had been a declining canal town in a floodplain. Its luck finally ran out in the early 1950s, when the town was abandoned, and much of it was razed, then flooded to create the Conemaugh Dam.

"I found some leads that suggest there might have been another swamp murder victim—a Matthew Easton from Livermore," Seth replied since in this case, the truth was the simplest explanation. "It would be a coup for my book if I could prove that."

Alex leaned back, stretching one arm out along the back of his side of the booth. "Gonna be hard to find out much since Livermore's been underwater for almost seventy-five years."

"What happened to the records? Birth and death certificates. Marriage licenses. All that stuff had to go somewhere," Seth pressed.

Alex cocked his head, thinking. "I know a guy in Blairsville, which is near where Livermore used to be. He might be able to put me in touch with someone who knows where the official records went. I'll give it a shot—you want some weird stuff," he added.

Seth managed a smile he hoped looked sincere. "Writers. What can I say? We're a strange bunch."

"Your cash isn't counterfeit. That's good enough for me," Alex said. He finished his coffee and stood. "I'll let you know what I find out. If the quality isn't too bad, I can scan and email them, save you a trip."

"I'm back and forth, so it'll work either way," Seth told him. "Thanks for the good intel." He dawdled a bit, letting Alex leave ahead of him, the better to observe the investigator. As soon as Alex left the coffee shop, he made a call. From the change in his expression and body language, Seth could tell it was personal, not professional.

And if I had to guess, it's his significant other, Seth thought. *Interesting. Wonder whether it's someone else in law enforcement, or completely out of the business?* It didn't matter—Seth had someone waiting for him at home, but he couldn't help the idle speculation. He'd always found that the more he knew about the people around him, the safer he felt.

Especially now, when they had a killer to stop.

4

EVAN

Evan spent the first hour after Seth left looking up anything he could find online about Brandon Clarke's family. He'd invested in a membership to a genealogy site, and by plugging in a few details about Brandon's immediate family, Evan got a wealth of information back.

He went looking for the oldest male in each generation, all the way back to 1900. It wasn't difficult to see where the witch-disciple had cut lives short. Every twelve years, one of the Clarke men died before his time. Cross-referencing the deaths with the details Evan could find online gave him a list split between disappearances and obituaries that were extremely vague about the cause of death.

Evan sat back and took a drink of his coffee. It soured in his stomach as he thought about the loss and grief inflicted on the families of the deputies by Gremory's disciples who were intent on living long beyond their natural span.

On impulse, Evan opened a new family tree and typed in the details for his own family. The tree populated quickly, making him wonder if Seth had used a similar program to find him. A month ago, that would have raised his hackles. Hell, he had accused Seth of stalking him and almost gotten himself killed by doing his best to get away—running right into the trap Corson Valac had set.

Now, the confirmation that so many Malone men had died because a bunch of warlocks felt entitled to be immortal stoked a quiet fury. Evan's parents had been assholes about rejecting him for being gay. And, all right, his younger brothers hadn't come looking for him, either. But despite their failings, the thought that if he and Seth hadn't stopped Valac, the killing would have gone on, generation after generation of Malone men, made Evan want to throw up.

He traced the death dates back through time, a pattern that was easy to see once he knew what he was looking for. More than a hundred years of husbands, fathers, brothers, and sons taken before their time, families torn apart, leaving grieving loved ones behind. All because Gremory and his disciples lusted for power and magic.

His very religious family would never have believed in magic if Seth had tried to warn them. But a long-forgotten conversation made Evan sit up, eyes widening as the implications of the memory became clear. He remembered overhearing a conversation between his parents about why they had moved from Richmond to Oklahoma. They were fighting about the move, something his mother apparently had resented.

Evan's father had told her, *"I swear there's something evil in Richmond, something done long ago that put a curse on the Malones, and I need to outrun it, bury it deep in the blood of Jesus, and pray to the Good Lord to lift this burden from us."*

Details began to click in Evan's memory. He'd met his grandparents, who lived in the countryside not far from Richmond. They hadn't struck him as overly religious people, and neither had his uncle, the older brother who'd been the sacrifice in his generation. No, the crazy fundamentalist super-religion was new, something his father led them into in his own misguided attempt to run away from a threat he recognized on a primal level but didn't fully understand.

Evan's father had hoped that being devout and ultra-scrupulous would protect him and his family. And the outcome—their religion-fueled homophobia—might as well have delivered Evan up to his would-be murderer like a package with a bow on top.

A sob escaped from Evan before he realized tears had started down his cheeks. Shit, he didn't even know what he was crying about. Thinking about how swiftly the family he had always believed loved him had abandoned him always made Evan melancholy. Knowing the truth about the deaths he had heard mentioned at family gatherings just made him sad. And realizing that Corson Valac had been indirectly responsible for Evan being ostracized from his family stung more than it should have.

Suddenly Evan needed to get some fresh air, get out of the RV, which felt too small and constricting. He knew Seth would be gone for hours, so there was time for him to go out and come back—he'd leave a note, just in case. In the next breath, Evan decided that he needed to see Brandon Clarke in person. Not meet him—just see him, get a feel for the man whom he'd gotten to know through his social media posts and online footprint. He wouldn't try to warn Brandon—the man would only think Evan was crazy if he tried. But it suddenly seemed imperative that Evan see Brandon with his own eyes, just to make sure he was still safe.

Evan went back to his notes to figure out how to make that happen. Brandon worked nights as an EMT, so casually strolling by the volunteer fire station wasn't going to work. But he also pulled shifts at Kona Café, and nobody would notice if a stranger with a laptop walked in and spent a few hours drinking coffee and working remotely.

He powered down his computer and put it in his messenger bag, then wrote out a quick note to Seth telling him where he'd gone and that he'd be back soon and taped it to the fridge. Then Evan grabbed a flannel shirt to pull over his Henley, laced up his boots, and headed over to borrow the campground owner's loaner Toyota since Seth had taken the truck instead of the Hayabusa. Motorcycles and snow-covered roads didn't mix.

His phone buzzed just as he went to get into the Toyota. He didn't recognize the number and let it go to voicemail. After the call ended, Evan couldn't ignore his curiosity.

"Need help financing your new car? Time to replace your old ride with a new Camaro or Mustang? Get in on this great deal before it goes up in flames."

The caller was obviously recorded, but the message sent a chill through Evan. *I'm imagining things. There are a gazillion ads for new cars and cheap insurance on TV. I probably show up in a database as a male twenty-something, so I'm a prime target for a sports car...the part about "going up in flames" is just a turn of phrase. Just dumb luck my Camaro really did burn in the fire.*

Evan didn't completely believe himself, but after a few minutes, his heart stopped thudding, and he felt okay to drive. He pulled out of the campground and headed for Emsworth, a borough just outside of the city of Pittsburgh on the north side of the Allegheny River. Snow covered the lawns and the sides of the road, but the trucks and plows had been diligent in clearing and salting the driving lanes. It had been a long time since Evan had driven in snow, and he was grateful for the road crews' hard work.

He slowed as he passed the Emsworth Volunteer Fire Department, although it wasn't like Brandon Clarke was going to come striding out at that very minute. The gray cement block building dated from 1905, and it fit right into the mix of older homes, shops, and restaurants that made up the solidly middle-class neighborhood.

Evan carefully parked the Toyota, not wanting to explain any scratches or dents to the campground owner. Kona Café looked as down-to-earth as the rest of Emsworth. Instead of a glitzy, hipster vibe, the indie coffee shop looked more like someone's comfortable living room. Well-worn couches and love seats, overstuffed armchairs, scarred end tables, and retro-kitschy artwork made Evan feel immediately at ease. The music favored rock oldies rather than jazz or New Age, and the baristas behind the counter wore simple black t-shirts with the shop's name instead of fancy uniforms.

Evan glanced at the list of drinks and pastry items. What the selection lacked in the number of fancy options, it made up for with lower prices that drew a crowd of patrons from business-suited bankers to mechanics.

"What'll you have?" The man's voice broke Evan out of his thoughts. He found himself staring at Brandon Clarke, who smiled at him across the counter.

"Um...a skim latte, please," he replied, hoping he didn't look rattled. Brandon looked just like his social media photos—perhaps even a bit better looking. His red hair looked darker, and he had a few days' russet stubble, which was a stark contrast to his pale skin. But Brandon's green eyes were his most striking feature—a brilliant green Evan didn't realize existed aside from colored contacts.

"Coming right up," Brandon said, and if he noticed Evan staring, he ignored it.

Evan silently castigated himself. *Jeez, I must look like a creeper. And he probably gets hit on all the time. Way to make myself memorable—for all the wrong reasons.* With a sigh, he accepted that he might need to work on his approach for low-key stake-outs and surveillance.

Brandon brought a steaming drink back in record time. "Would you like a muffin to go with that?" he prompted. "The pumpkin cream cheese ones are my favorite. We don't have them all the time, so I always recommend grabbing them when you can." He managed to sound friendly and engaging without any hint of flirting.

"Sure," Evan replied, digging for his wallet. He paid with cash, including a nice tip. "Thanks." Brandon was already helping the next customer by the time Evan made his way to an armchair with its own side table next to one of the café's exposed brick walls. He pulled the table in front of him and juggled the coffee and muffin until he got his laptop set up, then settled in.

Kona Café did a brisk business. Over in one corner, a trio of college-age young women appeared to be doing a study session. Two mothers with small children tried to have a conversation while they kept their youngsters corralled. An older woman sat curled up with a book and a hot beverage at the far end of the room, while several other people shared the room's single table, working from laptops.

Evan chose a seat where he could easily watch the workers behind the counter and overhear their conversations with the customers. Mindful of people moving all around him, Evan restricted his browsing to looking for a Christmas gift for Seth. Everything he found either seemed too trite or too serious for having only been a couple for two months by the time the holiday rolled around. Then again, they were already living together and in love, so that meant they were committed while still getting to know each other. Awkward.

All the while, he kept an ear open for the conversation at the counter. Brandon greeted regulars by name, offering to get them their "usual" or suggesting the items on the Daily Specials chalkboard if the customer wanted something different. Although the café saw a steady stream of patrons, Brandon's energy didn't flag, nor did the huge grin and hearty welcome he extended to each person.

He's like the friggin' Energizer Bunny, Evan thought. Back when he tended bar, Evan tried to be sociable, although he had to force himself to be as extroverted as the job required if he wanted to make good tips. He remembered coming home exhausted, not just from the demands of being on his feet and running back and forth the length of the bar all night to keep up with orders, but with maintaining the energy level necessary to be the upbeat, engaging bartender customers expected as part of the Treddy's experience.

Is he really that bouncy, or just a good actor? As one hour passed, and then two, Brandon's cheerfulness never waned. Evan snuck a look, focusing on the man's eyes, the first place to spot deception. But what he could make out from his quarry's expression looked like Brandon sincerely enjoyed interacting with customers. A few of the patrons were grouchy and snappish, but Brandon deflected their bad mood with a quip or a compliment that mollified even the surliest.

A few men in EMT uniforms came in as a group. Brandon hailed them with a shout and a wave over the heads of the customers in line, and the men waved back. They talked and joked among themselves as they waited their turn, then ribbed Brandon good-naturedly when they reached the counter.

"Still bringing people back to life, I see," one of the paramedics, a dark-haired man with glasses, joked as Brandon handed him a large coffee.

"Yeah, that's me. Keeping the blood pumping one way or another," Brandon replied. "I'm pretty sure some of our folks wouldn't turn down a java IV if we offered one."

"Sign me up," another of his EMT buddies, tall and blond, built like a boxer, quipped. He looked tired, and Evan wondered if they were just coming off a long shift.

"Coffee makes the world go 'round," Brandon said, handing over another steaming cup. "Any of you guys working tomorrow night?"

"Ben is," the guy with glasses replied. "Kane and Stu also, I think. We're all still on days this week."

Brandon nodded, delivering cups for the other two EMTs who had come in with the group. "Nice to know. I saw my schedule, but I didn't take the time to look at who else was on it."

"Keep bringing coffee in to the station, and you can probably sweet-talk the scheduler into putting you on any shift you want," Ben said with a laugh. The paramedics took their drinks and headed out, still joking among themselves.

Evan sat back in his chair, watching the scene play out. From everything he had seen, Brandon Clarke worked hard, was well-liked, and seemed to be a decent guy. If Noson Thane had his way, sometime between now and Halloween, Brandon would be gruesomely murdered in an unholy ritual. All that light and life snuffed out to give a warlock serial killer an extension of stolen immortality.

His fists balled at his sides as Evan fought to keep himself from trying to warn Brandon about the danger. *I know what I would have thought if Seth had tried to warn me. I'd have figured he was crazy and called the cops on him. There's nothing I can do to prove the danger, and only a madman would believe me. Especially since right now, we don't even know Thane's new identity.*

Evan looked around the coffee shop, remembering that Corson Valac—in his cop persona—had become a regular at Treddy's, keeping his prey in sight. Was Thane a regular at Kona Café? Evan glanced at the other patrons, but no one seemed out of the ordinary. None of the others were paying much—if any—attention to the people around them, focused on their phones, books, or computers.

The frustrating thing was, Thane knew how to hide in plain sight, just like Valac had. Nothing about Valac, posing as a local cop, had set off Evan's alarms until it was almost too late. The witch-disciples had a century of practice to know how to blend in, evade notice, and track their intended victims like an apex predator. Maybe Thane wouldn't come to the coffee shop to keep an eye on Brandon—although Evan doubted it—but if not, he'd have created some plausible, unremarkable way to make sure Brandon remained in his sights. And Brandon would never even realize anything was wrong—until the killer struck.

Evan glanced around the shop once more, using the excuse of sipping his coffee. From what they'd learned of Thane from his known personas, he probably appeared to be in his early thirties to mid-forties, although the disciples had learned to master the use of disguise to hide their identities. Only a couple of the men in the café matched the right age, and Evan knew it was hoping too much that he'd happen into Kona Café at the same time as Thane. Still, it was worth a look.

Seth hadn't turned up a photo of Thane yet, and Evan recalled how successfully Valac had evaded the camera over his many reinventions back in Richmond. Still, remaining completely un-photographed in this century was impossible, and Evan knew they just needed to find the pictures that would help them put it all together.

Evan's computer pinged with new email. He saw notices for several updates to the genealogy website, a couple of notices for sales at sites he'd bookmarked as having Christmas present possibilities, and another email from a sender he didn't recognize.

"Phone destroyed by fire, flood, or accident? We can help."

Evan closed his eyes and took a deep breath. He didn't want to attract attention, but the email triggered a reminder of the apartment fire that had ruined all his electronics—and most of his possessions. He told himself that although he'd left Richmond and had a new phone number, he was still using the email address he'd had for several years, one he had used with online merchants for a variety of sites. Which meant his name popped up in databases and probably cross-referenced with public records by clever marketers.

I've heard people say that they get spammed by lots of companies when they get married or have a baby, all trying to sell them something for their new stage of life. Same with graduations and other big events. No one's psychic, or spying on me, or stalking me—no more than they are for everyone else who's online. It's just Big Brother, data mining…nothing personal.

Evan glanced at the time and decided he'd better head back to the RV. He wanted to be back before Seth arrived. Evan didn't intend to keep his trip to the coffee shop a secret, but he struggled with how to present it to keep Seth from fearing that he'd put Brandon—and himself—in more danger. He packed up his laptop and headed out. Brandon was joking with the other barista behind the counter, and their laughter carried all the way to the door.

He'd barely met Brandon Clarke, but that brief encounter was enough to convince Evan that the EMT/barista deserved far better than the fate Thane had in mind. If he needed any more convincing to sign on with Seth's quest to destroy Gremory's witch-disciple, meeting the next victim cemented his certainty.

Evan breathed a sigh of relief when he got back to the campground, returned the borrowed Toyota, and didn't see Seth's truck. Then he reprimanded himself. He was not sneaking around. Evan had every intention of telling Seth where he'd been, and he'd gotten an idea good enough that it should win over his lover should Seth prove to be grumpy about the side trip.

Once he'd set his boots aside and taken off his heavy coat, Evan set up his laptop at the table and pulled out the notebook he'd been keeping of sigils, spells, and useful materials to banish spirits or protect from evil. Not long ago, he would have laughed and considered the notes to be nothing more than prompts for a fiction story or a role-playing game. Now, that information made a life-or-death difference in their hunts.

Evan grabbed chalk and slate from his messenger bag and spent the next hour practicing sigils. Accuracy counted, coupled with speed. Sloppy sigils wouldn't work—or might have an unexpected effect, never a good thing in a fight. But he also had to be able to reproduce the sigil quickly under pressure, since a monster wouldn't wait for him to finish his masterpiece. That meant practice—and plenty of it.

Some of the sigils—like the one for "light," "fasten," and "silence" were easy enough to not only draw but also practice activating with his will and focus. Cross through the sigil, and it caused the reverse effect. Others, like "distract," "summon ghosts," or "sense undead" were ones Evan didn't want to risk actually using except in an emergency. He was pleased that he had gotten faster and better at making the marks and that pushing his energy and intention into the sigils no longer seemed clumsy and alien.

Seth was better with spoken spells, but the same graphic design abilities that helped Evan please his clients made drawing the sigils easier for him to master. Before he met Seth, Evan had never dreamed that magic of any kind really existed, especially not simple spells that could be learned by anyone given enough practice—hence the designation of "rote" magic. Now, magic was as much a given as the existence of monsters. Seth had turned his world upside-down and inside-out, and despite the danger, Evan wouldn't have it any other way.

The familiar rumble of the Silverado signaled Evan to put away his slate and notebook. Seth came inside with a blast of cold air behind him and looked around with concern until he spotted Evan.

"Hey. Everything all right? I saw the footprints. Did you need to go somewhere?"

Evan smiled self-consciously and ran a hand back through his hair. "I got a little claustrophobic after what happened last night," he admitted. "Needed to clear my head. And I got the idea of going down to Kona Café to see if I could get a look at Brandon Clarke."

Seth's eyes widened, but before he could object, Evan rushed ahead. "I didn't talk to him other than ordering a latte and a muffin," he said, raising his hands in appeasement. "I just observed. I wanted to get a sense for the guy beyond what was online."

When Seth didn't say anything, Evan grew nervous. "Um…honest, I didn't mess anything up. He didn't have any reason to notice me, and I didn't try to warn him or anything. I just sat there and looked around. Say something, please?"

Seth blinked, and his expression was hard to decipher. "I'm not upset," he said quietly. "I'm worried—because you might have been in danger, and because you're acting like I'm going to take a swing at you for going out. You're not a prisoner, for fuck's sake."

Evan lowered his hands. "I know. It's just…" How could he put into words that old defense mechanisms were hard to turn off? Surviving in close quarters with Mike had meant constantly apologizing, anticipating what might upset him and smoothing it over, hiding innocent things that seemed to set him off. He knew Seth wasn't Mike, that Seth hadn't shown any of Mike's controlling tendencies, but here he was, falling back on old patterns—

"It's okay," Seth said, pulling Evan out of his mental free-fall. "I just worry. You haven't had a lot of experience driving in the snow, and even though they keep the roads clear, there're still icy patches. And if Thane's keeping an eye on Brandon, it scares me to think that he could notice you, too."

"About that," Evan said, licking his lips nervously. "I have an idea. None of the people in the coffee shop looked suspicious today. But what if Thane is a regular so he can keep tabs on Brandon? Can you hack into the café's security cameras? Maybe if we could access a couple of weeks' worth of footage, we'd get to know the people who are there all the time—and then if you turn up a photo of Thane in one of his old personas, we might be able to figure out who he is now."

Seth stepped forward and pulled Evan in for a kiss. "You're really smart. And sexy. That's a great idea."

Evan returned the kiss, happy to have avoided an argument. As much as he still thought he was right in visiting the café, he knew Seth had a point about the danger. And if he expected Seth to be careful about running headlong into dicey situations, then he realized he owed the same caution in return.

"Want to tell me how your afternoon went?" he asked, pulling away with a grin. "Or would you rather play Twenty Questions—strip-tease edition? I guess right, you take off a piece of clothing. You fake me out, I have to strip. The first one naked wins."

Seth gave him a confused look. "I don't think that's how it works."

Evan raised an eyebrow. "In my book, the first one naked always wins."

Seth pulled him in for another kiss. "I like how you think."

Evan slipped a hand down between them, cupping Seth's groin. "So what's it gonna be?"

Seth sighed. "Another rain check. I thought we should go to another site before it gets dark. Thirteen Bends Road. Ghost cars, shadow men, disembodied voices—"

Evan rolled his eyes. "Cockblocked—again—by ghosts," he said with exaggerated resignation.

"I promise to make it up to you," Seth added in his sexiest voice, the tone that made Evan immediately hard. "All night long."

Evan adjusted himself. "Gonna be hard to outrun a ghost with a stiffy. Now I've got to think about shredded wheat or something."

"Shredded wheat?"

"Can you think of anything less sexy?"

CAMPBELLS RUN ROAD in nearby Harmarville, aka Thirteen Bends Road, didn't look like the kind of spot people would tell urban legends about. "Are you sure this is the place?" Evan asked. The road was curvy, tree-lined in places, winding past fields or large open lawns in others.

Seth shrugged. "Just trying to check out the most prominent legends, in case there's a germ of truth to them. Stories say there was an orphanage that burned down out here, but others said it was a mine collapse. Take your pick between dead kids and dead miners, but people say they've seen orbs and spotted ghosts that look so real, they talk to them and don't realize it's a ghost until it vanishes."

"You think Thane had something to do with the orphanage?"

"No idea. Unfortunately, there's still too much we don't know, so we've got to run down the leads we've got."

Seth pulled the truck off to one side of the road. Before he could get out, Evan put a hand on his arm. "Hold on a sec. Let me try something." He pulled his slate and chalk out of his bag and drew the "sense undead" sigil, then touched it with his fingertips and sent his energy and will into it until the symbol gave a faint silver glow. He kept the connection for several breaths longer, then lifted his hand away.

"The lore says that if there'd been undead, the sigil should have glowed red. So, either I did it wrong, or we're probably okay."

"I think you did just fine," Seth replied, and Evan warmed at the pride in his lover's gaze.

"There've got to be mediums in Pittsburgh, right?" Evan asked as they got out of the truck and started to walk along the edge of the road. "How come they don't lay all these ghosts to rest?"

Despite the reassurance of the sigil, Evan and Seth both kept iron knives in hand. Just in case, Seth had a shotgun filled with salt rounds, and Evan had his Glock. A cold wind rustled the dead weeds along the ditch and moved through the bare bushes in the undergrowth. Evan felt a sense of sadness settle over him that didn't feel like his own, as if he were borrowing someone else's emotions.

"It's listed in that database I told you about—the one of known haunts that haven't proven dangerous," Seth replied. "I would assume mediums don't just wander around all day looking for restless ghosts. They'd never get anything done. They focus on the ones who come to them or the people who want to make a connection—or the ghosts that cause problems."

The wind gusted, and Evan shivered. "I don't know if it's ghosts or not, but this place is fucking with my mood."

"Mine, too. They say the orphanage burned down in the early 1900s. What I've found about Ewing Carmody—Thane's name at the time—puts him over near McKeesport, by the Youghiogheny River. Pretty far from here, although I guess anything's possible."

Evan stared out into the strip of woodland along the road. The longer they stayed, the more he felt they were being watched. He thought about pulling out his slate and drawing in most of the "banish spirits" sigil, but Seth caught his eye and shook his head as if he guessed his thoughts.

"If we need it, I'll say the spell. I think we're all right, for now."

Unlike in North Park, no freaky blue mist rose, and no words appeared etched in the snow. But Evan kept catching a glimpse of movement out of the corner of his eye, only to turn and see nothing there. More than once, he thought he spotted gray shapes among the underbrush, but the dim light from a cloudy afternoon made it difficult to know for certain.

"There!" Evan hissed, pointing at the featureless figure of a man standing inside the tree line. He should have been able to make out the face of a living person at that distance, but while the form was right, the face and the clothing were grayed out.

"Cue the orbs," Seth said quietly, as balls of light began to rise from the snow-covered banks like misdirected fireflies. Some of the orbs were just specks, while others hovered like glowing soap bubbles before winking out and reappearing elsewhere.

"What do they want?" Evan gripped his knife, keenly aware of the salt and iron mixture in his pockets.

"Maybe just to be acknowledged," Seth replied. "Maybe us seeing them helps the ghosts stay connected here."

"Why would they want to stay?"

"Because they don't know how to go on? I'm the wrong guy to ask." Seth slowly turned in a circle, but if he saw more than the vague shadows Evan glimpsed, he didn't let on.

"We're trying to stop a man you might have known as Ewing Carmody," Seth called out to the spirits. "A bad man who hurt people. We want to keep him from hurting anyone else. If you know something, please tell us."

They waited in silence as the forest around them seemed to hold its breath. The orbs hovered and bobbed but made no move to come closer. Neither did the gray figures. Evan found himself holding his breath. Then, one by one, the orbs vanished. The gray man faded into the forest gloom, and the other shadows disappeared. Evan felt the bleak mood shift, and his feelings were his own again.

"I guess they didn't have anything to tell us," Seth said as they headed back. "Or they couldn't make themselves heard."

When they returned to the truck, the snow was unmarked except for their boot prints. Three small handprints—child-sized—stood out against the black paint in white dust.

"Maybe they found another way to get the point across," Evan said, pointing. "Three prints. That's not just saying 'we're here.' That's a message."

Seth nodded. "Fifteen. Now we just have to figure out what the hell it means and why it's important. I found a private eye. Maybe I need to go looking for a medium."

5

SETH

"This is my associate, Evan," Seth said as Alex Wilson sat down on the other side of the booth. He and Evan had already agreed that it would be better not to give any more information than necessary to the private investigator, and that included letting on that they were together. Evan had promised he was fine with the slight deception, but now, Seth noticed an uneasiness that made him wonder if his boyfriend had changed his mind.

"Nice to meet you," Alex said smoothly. He had another Manila file and a new flash drive. "I got ahold of my contact in Blairsville about your Livermore question," he said. "I can't say that the answer is exciting, more like intriguing."

"How so?" Seth asked, trying to take Alex's measure. The PI had balked a little at looking into Matthew Easton's connection to the drowned city of Livermore. Now, he seemed a bit more enthused.

"I went out to Blairsville myself to poke around because my contact said they had all the Livermore records that survived in the basement of the town library—undigitized, of course," he said, rolling his eyes. "And I stopped by the Conemaugh Dam on the way. The lake is pretty, but it's weird to think that underneath the water is a whole town. Like Atlantis—only on purpose."

That was a bit more poetic than Seth had expected of the investigator. "Is anything still visible?"

Alex shook his head. "Not now. Maybe after a drought. From what I found out, they at least partially razed the buildings, although that would have left foundations and basements, maybe more. The graveyard is up on a hill, beyond the area that was flooded. Of course, there are ghost stories about it, although most of them get the facts all wrong. It's much more exciting to talk about the 'lost city of Livermore' and how it was 'flooded by a freak storm in one awful night.'" He used air quotes to set off the descriptions he had probably gotten from a cheesy ghost-hunting site.

Alex took a drink of his coffee. "The real story is a lot less sexy. The town had been in decline for half a century since the canal system lost out to the railroads. Most of the people and businesses had gone. When the government decided to build the dam, everyone had years' worth of notice and got a buy-out. Practical—but not nearly as a good a story."

"Thanks for checking it out," Seth replied. He flipped through the folder. A few fuzzy old photos of a man he assumed was Matthew Easton appeared. One of them was a formal portrait. The other two were pictures of workers inside the Livermore Bank and Trust. The photos looked like something for a newspaper article, with a dozen young men dressed in serious suits and two dour supervisors standing in the background. The names of the men were hand-written in graceful script beneath the picture.

"I can't imagine how Easton got himself murdered and dumped in Hell's Half Acre," Alex said, frowning. "It's harder to find information about people back then than it is now." He raised an eyebrow. "Respectable folks didn't get their names in the newspaper often. Still, I tracked Matthew's birth certificate, baptismal certificate—St. Agatha's Parish—no death certificate, since he officially went missing. A few mentions for academics, and then he received some local commendations for community service work he did through the bank. Nothing to suggest how a guy like him ended up dead in a swamp."

Seth took a picture of the photo with his phone and then blew it up.

"This man," he said, pointing to one of the bank supervisors. "Thaddeus Ramey. Know anything about him?"

Alex gave Seth a look like he'd lost his mind. "No, not off hand. Did he end up in the swamp, too?"

Seth shook his head. "It's hard to tell with the hat he's wearing, but he reminds me of someone."

Evan gave Seth a sidelong look that said he'd caught the reason for his partner's interest. The blurry photo might have captured Noson Thane on film.

"Since that photo was from 1939, you're going back a ways," Alex said. "But I do have copies of a couple more pictures that the reporter apparently shot but didn't use in the paper." He reached over to shuffle the papers, pulling out two from the center of the thin stack. One had a picture of three men sitting stiffly at their desks, while the other caught the same three men outside on the bank steps.

"That's Ramey," Alex noted, pointing with the tip of his ballpoint pen. "The other two men are Ronald King and David Boson. They were all senior managers with the Livermore bank and very involved in the community."

Seth and Evan leaned forward, squinting to make out Ramey's features. The interior shot at his desk had Ramey looking down at the crucial moment the shot was taken so that he wasn't looking directly at the camera, which made it impossible to see his features. In the outdoor picture, the brim of Ramey's Fedora shadowed his face.

"I'd like you to go back to the archives and see what you can find on Ramey," Seth said. "Send me your bill for the time you've put in so far. Something about this guy—my gut says he's got a story."

Alex gave Seth an appraising look. "I'm happy to look into anything you want," he replied. "But maybe if you could tell me a little more about the project you're working on, I could be more helpful."

Evan's hand tightened beneath the table on Seth's thigh, a warning. Seth gave a pleasant smile and did not look over at Evan. "You know how it is with journalists—we never want anyone to beat us to the scoop," he said. "I want to take a look at the murder swamp story from some angles no one has viewed it from before, and that means details about the victims and the people around them. How did the killings go on so long? Did the police miss crucial evidence? How did the killer get away with so many deaths without being caught?"

Alex drummed his fingers on the table for a moment. "I guess I'm just used to people with a less...academic...interest in crime," he said. "I'm a former cop. What PI isn't? My clients usually want me to track down evidence on someone who can get convicted and thrown in jail. You're chasing ghosts."

Alex had no idea how right he was, but Seth didn't dare enlighten him.

"There's actually a niche readership interested in True Crime classics," Evan spoke up. "Unsolved murders or high-profile deaths—the Black Dahlia killings, the Zodiac Killer, Jimmy Hoffa's disappearance." Seth was impressed at Evan's enthusiasm, and a little weirded out.

"Really?" Alex looked surprised.

Evan nodded. "Everyone wants to be the one who finally solves the crime, after all these years, I guess. I mean, everyone still talks about Jack the Ripper, and it's been over a hundred and fifty years. People still don't know for sure who he was."

He leaned forward with his best bartender smile. "Think about it. People watch *CSI*, and all those detective shows on TV, and there are these real-life—gruesome—unsolved mysteries. Now and then, you see an article about how a chance speeding ticket or a bit of trace DNA catches a serial killer who got away with murder for decades. Readers want to believe that they might be the master armchair sleuth who finally puts all the pieces together."

Evan lowered his voice conspiratorially. "Did you know, there are even services people pay to join that will send them a box of fake clues every month so they can join the fake hunt to catch a fake serial killer?"

Alex's eyebrows rose. Seth looked at Evan with equal surprise. "No shit?" Alex asked.

Evan nodded solemnly. "Yeah, and those box subscriptions aren't cheap. So this book...the murder swamp isn't as well-known as some of those other killings. It's fresh—you know what I mean? Not something that's been talked to death. So we're kinda keeping the details hush-hush because we don't want anyone to beat us to the gate."

Damn, if Seth hadn't known the truth, he would have bought

Evan's story hook, line, and sinker. That made him a little uncomfortable. He sometimes had to shade the truth when it came to hunting because normal people—and cops—definitely weren't believers in the supernatural. It never gave him pause because he wasn't trying to deceive anyone to cause them harm. Still, a lie was a lie, and he remembered how much it had strained his early relationship with Evan when his lover discovered that Seth had not told him the entire truth. Realizing that Evan was skilled in selling a story put the shoe on the other foot and made Seth squirm a bit internally.

"I guess I can see that," Alex allowed. Evan sat back, hiding his triumph, although he bumped Seth's leg under the table. "Thrill of the chase, even if there's no one left to bring to justice."

That wasn't quite true, but Seth knew Alex wouldn't believe the whole story.

"And there's another set of records that we could use your help on, for a project we're just starting," Seth said. "About Dixmont Hospital."

"I can't access medical records, even if they still existed," Alex said, eyes widening.

Seth quickly shook his head. "No, that's not what we need. Places like that have so many urban legends around them. Ghost stories, tall tales, that kind of thing. There was a doctor who might have worked there in the fifties or sixties—Roy Moser. There's not much about him online, and I was hoping that, as with the Livermore issue, you might be able to find some information in the non-digitized archives."

Alex tented his fingers and weighed his words before he spoke. "That's close enough to modern times that people from back then could still be alive. Maybe not Dr. Moser, but his close relatives or those of his patients. I'm hoping your publisher has a good lawyer. You don't want to find yourself on the wrong end of a lawsuit."

"We're not looking to cause any trouble," Evan said, working that million-watt bartender smile again. Evan wasn't exactly flirting with Alex, but his attentiveness made Seth a little jealous, even while Seth's upstairs brain recognized the value in Evan's diversion. "We definitely don't want any legal problems. Right now, we're not even sure Dr. Moser really existed. He might just be an urban legend. So that's the first part—finding out if he was actually for real."

Alex rubbed his jaw. "I guess I can do that. What you do with the information is on you—but people around these parts are still a bit protective about what happened at Dixmont," he added. "Aside from the ghost hunters, that is. The buildings are gone, but plenty of people had relatives there, so tread lightly."

"Got it," Seth promised with a smile. They wrapped up the meeting with a plan to reconnect in a few days. Seth and Evan let Alex leave first, pausing to finish their coffee and settle the bill.

Now that Alex was gone, Evan looked restless, maybe even upset. Seth gave him a curious look, but Evan only responded with a curt shake of his head, and Seth gathered that the other man didn't want to say anything where they could be overheard. They paid their check, got coffee to go, and headed out to the truck.

"I'm worried about bringing in an outsider," Evan said as soon as Seth had the Silverado on the road. "Alex could cause trouble."

"He doesn't have our full names. I pay cash. He has no idea what we're really doing with the information, or how to find us. The phone number he's got isn't going to give anything away, and neither is the email I gave him."

Evan's leg jiggled, a sure tell that the other man was upset. "He's a private fuckin' investigator," he replied. "He knows how to dig up dirt. It wouldn't take much digging to blow our cover."

Seth dared a glance at his boyfriend. Evan looked worried, maybe even a little angry. "If there were warrants out for us after what happened in Richmond, Milo and Toby would have given us a head's up. They have alerts set for that kind of thing. So do I. Nothing tied us to the fight in that tunnel. If he tracks me, he'll find out about Jesse and maybe that I spent some time in that hospital, but I didn't do anything wrong, and there's nothing on me except rumors. If he IDs you, there's even less to go on. He'll find out about the apartment and the fire at Treddy's, but you're not even a missing person—you still keep in touch with your old boss. So there's no story."

Evan didn't look convinced. "I just think he could become a problem. I wish you hadn't asked him to look into more stuff. I could do it. Now that I can drive the truck, I can hunt down those archives, and you wouldn't have to pay me."

Seth tried to figure out how to diffuse the tension. "I know it's a risk, using Alex. But there's no way he can confirm or debunk that we're working on the book. There's no publisher to call, no newspaper editor to check up on us with. Nowadays, you say you're writing a book, and you write one. It's not like it used to be."

"I know," Evan said. He ran a hand over his mouth, and he was still bouncing a bit in his seat. "It's just...I spent so much time worrying that Mike would find me, it's hard to give anything out. And now we're flying under the radar, and attracting attention from the cops would be a bad thing—not like it's ever a good thing. What if someone traced the casings from the shots you fired at Valac? Or Jackie?" he asked, getting more worked up.

"Hey," Seth said in a quiet voice. He reached over to put his hand on Evan's thigh and gave a squeeze. "The tunnel collapsed with a big, fiery explosion, remember?"

Evan looked away. "Not really. There was a loud noise, I fell down, and you were on top of me. I wasn't paying attention to anything else because I thought we were both going to die."

"Yeah, well. So did I for a few minutes there. But my point is, no one had any reason to poke around in the tunnel debris, and there wouldn't have been much left if they did." He cleared his throat. "And even if they did find casings, the gun was unregistered, bought under the table from another hunter. There's no paper trail."

"I'm not sure that makes me feel better, actually," Evan said with a sigh. "I'm still adjusting to being an outlaw."

Seth stiffened. "I didn't know you felt like that." Shit. He thought Evan was getting used to the "new normal" of the two of them hunting together, but had he been wrong? Was Evan still on the fence about their future? He couldn't blame him if he were—a lot of hunting involved living in the shadows, staying off the radar, avoiding a footprint that could be traced. Some lawbreaking—hacking computer files, picking locks, breaking and entering, trespassing, and other infractions —went with the nature of the job. That's why only people whose loss and grief led to obsession usually got into the work, and those who did rarely looked forward to a long life. Milo and Toby were the exceptions to the rule.

Evan's hand closed over his. "I'm sorry," Evan said. "I didn't mean that the way it came out. Well, I guess it's kinda true, the outlaw thing. But I understand why it has to be. And why it's important. Because if we don't stop the witch-disciples, who will? No one's done it in a hundred years, and they'll just keep on killing unless we do something about it."

He let out a long breath. "It's not just because of what they did to Jesse, or what Valac tried to do to me. When I went to the coffee shop and I met Brandon, he was so alive. Seemed like a genuinely good guy. And Thane would carve him up as a sacrifice to level-up his own power without a second thought. Not just Brandon, but all the other deputies' descendants. And you," he added quietly.

Seth gave him a curious look, unwilling to speak and break the moment.

"You haven't caught the disciple that killed Jesse. He meant to kill you. So if we don't get all the warlocks, he'll come back for you the next time the cycle goes around." Evan's hand tightened around Seth's. "I'm not going to let that happen." His voice had gone from angry to resolute. "So quit worrying. I'm staying right here, with you."

Seth hadn't realized how tense he had gotten until he heard those words. His shoulders loosened, and he felt like he could breathe again. "You're right, about the risk with Alex," Seth admitted. "But I figured you were more valuable chasing down the stuff you've been looking at —the kind of thing you need to know the whole story to understand. And I've got a full plate of my own pieces that can't be farmed out."

Evan nodded. "So the pieces you've given Alex make sense. Just… have a plan in mind in case he double-crosses us, or freaks out."

"Already working on it," Seth promised, giving Evan's hand a squeeze.

"Where are we going?" Evan asked, noticing that they weren't headed back to the campground.

"Would you believe, Zombieland?" Seth replied with a smirk. Evan raised his eyebrows and tilted his head, waiting for the explanation.

"What is that, some kind of freaky amusement park?"

Seth laughed. "Nope. It's actually back near New Castle and West Pittsburg—and the murder swamp. Hillsville, Pennsylvania. Another place with urban legends that might have something to do with one of Thane's different identities, since we know he was in the area when he was Andrew Wiegand—and maybe even afterward, if my hunch about Livermore pans out."

"You think Thaddeus Ramey, the bank manager, was Thane."

Seth nodded. "Maybe. That would fill in the 1940s, and it would be after he dropped his Wiegand persona. When I said Ramey reminded me of someone, it was Dr. Brunrichter. Some people say Brunrichter didn't actually exist—which would strengthen the case for him being Thane—because there's so little documentation. But I found a single picture, supposedly taken at an event he attended before the Congelier House debacle, of a man who've supposed to be Brunrichter. It's another lousy picture, and he's not exactly front and center, but the build, the way he stands, what I could make of his features—it could be the same guy."

"And if Alex hits pay dirt on Dr. Moser, that brings us up to the 1960s," Evan supplied.

"Yeah, still fifty years behind where we need to be, but it's progress. I think I have a lead on what Thane might have been doing in the seventies and eighties. No big surprise—a cop."

"Fuck." Back in Richmond, Valac's most recent persona had been a police officer, which gave him plenty of leeway and a built-in level of community trust to cover his actions.

"I'm running a program trying to ID any cops in the surrounding area that just disappeared," Seth said. "It's slow-going because Thane didn't stay in the city proper. He moved around to these little towns— Livermore, West Pittsburg, Gibsonia out by Blue Mist Road. That's a lot of ground to cover—as I'm sure he intended," he added, frustration clear in his voice.

"We should have time. We're still early."

Seth shifted in his seat. "My gut keeps telling me Thane is going to make his move before Halloween. I don't want to chance it. I feel like time's already running out."

"Then we'll just have to beat him to the punch," Evan said. He took in the scenery around them. "Now...tell me about Zombieland."

~

"THIS IS A BIKE TRAIL?" Evan turned in a slow circle, taking in the wooded area and the concrete railway bridge over Coffee Run, a sluggish, brown creek. The Stavich Bike Trail ran through Robinson's Crossing, near the Mahoning River. The area around the trail looked less like woodlands and more like the abandoned remains of old industrial grounds slowly being reclaimed by the forest.

"Now it is," Seth replied. "But the area's been the site of some murders and bodies left in shallow graves—they caught the killers in those cases, but that kind of thing leaves a mark on a place. Or an energy signature that attracts assholes to a place where murder's been done before."

"Okay," Evan replied, with a look like he was trying to figure out a sinister connection. "You're gonna have to clue me in."

"There are lots of local legends about a glowing tombstone over in the St. Lawrence Cemetery, unexplained bobbing lights over by the Hilltown Bridge, and eternal flame 'zombie torches' in the woods."

"Seriously? Zombie torches?"

Seth chuckled. "Those I can explain away. Gas vents to what remains of some old oil and gas fields that were abandoned back in the fifties. But what caught my eye more than that was the legend of the Blood House witch and the Hook Man."

"You mean like in the movies? The guy with a hook for a hand who creeps up on teenagers making out on some dark back road and scratches at the window with his bloody hook before he smashes the glass and carves them up as a warning not to have sex?"

Seth just stared at him. "Jesus, Evan. What movies have you been watching?"

"Pretty much every teen slasher flick ever made. You know—don't be a camp counselor who sneaks off into the woods to make out with one of the other hot staffers because some guy with a weird athletic cup on his face will kill you."

Seth covered his face with his hands. "That's not a cup. That's a hockey mask. You really don't pay any attention to sports, do you?"

"As little as possible, and none now that I don't have to work at the bar," Evan replied cheerfully.

Seth gave an exasperated sigh, but his grin was fond. "So, Hook Man. Maybe not quite like the movies, but you've got the gist of it. Didn't get a lot of details about the witch, except that the stories say she carried off children and ate them."

"Or sacrificed them to get a power boost from a dead master warlock," Evan said. "In other words, Thane snatching victims for his ritual."

"Possible. Especially given that we're close to places we know he was, in New Castle and the swamp."

"You're not going to try to summon the Hook Man, right? Because I am not going to get sexy with you out here in the woods just so we can see if he shows up. I can't imagine he's going to like two guys going at it any more than he likes straight couples getting hot and heavy in the back seat."

Seth just shook his head. "You really are adorable. No, we're not going to summon Hook Man, and much as I'd like to sex you up anywhere, anytime, I don't want to get frostbite in sensitive places."

They walked up and down the bike trail, crunching through the unbroken snow. At this time of the year, the greenway seemed lonely and a little sad, dormant until warmer weather beckoned cyclists once more. Despite that, Seth didn't feel the same pensiveness steal into his thoughts that he had sensed on Thirteen Bends Road or some of the other sites.

"I'm not getting the heebie-jeebies, which is strange," Evan remarked as if he guessed Seth's thoughts. "At the other places, I felt like we were being watched. But here, it just feels like we've gone for a walk in the woods. The very, very cold woods," he added with a side-long look at Seth.

"Same here." Seth kicked at a stone and walked closer to the trail's edge, peering into the thin underbrush. No snow-covered old house foundations or crumbled cement steps, no depression in the ground to show where a driveway had once been. Just rusted pipes rising to mark the gas wells.

"If you're out there, show yourselves," Seth called. "We're trying to catch the bad man who harmed you. Thaddeus Ramey. Andrew Wiegand. Noson Thane. Tell us what you know so we can stop him."

They waited in silence, standing back to back so they could watch all around. Nothing moved. Seth had a grip on his iron knife, and Evan had a sawed-off with salt rounds. A faint wind off the river stirred the tall, brown weeds. Overhead in the bare trees, a bird tweeted, and squirrels scolded them.

"I don't think anyone's coming," Evan murmured.

"Me, neither." He didn't know whether to be frustrated, disappointed, or relieved. "So either the legends about this area are just that —stories—or the ghosts have moved on. I'm not getting any vibes that there's anything here except us and the squirrels."

"Well, we got a nice walk," Evan replied. They remained alert on the trek back to the truck, but when they arrived, they found that nothing had been disturbed. No mysterious writing, no marks.

"I feel a little cheated," Evan said as he got into the truck.

"I know what you mean. Not that I wanted to fight off a bunch of vengeful spirits, but I keep hoping that we're going to find the missing piece that makes everything else fit together. And I guess it isn't here," Seth replied, starting the truck and turning around. He surprised himself as much as Evan when he stopped.

"When you borrowed Mrs. Kelly's Toyota while I was out, did you really think I was going to throw a fit?" Seth asked. "Because if I made you think that, I'm sorry." The stillness of the woods around them had given him time to think while they waited, and Evan's reaction weighed on his mind.

Evan shifted in his seat and looked away. "I didn't know how you'd react," he replied quietly.

Seth watched Evan's profile. "I meant what I said about not wanting you to feel stuck. You're a good driver. I'm going to worry, regardless."

Evan sighed and slumped a little in his seat. "I don't have a good feel for moods," he confessed. "I mean, when I worked at the bar, it was different, because I wasn't emotionally involved. I seemed to do all right reading total strangers. But my family kept feelings bottled up, and they didn't usually say what they meant or say things directly.

They kept secrets because they were taught to be ashamed of everything. And then Mike—"

Evan blinked back tears, and Seth froze, uncertain whether to reach out for him or remain still. He ended up staying where he was, barely breathing.

"Mike's mood swings were pretty intense, and they could come out of nowhere. I never knew whether he was going to laugh or take a swing at me, and it could vary day by day. So I guess I just fell back on old habits when you started asking whether I'd gone out. I'm sorry. I didn't really think you'd hit me."

Seth forced himself to relax. He dared to slide his hand close to Evan without touching, and Evan covered it with his own. "Good. That's good," Seth said. "I just thought I should ask, in case I did something—"

"It's not you," Evan said. "It's me. And I am so fuckin' tired of having Mike's ghost follow me around." He managed a watery smile. "Think any of your witchy friends could do an exorcism?"

"I think he either has to be dead or a real demon for that to work," Seth replied, his voice hoarse from unshed tears. Damn, he hated to see Evan torn up like this, hated the feeling of helplessness that the revelations about Evan's past caused for both of them.

"Close enough to the demon part," Evan whispered.

Seth cleared his throat. "Look, maybe getting out of the trailer a little more would help. It's overcast all day, and the RV isn't very big. You're used to having lots of people around at Treddy's, and it's got to be a big change being just the two of us all the time. So maybe going back to Kona Café and keeping an eye on Brandon is the way to go. Stay low-profile, watch the other regulars, see what you find out. And in the meantime, we'll find the security cam footage and start going through it. Maybe we'll catch a break."

Evan turned to face him, and his smile was confident this time. "I like it being just the two of us," he said, giving Seth's hand a squeeze. "But I agree—going back to the coffee shop feels right to me. I'll make sure I have my phone and pepper spray or some kind of weapon that won't get me arrested," he added with a smirk. "You're right—the gray days are getting to me."

"Welcome to Pennsylvania in the winter," Seth replied. "If it's anything like Indiana, it'll stay this way until April."

Evan shuddered. "Fuck that. We had pansies blooming all winter in Richmond, redbud trees in February and azaleas by late March. I hope the rest of the witch-disciples have the decency to go someplace with better weather." The look in his eyes was still troubled, but his smile seemed genuine.

They drove out of the parking lot, and it occurred to Seth that while they hadn't run into any vengeful spirits, perhaps in another way, they'd confronted a ghost of a different kind, after all.

6

EVAN

"I ADMIRE A MAN WHO KNOWS WHAT HE LIKES." BRANDON TOOK EVAN'S order for a mocha latte, hold the whipped cream, and grinned.

"I don't know whether it's knowing what I like, or being stuck in a rut," Evan admitted. It was the third day in a row that he'd come to Kona Café, and he found himself looking forward to the friendly vibe of the place, as well as his interactions with Brandon. In another situation—one without a crazy, homicidal witch-disciple—he could imagine them getting to be friends. Seth would like him, Evan decided.

"Oh, now don't say that," Brandon replied. "Nothing wrong with liking what you like. But if you ever feel adventurous, we have some really good combinations you won't find anywhere else," he added. "Something for every taste."

"I'll keep that in mind," Evan promised, looking at the sweets in the pastry case and trying to talk himself out of a particularly gooey treat. Despite the snow, he and Seth had still gone for an early morning run, although they took their sparring to the campground's community room, which was deserted this time of year. He wondered whether he had burned off enough calories from the workout and the cold to let him get away with the confection and reminded himself that if he ate one every day that he came to the shop, it would add up.

"See something you want?" Brandon asked as he frothed the milk for Evan's latte.

Evan sighed. "Yes, but I'd better not. At least, not every day."

"Something to look forward to, then," Brandon said, bringing the drink back to the counter. "We have that selection every Monday and Wednesday. Or until the bakers change out the menu for spring. Keeps people interested."

Evan had already sampled the baked goods on a prior visit so he could attest to how delicious they were. "I'll remember that," he promised, taking his drink and leaving a tip. The shop was surprisingly quiet today, and for once, there was no line behind him.

"So what brings you to Emsworth?" Brandon asked, leaning on the pastry cooler. "Or have you always been in town, and just found your way to good coffee?"

Evan hated to lie, but he could hardly tell the truth. "Just moved in a week ago," he replied. "Getting to know the area. And I never pass up a good cup of coffee."

"I'm Emsworth born and bred," Brandon said, with the kind of candor that came as part of an optimistic outlook and a belief that people were generally good. Evan's experiences had badly tarnished both for him, and he found Brandon's openness refreshing even as he worried it might get him hurt. Then again, the man was old enough to make his own decisions. "Family's been in the area for over a hundred years. Moved here from the Midwest and never looked back."

Evan's heart thudded as he realized that he quite probably knew more about the reason for that move than Brandon himself. "Really?" he managed. "Must be a great place to live." He hoped his voice sounded steady.

Brandon nodded. "I left for a while when I went to college—Penn State, go Nittany Lions—but I knew I wanted to come back here when I finished." He looked wistful, and Evan wondered if it was because he was still doing the EMT work part-time. "I lucked into the job here, and it's a lot of fun. Nice people. It's just coffee," he said, looking down as his cheeks pinked a bit, "but I figure that I can make everyone's morning better by being cheerful. I know that sounds silly—"

Evan shook his head. "No. I get it. I used to tend bar. People would tell me stuff I couldn't believe, and I realized I was the only person they felt they could talk to. It's not silly. Having a smile and a friendly face start off your morning is way better than road rage. I'm sure it makes a difference all day long for some folks."

"My grandma was always telling me to 'bloom where you're planted,'" Brandon said, moving to wipe down the espresso machine during the rare lull. "I don't think I'll be a barista forever, but it's a nice gig for now."

"I knew I wasn't going to be a bartender for the rest of my life, but it was what I needed at the time," Evan confided, finding it easy to talk to Brandon.

"What are you doing now?" Brandon asked. Evan felt his smile go brittle.

"Graphic design," he replied. "It's nice to be able to work from anywhere." He glanced down to the computer messenger bag he carried.

Brandon nodded. "I see a lot of folks in here, working remotely. Not something I can do. My other job is being an EMT."

Evan relaxed as he realized Brandon wasn't going to probe about his reasons for leaving Treddy's. "That must be exciting."

Brandon frowned. "I'm not sure that's a word I'd pick. Nerve-wracking, when we need to get someone to the hospital and traffic is moving too slow. Happy, when we get to deliver a baby or save a life. Then there are other nights—" He didn't have to finish his sentence.

"It's important work," Evan said before Brandon could feel embarrassed. "You make a difference. Most people can't say that."

"Oh, I figure everyone makes a difference somewhere, to someone," Brandon replied. "Maybe we just don't realize it." The bell above the door jangled as a customer came in, Evan's cue to find a table.

"Thanks!" Evan said, grabbing his cup. "Enjoyed the chat." He retreated to the table he had begun to think of as "his" and set up his computer. Today, he had some design work to do for clients, and that lifted his spirits. No matter how scary or chaotic the hunting side of his life seemed, Evan was making real progress on two things that meant a lot—his relationship with Seth and his dream of earning a living from his art and photography skills.

Evan sipped his coffee and looked around the coffee shop. Now that he had an idea from the old photos of what Noson Thane might look like, he scrutinized the other patrons, but no one resembled man from the pictures. Everyone was either too old, too young, the wrong build, or female. He wasn't sure whether to feel disappointed or relieved. Disappointed because he wanted to get a lead on Thane's current identity. Relieved because Evan had no illusions about his ability to go up against a dark warlock on his own, and he knew he wouldn't be able to protect Brandon or himself if Thane decided to make his move.

He sat back, trying to imagine the man in the faded pictures in modern clothing, without his Fedora. Would he be bald or have hair—or wear a ball cap? Had he gone upscale in this persona, or was he slumming as a regular Joe?

Evan glanced up at the security camera facing the seating area. Seth had hacked into the café's system and downloaded a month's worth of video—as much as the archive retained. They'd made popcorn and watched several days of recordings but hadn't spotted anyone yet who might be Thane. It wasn't the most exciting viewing, even when they sped up the replay. Then again, they still had most of the video to go through yet, so Evan kept hoping they'd catch a break.

The coffee was strong, hot, and sweet—kind of like Seth, Evan thought. He enjoyed his drink and let his mind wander. Among many yet-unanswered questions was what Thane was using for an amulet and an anchor. In Richmond, Corson Valac had worn a necklace with magical power and stored some of his essence in a sealed container hidden in a mausoleum. Toby and Milo had told them the amulet and anchor could be anything, depending on the whim of the witch-disciple. But it was important to figure out because destroying the anchor and separating the disciple from his amulet would seriously weaken the warlock's power.

He called up the old photos on his phone, settling back into his chair against the wall so no one could see. The pictures of Thaddeus Ramey were little help since a medallion or charm could be hidden under his starched shirt. Otherwise, the only visible elements were his hat, his watch, and what looked like a tie-tack. The timepiece caught

Evan's eye, since he had a fondness for snazzy wristwatches, and it reminded him of one his grandfather wore. Evan huffed in disappointment and closed the picture. Ewing Carmody and Andrew Wiegand had been working men, and no photographs of them had surfaced yet. Evan resolved to ask Seth about the Brunrichter picture. Maybe Alex would find something on Dr. Moser, or Seth would unearth photos when he found details of Thane's cop identity. It galled Evan to hit another dead-end.

Simultaneous beeps and buzzes told him he had a text message and new email. He glanced at his phone first. *"Welcome to Emsworth! Take $1 off your next hot drink at Kona Café,"* the text message read. *That's weird. I haven't signed up to anything with my phone number,* Evan thought.

One of the emails was from Seth—additional information for Evan to sift through in a more private location. Another was an inquiry about pricing from Evan's website. The third email sent a chill down Evan's spine.

"Did you enjoy your visit to Hillsdale? Rate your experience in St. Lawrence Church Cemetery."

Evan stared at the email and felt the blood drain from his face. He'd seen other emails pop up inviting him to add ratings after he made an online purchase. But he hadn't even had his computer with him when he and Seth drove out to Hillsdale. They hadn't stopped to talk to anyone or even gone to a local drive-through. *Shit. How did that happen?*

Evan walked the few steps to the counter, bringing his phone with him. "Can I use this coupon on a drink today?" he asked when Brandon came over.

Brandon studied the image, puzzled. "I've never seen a coupon like this before. That's really weird." He called over to the other barista who was restocking the fridge. "Hey, Bree? Do you know anything about a phone coupon?"

His co-worker, a dark-haired woman in her early twenties with a set of piercings down her left ear and a small ring in her right eyebrow, came over and stared at Evan's phone. "Nope. Then again, Rich forgets to tell us sometimes when he signs up for a great 'deal' of a promotion." She used air quotes, and her tone suggested the bargain was likely to be anything but a good investment.

Brandon looked up at Evan apologetically. "I'm afraid it's probably a scam," he said. "But I've got discretion to offer a discount, so let me knock a buck off your refill and call it square, okay?"

"Thanks," Evan replied with a smile, appreciating the gesture. "But you don't have to—"

Movement by the door caught his eye. Alex Wilson walked in, carrying an insulated lunch bag. He went around to the end of the counter, and Brandon met him with a broad grin.

"You left this in the kitchen," Alex said, standing close to Brandon as he handed off the bag.

Brandon gave Alex a peck on the cheek. "Thanks for bringing it. Sorry you had to go out of your way."

"I don't mind an excuse to get some good coffee," Alex said with a smile. His expression and body language confirmed that they were a couple. Only then did he glance toward the register—and froze when he saw Evan.

"Hi," Evan said, hoping he looked less freaked out than he felt. Running into the PI here was likely to raise suspicions. Catching him chatting up the investigator's boyfriend—no matter how innocently—couldn't end well.

"Evan, isn't it?" Alex said. He smiled, but it was as cool as his voice.

"You two know each other?" Brandon asked, glancing from one to the next as if trying to pick up on a subtext he missed.

"We've met," Evan replied, hoping his expression didn't betray his nervousness. *I've got every right to be here, drinking coffee, like anyone else. Seth said he didn't tell Alex where we camped. He shouldn't know I'm not close to home. For all he knows, we just live up the road. Stay cool, don't blow it.*

Brandon set the refill coffee on the counter, and Evan slid the discounted payment to him in return, putting the "coupon" dollar into the tip jar.

"Just thought I'd get some fresh air and a change of scenery," Evan said since Alex kept looking at him as if his stare might wring a confession. "And good coffee." He hoisted the cup like a visual aid. "Nice to see you again," he said to Alex. "Thanks," he added with a nod toward Brandon. He walked the few steps to where he'd left his laptop, which he'd made sure to keep an eye on.

Evan sat back down, opening his browser to look for Christmas presents for Seth since he felt too rattled to do anything else. Alex and Brandon talked for a moment at the counter until more customers filed in. Then Alex's tall frame appeared, looming over Evan's chair.

"Somehow, I had the impression you and Seth were out in the suburbs," Alex said. His inflection sounded disinterested, but Evan wasn't fooled. Alex was an ex-cop, and he knew how to question a suspect. Evan felt certain his presence at the place Alex's boyfriend worked sent up a red flag to the investigator, especially since he was sure Alex already harbored doubts about their "research" project.

"Not too far away," Evan replied, hoping he sounded pleasant and not spooked. "I found this place on one of the rating sites—a thousand satisfied coffee drinkers can't be wrong!"

"Hmm," Alex said. "You guys travel a lot for your work?"

"Enough to rack up some nice hotel reward points," Evan said with a smile. He had experience fending off overly personal inquiries by barflies that couldn't take "no" for an answer, and doing so without ruffling feathers. Now he called on that ability to deflect Alex's concerns, although from the suspicion in the other man's eyes, he didn't think he had completely succeeded.

Is he jealous? Does he think I was flirting with Brandon? Evan remembered that he and Seth had avoiding appearing like a couple when they met with the private investigator. Now, he wasn't as sure that had been a good idea, but there was no way to fix it without making the situation even more awkward.

"I'll tell Seth I ran into you," Evan said with his best customer service smile. "I know he's looking forward to seeing what you find out."

"Yeah," Alex replied. "I'm headed out that way now. I thought I might ask my partner if he has any contacts. He's been in the business longer than I have. No telling what he knows." The words were delivered in a neutral tone, but Evan's intuition picked up a hint of threat. He wracked his brain to remember anything Seth had said about the other investigator Alex worked for and came up blank. He didn't like the implication and felt more sure than ever that bringing in an outsider had been a mistake.

"Thanks," Evan replied. "I'm sure we can count on your discretion."

"Oh, believe me. I understand the need for keeping secrets." A glint in Alex's eye and the slight tightening of his jaw suggested that his intent wasn't quite as friendly as his voice. "I'll be in touch."

Evan watched Alex go and then glanced toward the counter, only to see Brandon look away a fraction of a second too late. No doubt he'd been watching Evan and Alex interact and trying to figure out what the fuck was going on.

The coffee no longer tasted as good, and he no longer felt comfortable in the café. He gathered up his things, tucked his laptop into his bag, and grabbed his cup. Evan gave a casual wave to Brandon, who returned the gesture but looked confused, maybe even a little worried. Fearing he'd just fucked everything up, Evan hurried to the Toyota and headed back to the campground.

"THERE'S no reason for Alex to make anything more out of it than you crossed paths unexpectedly," Seth said an hour later when they were back in the truck on their way to check out what remained of Livermore for themselves. In addition to the lead on Thane's persona as Ramey, legend held a witch responsible for the town's decline and "drowning." Alex might be checking out the archived records, but Seth and Evan were going to put boots on the ground and see what they found.

"I couldn't shake the feeling that somehow, he thought it was suspicious for me to be there."

"The guy chases cheating spouses, deadbeat dads, and insurance fraudsters all day. He's probably suspicious of his own mother," Seth countered. "That kind of thing eats away at a person after a while, makes them see shadows everywhere. Or else he's just a jealous bastard who thinks everyone's hitting on his man."

"Not my type," Evan replied. "I'm off the market."

"Good to know. So am I."

Evan frowned. "Oh, I've been getting some spammy emails and texts. Can you check that my GPS didn't get activated somehow?"

"Sure, just remind me when we get back," Seth replied.

They fell silent for a few minutes. "You find anything else out about the cop—Thane's old ID?"

"The search I ran gave me a short list, and I'm still checking them all out, but my money's on a guy named Kendrick Higgins." Seth sighed. "It was easier when Valac got cute about keeping his initials the same. Thane apparently doesn't have the same hang-up. But what I've found so far squares with the pattern—has no footprint before he shows up in 1972, disappears again in 1989."

"Ballsy bastard, sticking around for so long without switching IDs."

Seth shrugged. "Different warlock, different approach. I think this guy likes taking risks, and he's gotten away with it for so long without anyone looking, I'm hoping he's gotten a little careless."

"You think Alex will still turn in the report you asked for?" Evan said, drifting back to the previous topic.

Seth frowned. "He'd better. I'm paying him."

"What about mentioning it to his partner?"

"I imagine they trade information all the time, bounce things off each other. Sorta like cops—it's still confidential if it stays within the unit. I'm not going to worry about it—at least, not yet."

The drive to Livermore didn't take as long as Evan expected. "If the city's underwater, what do you think we're going to find?" he asked.

"Not sure. There's a cemetery and some old bridges. Also, an abandoned tunnel."

"Oh, joy." Valac had chosen the long-disused Church Hill Tunnel in Richmond for the site of his final ritual, and Evan still saw it in his nightmares.

"As long as Thane isn't around, it's just an old tunnel," Seth reminded him.

"Yeah. I know. It's fine," Evan said, not wanting to let on that the thought bothered him. *I can't go through the rest of my life letting that bastard make me afraid,* Evan thought, drawing on the stubborn streak that had always been a mixed blessing. *Not of Valac, and not of stalker-Mike. I won't let them take my sanity away from me.*

They parked near the cemetery, a lonely collection of old tombstones and obelisks dating from before the 1950s back into the late 1800s. The graveyard sat atop a hill overlooking what had once been the town of Livermore and was now a man-made lake. Evan didn't know whether the spot was really haunted or not, but it felt desolate and forgotten.

"Someone's still paying to have the place mowed, or it would be hip-deep in old weeds," Seth observed.

"Maybe it was part of the deal when the townspeople sold out to the state," Evan mused. "People who were homeowners back then would be getting pretty old now, so they've probably hired out the maintenance." In another decade, or when the money ran out, the Livermore cemetery would look like many of the other old graveyards he and Seth had visited—overgrown and derelict. He couldn't blame spirits that hung around for feeling annoyed over being forgotten.

A ping on Seth's phone drew his attention. "Alex sent me a new file," he said. "Signal's not strong enough out here to download the attachment." He met Evan's gaze. "So, whatever he took out of your run-in at the coffee place, he still delivered the work."

"Very professional," Evan replied, unconvinced. Seth chuckled, but let it go.

They went back to the truck and drove down farther into the park. The massive cut-stone footings for bridges and trestles still remained, jutting up from the water, though the trains and track were long gone. As they followed the trail toward the reservoir, they passed several bridges made of the same hand-hewn blocks of stone. On a winter afternoon, they gambled no one would be around to notice their intrusion with the truck.

"I can't even imagine what it took to build those," Evan said as he stared at the stone archways, marveling at the solid construction that remained standing after a century of abandonment.

"Solid—and beautiful," Seth replied. "People back then intended for the things they built to last forever."

Despite the cold, the drive was pleasant and peaceful. Seth reached out a gloved hand, and Evan took it, enjoying the scenery around the snow-covered trail that in better weather might be alive with bikers and joggers, dogs and kids.

"No one actually drowned when they flooded the city," Evan spoke up after a while. "That's part of the 'curse' story, but it didn't happen. And for the record, they also didn't film that famous zombie movie in Livermore, either."

"Spoilsport," Seth teased. "I bet you're impossible to beat at trivia games."

Evan chuckled. "I used to work the upstairs bar at Treddy's sometimes when they ran weekend game nights. I think I've heard the trivia questions so many times, I probably memorized them. Those—and the karaoke songs."

"You're safe from me dragging you to karaoke night," Seth promised. "Unless you get nostalgic. Then you might be able to get me to go watch you—with suitable incentives and rewards," he added, giving Evan a lecherous wink.

"Good to know I can bribe you with sex. But I think you're safe from karaoke for the foreseeable future," Evan replied.

They fell silent for a while. "Since Alex was looking into Dixmont for us, I tried to track down the orphanage records," Seth said. "It helped that I could narrow it down to 1915—from the clue the ghosts gave us."

"And?"

"The historical association required a donation to dig out the boxes they had in their basement," Seth reported. "They were dusty enough to make me almost stop breathing a few times. A hundred years is a long time to store paper. But I found a mention in a ledger from 1915 that a 'Mr. Carmine' had come to pick up two of the older boys for work at the Union Sewer Pipe company in June, and that he came back for two more in September. No notation of the names of the boys he took or whether they ever came back."

"If they were teenagers, the orphanage was probably happy to be rid of them," Evan said with a sigh. "They would have probably tossed them out as soon as they were sixteen—maybe younger. And if Carmine was Carmody, he might have made it seem like a good job opportunity."

Seth nodded. "If the boys were ready to age out of the system, no one would have noticed if they never came back. And if Carmody wasn't sent by Union Sewer Pipe, then the company would never have realized the boys didn't arrive."

"One more way Thane's gotten away with murder all these years," Evan said.

By now, they were closing in on the Bow Ridge tunnels, two abandoned and blocked railway passages. Evan supposed that the road would have been pretty in the summer, lush with trees and bushes in full leaf. But today, the unbroken cloud cover and chill wind was starting to weigh on Evan's mood.

"Too bad it's winter," Seth remarked. "I bet this is gorgeous in the spring. There's plenty of wild rhododendrons and mountain laurel," he added, with a nod toward bushes on the hillside. "It wouldn't seem quite so deserted in bloom."

"If Thaddeus Ramey was in Livermore in the 1940s, then he would have known about the plan to flood the town before it happened," Evan thought aloud. "Which means that if he had anything valuable here—like an anchor—he had time to move it so it wouldn't be stuck at the bottom of a lake."

"We hope," Seth agreed. Back in Richmond, Seth and Evan had originally thought Valac might have buried his anchor in one of the burial plots of his false personas. Then Seth realized that the witch-disciple might have his own reasons for wanting to be able to retrieve his anchor a little more easily than needing to dig up a grave. "Because if it's down there, there's no good way to bring it up."

"I doubt he hid it at the orphanage," Evan replied. "And I'm not sure he ever was in Zombieland. I guess it could be in the ruins of the 'witch house' on Blue Mist Road. How about the Union Sewer Pipe company? Is there anything left of it?"

"Haven't gotten to check it out," Seth replied. "From what's online, I'd say it's just ruins. So—it's a possibility."

"Do you have any idea what we're looking for? Because if he left anything here, and it's not underwater, it's likely to be in the cemetery, near the support footings on one of those bridges, or in the tunnels," Evan said.

"Or it could be somewhere around the old Dixmont property. The mental hospital was torn down in 2006, but there are still some outbuildings and maintenance structures standing," Seth answered. "Dixmont is a contender—it was built in 1864, so it would have been around when Thane came here around 1900. I don't think he'd have hidden something in a private home—like the witch house or the Congelier mansion. Too vulnerable and the ownership would change frequently." Seth shook his head. "I think he'll pick somewhere institutional, industrial—more permanent."

"If Thane—Ramey when he lived in Livermore—killed Matthew Easton after he came here, he took a chance hauling him all the way back to the murder swamp."

"You're assuming he would have killed Easton here and taken the body to bury. If he lured Easton to travel with him—maybe even by train, which would have been fairly quick—he could have killed Easton in the swamp and come back alone," Seth suggested. "Maybe Thane had a 'type' for his extra killings. Most serial killers do. Blond, brunette, ginger, certain build, temperament. Easton was just the unlucky one to draw Thane's attention."

"Or he's the one we found out about," Evan pointed out. "The records from back then are spotty. Thane probably didn't make a habit of picking his 'battery-charger' sacrifices from groups that would get noticed."

"And when he was working on the railroad as Wiegand, he had his choice of hobos and transient workers," Seth added. "But as a bank manager in a small town, he had to be careful to cover his tracks. Easton went missing right around the time Wiegand became Ramey. So maybe he relied on old habits while he figured out his new environment."

If anyone had told Evan six months ago that he'd be trying to second-guess a century-old mass murderer, he'd have laughed out loud. Now, solving the puzzle was not funny at all.

Seth stopped the truck, and they got out. "There's the first remaining tunnel," Seth said, pointing to a tangle of underbrush on the slope of the Bow Ridge Mountain. "The original tunnel from 1820 is completely underwater. This one was built in 1864. You can see where the railroad bridge was." He pointed to the massive support pylons that remained, still rising from the Conemaugh River.

They scrambled up the incline. Behind the scrub vegetation, the arch of the old tunnel was still clearly visible. Snow drifted against a chain-link fence that blocked access, though a determined vandal would be able to climb over the barricade. Icicles formed stalactites from the ceiling and frozen stalagmites from the ground. Evan felt his heart begin to race at the sight of the dark passageway.

"The other end of this tunnel is underwater," Seth said. "So it's plugged about ten feet in."

"I'll wait here and keep watch," Evan volunteered, leery of getting too close to the tunnel. Seth gave him an appraising look, then nodded and hiked on while Evan stared out over the river, tracing the path where the railway bridge had once been.

Seth was back in minutes. "Not much of a hiding place," he said. "Very shallow. Then again, it's been abandoned for a long time. I'll come back another time to dig around if a better possibility doesn't show up."

"There's another tunnel?" Evan asked. He didn't like the way his heart rate quickened in fear at the sight of the dark expanse, and he hated his reaction. Seth needed his help. There was no way Evan wanted Seth to come back and poke through a deserted tunnel by himself. *I need to man up. Grow a pair. It's just a fuckin' empty hole in a mountain.*

"Yeah," Seth replied, and if he noticed Evan's battle with himself, he didn't say anything. "This tunnel was only wide enough for one set of tracks, and there was too much traffic. So in 1907, they built the other tunnel and a new bridge."

The new bridge was still standing, an impressive arch bridge with a slight curve. "You can still drive on it, although it dead ends in the tunnel," Seth added. He and Evan climbed the hillside to the point where the tunnel met the mountain. Unused tracks still remained, leading nowhere.

This tunnel was much wider, with an iron gate that ran from the top of the arch to the ground and side to side with a locked door in the middle. Where Evan could easily see the cement plug in the first tunnel from a safe distance, the 1907 passage stretched into darkness.

Suddenly, Evan couldn't breathe. He could smell the mold and dirty water that ran through the Church Hill Tunnel where Valac had nearly killed him. It all came back—the candle smoke, the tang of blood, his helplessness at being bound and magicked, the certainty that he was going to die.

"Evan!" Seth gripped him by the shoulders and shook him gently. "Hey. Come back to me. You're safe. I'm here. Valac's dead. He can't hurt you."

Evan took in a huge gasp, then began to cough violently as his lungs spasmed with the frigid air. He doubled over, as Seth caught him, supporting his weight, murmuring all the time in a low, comforting voice.

"I'll be all right," Evan insisted as Seth helped him straighten up. "I'm over it now." He wasn't. His heart pounded like a jackhammer, and despite the cold, sweat ran down Evan's back. His mouth had gone dry, and he wanted to throw up. Thoughts spiraled on a non-stop loop: *Run, fight, trapped, going to die...*

"Bullshit. I know a panic attack when I see it." Seth started to turn Evan away from the tunnel and back toward the road.

Evan tore out of his grip. "I said I'll be all right!" He nearly stumbled, but caught himself, avoiding Seth. "I need to get over this, or I'll be running my whole life."

Seth held up both hands in appeasement. "It's only been a little over a month," he said quietly, holding Evan's gaze. "Guys I was in the army with took years to get over a bad incident. Hell, Toby told me stories about guys he served with in 'Nam who were still coping with PTSD decades later. There isn't an expiration date on trauma. We'll get through it."

"I'm not going to be useless when you need me to watch your

back." Evan felt his breath closing off again, made worse by the cold air that seared his lungs.

"You're not useless—"

"Yes I am!" Evan shouted. "Fuckin' useless, How'm I gonna keep you safe when I can't…breathe." He felt tears start in the corners of his eyes. Seth stepped closer, opening his arms to embrace him, but Evan staggered backward. "You need…a partner. Not someone…who can't even look at a tunnel without having a breakdown." His chest heaved with the struggle to get enough air, and his heart thudded hard enough that he thought he might pass out.

"Evan. Listen to me," Seth said quietly. He kept his arms wide but didn't come closer. "I know what it feels like—"

"You don't—"

"Yes, I do," Seth countered. "That six months I spent in the psych ward after Jesse died? You think I was on vacation? Man, I was a mess. Couldn't sleep because I'd wake up screaming. Couldn't keep food down. Every time I closed my eyes, I saw him hanging from that tree, messed up. All the blood." Seth raked a hand through his hair, looking distraught at the memory.

"They said I screamed his name in my sleep. I'd wake up with my throat raw. They gave me drugs. It only helped a little. On good days, I'd just sit in my bed and rock back and forth. On bad days, they had to tie me down." Seth's eyes were wide and haunted.

"But you got out," Evan argued. "You got better."

"I learned to function," Seth corrected. "Therapy helped—except they didn't believe what really happened. But even when they let me out, I was still messed up. Drank too much. Jumped out of my skin at strange noises. I probably wouldn't have lasted long if I hadn't run into Toby. I have the feeling he's got his own ghosts. He took me in. Taught me to hunt—and showed me how to cope. Pretty sure he saved me."

Tears ran down Evan's face. "I'm no good to you if I can't do what has to be done."

"How about all those hunts we've done?" Seth argued. "You handled yourself just fine. Baby, everyone's got triggers. And you don't know what they're gonna be until they hit you." He took a step closer, and another step, until Evan collapsed into his arms, sobbing.

Seth tightened his grip, one hand on the back of Evan's head, pressing him into his shoulder, the other on his lower back, holding him close. "You're everything, babe. I need you. Love you. Can't do this without you. And you know I fall apart sometimes, too. Got my own triggers. You've seen it."

Evan sniffled and nodded. He'd seen Seth thrash awake from nightmares that left him sweat-soaked and shaking. Those nights, Evan had been the protector, comforting, encouraging, murmuring his love and proving it with his own warm body.

"So we hold each other together, okay?" Seth said in a low voice, lips against Evan's ear. "That's what partners do. I'll cover for you, and you cover for me. No shame. I think you're strong and brave and you've come so far. Hang in there with me. It's gonna be all right. We can do this, as long as we stick together."

Evan stayed in the warmth of Seth's embrace until his breathing slowed and his heart calmed. He finally pushed back from where he'd nestled against Seth's parka and wiped the back of his hand over his wet eyes. Even in the cold, he was certain he'd gotten blotchy from ugly crying.

Seth ran the back of his knuckles gently down Evan's jaw, tracing the pad of his finger across his lips. "That's my boy," he said in a fond voice that made Evan's throat tighten. "You ready to go back to the truck?" Evan nodded, feeling the crash from the earlier spike of adrenaline. Seth took his hand, and they made their way down the incline to where the Silverado was parked. They got in, and Seth leaned over for a reassuring kiss before he put the truck in gear.

"Let's go home. I've got a frozen lasagna we can cook. No more investigating tonight. We'll watch something stupid on TV and curl up on the couch," Seth promised. "Gonna hold you all night long."

7

SETH

Seth found excuses to hang around the RV the next morning, checking his email, working on a project for one of his security clients, and watching a few hours of the exceptionally boring security footage from Kona Café. All the while, he tried to assess how Evan was bouncing back from the panic attack at the tunnel while trying not to look like he was looking.

"You're doing it again," Evan said with a sigh, glancing up from his own computer.

"Doing what?"

"Pretending not to stare at me when you're staring at me," Evan replied. "I'm fine."

"Didn't say you weren't."

"You didn't have to say it. You're hovering."

"Am not. I had stuff to do. Real people stuff."

"Real people stuff?" Evan asked.

Seth managed a self-deprecating smile. "Yeah. That's what I call stuff normal people do—you know, pay bills, answer email, do dishes. Things that aren't monster hunting."

Evan reached over and took Seth's hand. "I appreciate how you talked me down yesterday. I'm sorry I freaked." He shook his head before Seth could launch into reassurances. "I know—it's gonna take time. And, I feel better now. You were wonderful," he added, giving Seth's hand a squeeze. "But you need to give me some space to put myself back together."

"You sure?"

Evan nodded. "If you want me to believe you'll trust me to watch your back, then you have to trust me to handle my own shit."

Seth knew Evan was right, but that didn't mean he had to like it. Evan brought out a protective streak a mile wide in Seth, and he knew he had to temper that in order not to take away Evan's independence.

"Okay," he said, sitting back in his chair. "What do you want me to do?"

"Go to Dixmont, like you planned to do today," Evan replied.

"All right. But what about you?"

Evan smiled. "I'll borrow the loaner car again. I got talking to Mrs. Kelly in the camp office. She said I'd be doing her a favor if that old Toyota got driven occasionally during the winter and told me to just stop by and pick up the keys whenever I needed it. So I'll go down to Kona Café after I watch some more of the video. I'm sure we're going to get a lead on Thane from the footage; we just haven't watched long enough."

Seth admired Evan's resolve. "All right," he agreed, although he wanted to stay beside his lover all day to assure he really had recovered. "I'll go over and check out the Dixmont cemetery, maybe one or two other things." He held up a hand to forestall Evan's objection. "Broad daylight, I'll go armed, and it's not anywhere I expect trouble. Just covering territory," he said. "Then tonight, let's take a break. Go into town, find a nice restaurant, maybe go to a movie. A date. We haven't done that in a while."

"Do we get to come back and have wild, sweaty sex?" Evan asked, with a hint of a wicked smile.

"Always," Seth assured him. "Wild, sweaty sex is the second-best part."

"Second best?" Evan asked, raising an eyebrow.

Seth grinned. "The best part is waking up next to you in the morning and getting to do it all over again."

Evan practically pushed Seth out of the door, promising to take his pepper spray with him, to keep his phone handy, and to let Seth know if he intended to make any detours. It took all of Seth's willpower to go, but he knew that if Evan was going to fight his fears, he needed to know that Seth believed he could do it on his own.

He fell back on a tried-and-true solution to keep himself from dwelling on Evan's reaction, by throwing himself into investigating what remained of Dixmont. Ironically, the old hospital property wasn't far from Emsworth, where Kona Café was located.

In its heyday, back at the time of the Civil War, Dixmont State Hospital was at the cutting edge of "humane" treatment for mental illness. It advanced treatments that were enlightened for its time, although woefully inadequate in retrospect. Before its decline, the sprawling campus had eighty buildings and nearly two thousand resident patients, along with hundreds of staff.

Financial problems, aging infrastructure, and changing ideas about appropriate treatment eventually led to the hospital's closure. Its massive buildings sat empty and fell into disrepair. Vandals and thrill-seekers hastened the decline. Stories and rumors circulated, and ghost hunters flocked to the site, regardless of attempts to keep out trespassers. Attempts to salvage the old buildings collapsed in the face of massive costs. Finally, all of the main buildings were razed in preparation for a deal to put in a retail mega-center that, eventually, also fell through.

And so the old Dixmont property stood vacant, still a ward of the state, awaiting a chance at reinvention. Seth parked a distance from the fence where his car wouldn't alert the police that a trespasser was on the grounds and hiked in.

Looking out over the empty land, it didn't take much imagination for Seth to picture the main building that ran the length of the ridge—a four-story brick Victorian institution with an even taller central section and tower. It had been a self-sustaining community with farms, a railroad station, post office, and water treatment plant. Now, practically nothing remained except ghosts and rumors.

Seth kept his gun handy, as well as an iron knife and a gear bag with salt and other weapons. He couldn't shake the feeling that he was being watched, although he'd kept a careful eye out for anyone following him and had doubled back on his route several times.

His phone vibrated in his pocket, and Seth glanced at it, worried something had happened to Evan. An alert popped up, letting him know that one of his research programs had completed its analysis. He thumbed the screen open and looked at the results.

"Fuck," he muttered, staring at the message as if it might magically change. *"New Beginnings, Inc. dissolved in 1995, and any remaining assets moved offshore that same year. No further information is available."*

Seth kicked a rock and let out a torrent of frustrated curses. In Richmond, tracking Valac's assets had helped to discover his current persona. New Beginnings, a real estate and investment holding company, had links to Thane's previous identities at least from the 1940s, including Thaddeus Ramey. The company was involved in a mortgage and house sale for Dr. Roy Moser in 1950 and again in 1969, and for Kendrick Higgins, a Gibsonia police officer. It had handled real estate transactions for an investment banker named Conrad Bennington in the early 1990s—a lead Seth had yet to follow up. But with the company's dissolution and move out of the country, he had hit a dead end.

He jammed his phone back in his pocket and paced, trying to let off steam. Worry about Evan had him keyed up enough already, and now that the New Beginnings lead had fizzled, Seth realized how much he had pinned his hopes on it turning into something solid that might lead them to Thane's current persona.

Seth forced his feelings down, switching into what he thought of as "soldier mode"—cold, rational, analytical, hyper-vigilant. He'd unpack his worry and disappointment later. Now, he didn't have the luxury of venting or the time to waste spinning his wheels. There had to be another way to track Thane's real estate and investment transactions, and Seth would figure out how to mine that data stream for the information he needed. Right now, he needed to keep his mind on what he could learn from the remains of Dixmont State Hospital.

Dixmont's cemetery held the remains of more than a thousand lost souls who had died during their stay. Weathered stones held only numbers, not names. Even in death, the patients of Dixmont remained unacknowledged. Seth's steps crunched through hardened snow and dry leaves, but the old graveyard wasn't as unkempt as he feared. From what he'd seen online, volunteers periodically did a cleanup, a small nod toward restoring the dignity of those who had been pushed aside so long ago.

If there weren't ghosts here, there should be, Seth thought. In addition to its civilian patients, Dixmont served soldiers from every conflict from the Civil War through Vietnam. Back then, they called it "shell shock," "soldier's heart," or "battle fatigue" when a soldier returned from a war broken in mind and spirit. Places like Dixmont might have offered treatment, but few in those days offered compassion.

Seth remembered the dark days after his brother's death. The cops had dismissed Seth's traumatized ramblings about a supernatural cause and decided that he and Jesse must have stumbled onto a drug deal gone wrong. The police had taken a long, hard look at Seth as a suspect before finally clearing him—although the local rumor mill never did. His overwhelming grief and the trauma of what happened that night landed Seth in the local psych ward, on suicide watch, under observation. That's where he'd been when a car accident killed both of his parents, sending him into a darker spiral.

Those days were a fog of pain, turmoil, and medication. But what hadn't faded with time was how alone Seth had felt, more isolated by experiences no one else could understand than by the walls and locked ward. When he had recovered enough to strategize, he'd started telling the doctors what they wanted to hear, even if it meant lying through his teeth and recanting his testimony. Doing so broke his heart and seared him with fury, but he knew that he could never get justice—and vengeance—for Jesse until he won back his freedom.

That's when he discovered what many of his armed forces colleagues already knew—he'd earned his walking papers from the treatment center, but getting his freedom from the demons in his mind would be a life-long struggle.

Hunting down and destroying the witch-disciples wouldn't bring Jesse back or heal Seth's pain. But he could stop those sons of bitches from killing more sons, brothers, husbands, friends, and fathers. He could mete out justice that was long overdue. He could protect people who had no idea they were in danger when he had failed to protect a brother he had loved more than his own life. And now, he could make sure that Evan stayed safe, no matter what it took.

He'd failed once. He'd be damned if he would fail again.

By the time Seth had walked the huge property, getting a look at the remaining outbuildings, hours had passed and he was cold to the bone. Dixmont's ghosts had remained silent, ignoring his repeated invitations to pass along any clues about Dr. Moser, and even his "summon spirits" spell failed to rouse more than baleful specters intent on keeping their secrets. He finally headed back to the truck, starting up the engine and shivering until the heat kicked in.

Well, I know where the anchor probably isn't. While Dixmont might have made a good hiding place at one time, the site's future was too precarious for Thane to count on it as a secure hiding place for his precious anchor. Even at its height, Dixmont would have been a hive of activity, staffed around the clock, providing far too many opportunities for the anchor to be discovered.

Gradually, the cab grew warm, and Seth stopped shivering. He checked his phone for directions, then headed for his second stop—a place near McKeesport with the charming name of "Dead Man's Hollow." The Union Sewer Pipe plant burned in 1925, but its ruins remained. The area had also been home to a brick factory and a quarry, along with coal kilns. But despite its industrial roots, Seth's research had turned up how the location had earned its ominous name.

Legend held that at least one dead man had been found hanging from a tree near the old plant. Some claimed there'd been a deadly dynamite explosion nearby or that bank robbers had stashed their loot amid the ruins. The old pipe plant had been plagued with bloody casualties, including a man being cut in half while trying to escape an elevator that had gotten stuck.

Seth already knew that Ewing Carmody—Thane's first new identity after Gremory's death—had worked at the pipe plant. The fire that destroyed the factory had been so long ago that few people remembered it, and the area had been deserted for decades. To Seth's mind, that made it a likely suspect for a place Thane might stow his anchor.

The drive between the old Dixmont site and Dead Man's Hollow took less than an hour. Seth kept an eye on the traffic around him, alert to any possibility that he was being followed, but saw nothing. He checked his phone before he left to make certain that he hadn't missed any calls or texts from Evan and didn't know whether to be relieved or concerned that there were no messages.

Shit. He wanted to ask me something about his phone, and with the panic attack and all, I totally forgot. Seth sent himself a reminder so he could fix whatever had gone wrong that evening.

To Seth's amazement, the formal name of the nature preserve that included the old ruins actually was Dead Man's Hollow. Legends about the area remained, despite its new owners' efforts to shed the park's haunted past. The old industrial site now boasted hiking and bike trails and guided nature walks. It also permitted hunting, so Seth was careful to grab a bright orange safety vest before he ventured from the truck.

Before Jesse died, Seth used to find comfort in the silence of a forest. He and Jesse loved going camping. While the military life had cured Seth of his fondness for sleeping in tents, he had to admit that tramping around in the woods was one of the good parts of hunting monsters. Despite the danger, he found a sense of peace in the solitude and the beauty.

Now, Seth found himself on high alert. Something about the area felt "off," and he had learned long ago to trust his gut.

Snow blanketed the stone walls of the old factory and the broken steps of a long-vanished building. By the look of the parking lot when he had pulled in, no one had been out to the park in several days, so Seth didn't worry about having his gun in hand as he explored. The heft of the gun made him feel slightly better, though he felt certain that any threat here wouldn't be from a bear or wildcat.

This time, Seth didn't rely on calling out to the spirits for an answer. Given Carmody's close ties to the factory and the four missing orphanage boys, Seth decided it was time to start with magic. He had no native magical ability, but where Evan found he could will power into sigils, Seth had discovered that with a great deal of practice, he could focus his energy into spoken words.

He'd only used a "summon spirits" spell like the one at Dixmont a few times—most notably, the night he'd begged Valac's long-dead victims to help him rescue Evan. Working the spell posed a risk, especially without someone to watch his back. It also drained his energy rapidly. But while Seth felt certain Thane had used the pipe factory as a cover for his false identity, he was less sure the witch-disciple would have made it the hiding place for his anchor—especially now that it had become a public park.

Seth hiked across the terrain until he was in sight of the ruins, and then stopped and took several deep breaths to center himself. He visualized his breath, blood, and life energy as a burning glow inside him, and drew from that force to speak the arcane words that focused his will and created a magical summons to the spirits of the dead.

When Seth opened his eyes, he saw the hollow ringed by gray specters, most of them men in the work clothes of a century past. They watched him warily, silent and curious.

"A man named Ewing Carmody worked here," Seth said to his ghostly audience. "He killed people—many people. Worked dark magic to keep himself alive. I'm going to stop him, but if you know something useful, I need your help. Please. He's going to kill again soon."

Before the ghosts had a chance to consider his plea, a deep growl echoed from the rocks and ruins. The ghosts blinked out of sight, and a massive black form sprang over a ridge behind the remains of the old factory.

Seth reacted before he had time to process what he saw. He brought the Glock up and fired, getting off several shots as the huge beast launched itself into the air.

"Shit!" Seth cried, throwing himself to one side to avoid being crushed by the creature's weight or impaled on its sharp claws. He rolled and came up firing, but it felt like he was using a pea shooter against a rhinoceros. His shots hit center mass, but they didn't slow down the beast, which lowered its head and growled, a rumble that cued every primal instinct in Seth to run.

What the fuck is that thing? Nothing natural—that was certain. The creature had a squashed, bat-like nose, long fangs, and glowing, blood red eyes. A thick coat of matted, coarse black hair covered its bulky body. Seth guessed it was easily the size of a grizzly, but this was no bear. And while blood soaked its heavy coat, it had taken half a dozen high-caliber shots and still kept coming.

Black dog. Hellhound, Seth's memory supplied. *I am so screwed.*

He backed away as the monster advanced. Seth desperately searched his memory for how to kill the creature. He shot again, aiming between the eyes, but the hellhound lurched to one side, and the bullet grazed its ear.

When all else fails, cut off the head. Few things—with the exception of cockroaches—could withstand decapitation. The only problem was, to get close to the monster's head, Seth had to go past those sharp fangs.

Seth spoke his fire spell and sent a blast of orange flame at the creature. He didn't wait to see what happened; the smell of burned hair told him his aim was true as he dodged out of the way of a huge paw.

He hit the ground and felt his jacket tear as one of the claws snagged in its fabric. Desperate, Seth drew his Ka-Bar and rolled beneath the monster, slashing at its underbelly as he went. He couldn't tell if it made a difference.

"Hey, asshole! Over here!" A man stood several feet to the left of the creature, waving his arms like a madman to attract the monster's attention. Seconds later, Seth heard another man's voice chanting in Latin and recognized the words from the Rite of Exorcism.

Seth stumbled away, wary that the hellhound would follow, but it charged toward the waving man, then suddenly froze, transfixed. In the next breath, the creature vanished in a coil of green and black smoke.

"What the fuck?" Seth gasped, adrenaline surging through him in the aftermath of the fight.

"This isn't a game!" The man who had risked the beast's attack strode down the hill with a furious expression. Seth sized him up as a threat automatically. The moves were military, even though the blond fade haircut was not. The guy was an inch or so taller than Seth but probably had him matched for muscle mass. The second intruder had longer, crow-black hair and a tall, lean build. Seth knew how to size up an adversary and bet the second man had a martial arts background.

"Who the hell said I thought it was?" Seth demanded. "Maybe you didn't notice, but I was fighting that damn thing off!"

"And losing," the blond man snapped. "Fucking amateurs! Come out on a lark ghost hunting and get in over your head."

"Thanks for the distraction. Now get the fuck out of my way," Seth said, in no mood to argue with a stranger, even if the man had saved his life. He swung around to glower at the taller man.

"Why did an exorcism work? That thing was real and solid."

"Does it matter? You're alive. Go home and stay out of trouble."

Seth looked from one man to the other. "Seriously? You gonna tell me what the hell you were doing out here?"

"Saving your ass," the blond retorted. His partner leveled a glare at him, but the man crossed his arms, unrepentant.

"Fine," Seth said, sheathing his knife but keeping his Glock in hand. "Fuck you. And for the record—I had it handled." He strode off for his truck before the other men could reply.

A black Crown Victoria sat in the parking lot, with less snow on it than Seth's truck. No one was likely to show up by accident at Dead Man's Hollow on a cold December Wednesday, which meant the newcomers had to have been following him.

He pulled out of the lot as quickly as he could without fishtailing, but his heart kept thudding. Seth needed to talk to Milo and Toby and Simon because he'd heard of black dogs as omens, harbingers, and real creatures, but as demonic hounds? That was new.

That meant as much as Seth wanted to believe he could have successfully defended himself, maybe he'd needed help after all. But how had a demonic entity come to be at a public park? Surely if there had been a rash of attacks on hikers by huge black hellhounds, someone would have noticed.

Unless Thane knew Seth was tracking him and decided to leave a trap. And if Seth had brought Evan with him, one or both of them might be dead by now.

"Shit. Fuck. Damn," Seth muttered, slamming his palm on the steering wheel. The hunt for the witch-disciple had just taken an unexpected turn, and Seth feared he and Evan—and Brandon—had just become the prey.

8

EVAN

EVAN WATCHED SETH PULL OUT OF THE CAMPGROUND WITH MIXED feelings. Seth had been wonderful about his panic attack the night before, comforting and supportive. Nothing he said or did made Evan feel weak or like Seth had been disappointed in him. Still, Evan couldn't help feeling ashamed and humiliated at breaking down like that over a tunnel—a stupid, freaking tunnel.

He leaned back against the wall and covered his face with his hands. Seth was right—the trauma of having barely evaded a killer was too raw, too fresh for him to have put much distance between himself and that awful night. People took years—decades sometimes— to learn to cope with horrific experiences, and that wasn't factoring in anything supernatural.

So why did he still feel like he'd failed?

Evan went to the kitchen and made himself a cup of tea. He felt too jangly for coffee, but the aroma of a cup of mint tea with just enough sugar helped calm him, and Evan breathed in the scented steam and let it fill his lungs.

Fuck anxiety. He had work to do.

Evan sat down at the table and loaded the Kona Café security video onto his laptop, picking up where he and Seth had left off the night before. Two more of the weird "coupon" emails came up, but he ignored them, and the new, unwanted texts on his phone as well. *Fuck. I meant to show those to Seth last night before I fell apart.* He didn't have time to get distracted, and he wasn't going to risk shattering his recaptured equilibrium worrying about junk mail.

Even with the video moving at twice normal speed, watching was tedious. The faces of the coffee shop's regulars had begun to look familiar, and Evan could place many of them from his limited time visiting the shop. He recognized the mothers who gathered for a sanity break as their toddlers played or napped and the college students who used the café as a place to study. Even some of the business people who used the shop to "office" were familiar from his visits.

Evan spotted Brandon and Bree behind the counter. Some of the footage covered times when Brandon wasn't working, but Evan sped through them, going with a hunch that if Thane did show up, it would be to stalk his intended victim, not just scope out the café.

He was about ready to quit watching for the day when a newcomer walked in the café door. Evan's eyes widened, and he froze the video.

This man wore a ball cap instead of a Fedora, but he had the same build as Thaddeus Ramey and the man in the blurry photo of Adolph Brunrichter. The angle of his head and the shadow of his visor meant the video didn't capture his full face, but the jaw and shape were a match for the two men from the older photos.

Evan felt a surge of triumph. He took a screenshot and sent it to Seth's email. The stranger came in, ordered coffee, and then sat reading a book for half an hour. He kept his head inclined or held his book, so the camera never got a complete shot of his face, something Evan felt certain wasn't an accident. He watched as the man finished his drink and threw out the empty cup, then left the shop. Evan had marked the place on the video and sent the clip to Seth as well.

Maybe the photos from this encounter wouldn't be enough for Seth to run a facial recognition scan and match the man with a name. But it confirmed, at least in Evan's mind, that Thane was watching Brandon, stalking him, and that suggested Thane might not wait until Halloween to strike.

Evan checked the time on the video and saw that it was much

earlier than he usually visited. That was okay; he didn't want to actually run into Thane. It also made sense—in the early morning rush, Thane was more likely to be overlooked.

He felt a sudden, urgent need to go make sure Brandon was all right. Evan gathered his things, turned off the lights, and dressed for the weather. Then he locked up and walked over to the camp office to see about borrowing the car again.

Mrs. Kelly's faded red Toyota didn't have the best shocks, but the winter tires kept a grip on the slick road, and the heater worked. Evan took it slow, letting other drivers pass him, and made it to Kona Café without a mishap. He parked a distance away from the other cars, leery of returning the loaner with damage, although its finish already had more than its share of scratches and dents.

Evan had worked out Brandon's schedule by hit-or-miss, and today should have been one of his days. But when he walked into the café, he saw an unfamiliar barista working with Bree.

As he waited in line, he kept an eye on the small kitchen, hoping Brandon would appear. But by the time he reached the counter to place an order, Evan was certain that the other man wasn't there.

"Sorry, I don't remember your usual order," Bree said, looking like she had already put in a hectic morning.

"That's all right," Evan assured her. "I'm fine with a skim latte today." He glanced at the other barista. "Looks like you got short staffed today."

"Brandon quit," she said. "Asshole. No notice, no warning. Didn't say anything to me yesterday." Bree seemed to suddenly catch herself and colored at the indiscretion. "Sorry. You didn't need to hear that."

"I know what it's like to have someone call off on a busy shift," Evan commiserated. "No offense taken."

Evan took his drink to a chair and glanced around at the café patrons. To his relief, the man he'd seen in the video wasn't present—but then again, neither was Brandon.

Shit. Had Thane made his move already?

On impulse, Evan looked up the phone number for the volunteer fire station and called. When the dispatcher answered, Evan asked for Brandon.

"Sorry. He's out and won't be in for a couple of days. I can take a message." Evan assured him that he would call back and hung up, more worried than before.

He debated what to do, then remembered that he'd put Alex Wilson's card in his wallet when they had met to discuss research. A different voice answered when the call picked up.

"Lawson Investigations."

"Alex Wilson, please."

"He's out sick. Won't be back for a while. Can I help you?"

Evan felt his heart speed up. "No. Thanks. I'll send an email." He ended the call, staring at the phone as if it had burned him.

What were the odds? Alex saw Evan interact with Brandon. Alex and Brandon were obviously together. Now, both men had suddenly called out. Not a coincidence. But Evan struggled with the reason. Thane might have taken Brandon, but he doubted the witch-disciple would make a separate grab for Alex unless he'd been a hostage to assure Brandon's compliance. Possible, but it didn't feel quite right.

Then Evan remembered how Alex had acted when he'd recognized Evan from the research meeting. Alex identified Evan with a project about a serial killer who never got caught. A project that Evan felt certain Alex didn't believe was exactly as Seth had presented it. Maybe he'd spotted Evan, seen him as a threat because of the research, and taken his boyfriend to safety.

Evan hoped so because none of the alternatives boded well.

He decided that he wasn't in the mood to do his work at the café after all. Evan dialed Seth's number, not expecting him to pick up. He left a voicemail instead. "Hey, Brandon quit his job at the coffee shop, and he's off indefinitely at the VFD. Alex is 'out sick,' too. Either they've done a runner, or they've been grabbed. I sent you a couple of emails, too. Lots to talk about. Heading back to the RV now. See you soon."

Evan headed for the borrowed Toyota. More snow had fallen while he'd been inside the café, and a few more cars had parked around him. He slipped between his car and a minivan beside it, opened his door with barely enough room between the vehicles, and put his satchel with his computer inside.

Before he could get in, the side door to the minivan slid open, and in the tight space between the vehicles, a man's body pressed up against Evan. The barrel of a gun jabbed against his spine.

"Move and I'll shoot you right here." Mike Bradshaw's voice chilled Evan to his core.

Fuck that. Evan had made up his mind long ago that getting in a car with an attacker would lead to far worse than what would happen out in the open, where someone might witness the attack. Evan pressed the electronic car key's panic button, setting off the horn and the alarm. That bought him a few precious seconds while Mike was startled to bring one foot back hard into his attacker's shin—not enough room to kick higher—and dive sideways, away from the gun.

The gun went off, shattering the Toyota's rear window. The open car door cut off escape from one direction, and Mike lurched forward, pinning Evan against the vehicle with his body. "You always were a pain in the ass," he growled as he jerked Evan's coat back and plunged a needle into his shoulder.

Evan gasped and struggled, trying to break free. The world spun, his heart thudded, and his vision tunneled. Mike caught him as Evan's knees buckled and dragged him back into the minivan that blocked the view from inside the café.

Evan tried to fight, but his body wouldn't respond. Mike kicked the Toyota's door shut and slammed the van's side door as he crawled inside. In seconds, he had Evan's wrists and ankles bound with zip ties. A stranger in the driver's seat threw the van into reverse and took off.

"My boss said I can't kill you. Anything else—well, that's up to me," Mike said as Evan's consciousness faded. "Your boyfriend won't come looking for you—not after how I'm gonna fix things. You and me, we're going to make up for lost time."

9

SETH

A DARK, EMPTY RV GREETED SETH WHEN HE RETURNED FROM DEAD MAN'S Hollow. He unlocked the door and found a note taped to the fridge letting him know that Evan had borrowed the loaner Toyota as they'd discussed. Still, something seemed off.

He checked his messages before he'd even gotten his coat off. The voicemail from Evan over an hour ago sounded as if his boyfriend had intended to head right back. Evan should have beaten him home, despite city traffic.

Seth stripped off his coat, boots, gloves, hat, and scarf, then checked texts and email. Two from Evan—a video clip and a screen capture— sent early, before he would have driven to Kona Café. He opened them and saw immediately what had captured Evan's interest. Tonight, Seth would see if the image had enough detail to use for a facial recognition match with social media. Now, he just wanted to know what the hell was keeping Evan.

Seth poured himself a cup of coffee, for warmth and to distract himself. He shared Evan's worry about Brandon and Alex. He tried to call Alex and got a recording. Maybe Alex had freaked out at seeing Evan and saw him as a threat to Brandon, but that seemed like a big leap. Could Alex or Brandon possibly have suspicions about the witch-disciple or, at least, about some hereditary evil stalking the Clarke men?

When fifteen minutes passed and Evan still wasn't back, Seth called. *I'm not checking up on him. He can come back whenever he pleases. I just need to make sure he's okay.*

The call went to voicemail.

"Dammit!" Seth stalked from one side of the living room to the other like a caged bear. Maybe Evan had car trouble—no telling what shape that loaner was in. But that wouldn't explain the lack of a "don't worry" phone call unless Evan's phone had gone dead. So, car trouble and a dead phone? Possible, although Evan wasn't usually careless about recharging. A cold slither of worry slid through Seth's belly. Evan didn't have a lot of experience driving in snow. Seth had no idea whether the Toyota had good tires. Even a good driver could wreck dodging the other assholes on the road.

A wreck wouldn't account for not being able to reach Evan by phone. Unless he'd been hurt...

The sound of a car pulling into the campground had Seth at the window, hoping to see the Toyota making its way to the campground office, with Evan at the wheel. Instead, the black Crown Vic from Dead Man's Hollow slowly made its way down the snowy side roads as if it were casing the place.

Seth's phone rang, and he felt his hopes rise, only to fall when it wasn't Evan. Mark Wojcik's number came up. "Hi Mark. This isn't—"

"Shut up. Those demon hunters I told you about? They wanted me to call you so you don't shoot them. Guess you've already met? They seem to think you four need to talk—"

"Evan's not answering his phone. I don't know where he is."

"Then you need to talk sooner rather than later," Mark replied. "Like I said before, Travis Dominick is an ex-priest. Brent Lawson used to be a Fed. They're pretty hardcore, but they know what they're doing. And they're good guys."

"Lawson? Aw, shit." Seth made the connection between Alex's partner at Lawson Investigations and the demon-hunting former Fed.

"What?"

"Brent's partner is missing, too."

"Then you've got your hands full," Mark said. "Just don't shoot them—at least until you've heard them out. Good luck. Hope Evan's okay."

A loud pounding came at the RV door. "Seth Tanner! We need to talk with you," a man's voice called.

He walked to the door and opened it just as the blond man from Dead Man's Hollow was about to bang again. "Come in. We've got trouble."

The two strangers shared a look suggesting that wasn't the greeting they had expected, but they bumped the snow from their boots and entered, glancing around at the interior of the RV.

"You live here?" the dark-haired man asked.

"In the RV? Yeah. Here in Pittsburgh? Just passing through." Normally, Seth would have been a little pissier about answering a personal question, but worry clawed at his gut about Evan.

"I'm Travis Dominick," the dark-haired man said, "and this is my hunting partner, Brent Lawson."

"Seth Tanner," Seth replied, shaking hands. "And you'll forgive me, but I'm worried that something's happened to my partner—my boyfriend—Evan. He's not back yet, and he should be." He looked at Brent. "He was staking out Kona Café, trying to keep Alex's boy Brandon safe. Now they're all missing."

Brent paled. "Alex isn't missing."

"He called out sick, last minute, didn't he?" Seth pressed. "And Brandon quit his job unexpectedly yesterday, and the VFD said he'll be out for a while."

"Whoa," Travis said, holding up a hand. "Can we start at the beginning? Wojcik said you and Evan were real hunters, but he didn't want to say anything about why you're in Pittsburgh. Maybe Brent and I can help."

Seth gestured for them to find a seat in the living room. Brent lingered by the door, placing a call. He spoke tersely to the person on the other end, promised to call back, and ended the conversation.

"Alex and Brandon are in hiding," he said, standing with his hands on his hips like he had too much nervous energy to sit. "Because they freaked out over your partner—"

"Evan."

"—stalking Brandon at the café."

Seth rolled his eyes, feeling his anger rise. "Evan wasn't 'stalking' anyone. He was trying to get a lead on the killer we came here to stop —the warlock who wants to make Brandon his next sacrifice."

"Maybe you should start at the beginning," Travis interrupted.

"First tell me how you happened to be at Dead Man's Hollow?"

Brent shrugged. "Alex is my associate—he's been working for me for a couple of months now so I can spend more time doing…this kind of thing. He mentioned something to me about his 'weird' client— wanting to know about the murder swamp, and then Livermore and Dixmont. I figured you were ghost-chasers, probably with some para-normal TV show, and likely to get yourselves killed. I followed you after you left your meeting with Alex and figured out where you were staying. Then Travis and I did a stake-out, waiting for you to move."

Seth sighed. "So I was right—I felt like I was being followed, but I didn't see anyone."

"Not our first rodeo," Brent replied. "And the old Crown Vic might still have a police engine, but on the outside, it blends into the scenery, so people don't usually notice it."

Seth knew it was his turn. He looked up to see the two men watching him expectantly and sighed. "Okay. Here's the story."

Brent and Travis listened as Seth told them almost everything. He started with the awful night Jesse died, walked them through how he'd discovered the truth about Rhyfel Gremory, his witch-disciples, and the blood sacrifice cycle. He explained how he'd gone to Rich-mond to save Evan and they'd ended up together, and why the trail led them to Pittsburgh, and Brandon.

Travis and Brent shared another look as if they'd worked together enough to guess each other's thoughts. "You don't know the current identity of this witch lord?" Brent asked.

Seth shook his head. "He was Noson Thane back when Gremory died. I've traced him up through the 1990s, to a guy named Conrad Bennington—"

"I've heard that name. Some kind of investment banker recluse, right?" Travis said, tilting his head as he thought.

"Just made that connection and haven't had time to follow up on it," Seth replied. "But we've got a guy we think is him—we just don't know the name he's using now." He showed Travis and Brent the blurry photos on his phone of Ramey and Brunrichter, and the screenshot from the café security video. "Alex was checking into a Dr. Roy Moser at Dixmont in the sixties for me before he bailed," he added with a glare in Brent's direction.

"Forget the doc," Travis said. "That's Cole Roberson. Commercial real estate guru. Loaded and connected. Bit of a diva—hates photographers, won't do interviews, does everything behind-the-scenes. Now I guess we know why."

"You'd better be sure," Brent warned. "That guy has a shit ton of security around him all the time, and he's a high-roller. You can't just walk in and shoot him and tell people he's a wicked witch."

"Hadn't planned on strolling into his penthouse and capping him," Seth muttered. "We thought he was likely to make his move on Brandon early—before Halloween—and we thought if we could get close to Brandon, we'd be able to protect him."

"But you spooked him instead," Brent finished. He looked up at the ceiling like he was gathering his thoughts, and probably his patience. "Okay. Alex and Brandon are safe, for now. They're at a cabin I own that's more of a safe house. Evan's definitely not with them, and Alex didn't know where he might be."

Seth's skin itched, wanting to *do* something to find Evan. He got up abruptly.

"Look, I can't sit here. Something's gone wrong. Evan isn't answering his phone, and he isn't home. I've got to go down to Kona Café and see if I can figure out what happened to him."

"We'll go with you," Travis said.

Seth opened his mouth to argue, but something in Travis's expression made him hesitate.

"You're a good fighter," Travis said. "But so are we—and I'm also a clairvoyant medium."

"Like Simon Kincaide."

Travis nodded. "Yeah. Simon and I have a lot in common. The point is, if I see the location, I might get a vision. No promises—it never happens on cue. But...it's possible. And while you and Brent check in with the living, if there are ghosts around, I can see if they can tell us anything."

Seth's heart clenched. Ghosts? *Please, not Evan.*

Travis must have guessed his thoughts because he gave Seth a compassionate look. "If Evan was dead, with the bond you two have, he'd be trying to contact you. But there are ghosts around us all the time—a 'cloud of witnesses'—and sometimes, they're willing to be snitches."

They all turned as a gentle tapping sounded at the RV's door. Seth went to answer, and behind him, Brent and Travis took up defensive positions. He was certain they were both armed, though they kept their weapons down.

Mrs. Kelly stood on the step, huddled in so many layers Seth could barely see her face. "I'm sorry to intrude," she said, "but do you know if Evan is home yet? He borrowed my Toyota, and it isn't back in its spot."

Seth plastered on his best fake smile. "He ran out of gas. We're going to go pick him up. We'll bring the car back."

"Thank you so much," Mrs. Kelly gushed. "One of the other campers has it signed out for tomorrow morning, and I was worried that maybe he'd parked it someplace and I couldn't find it."

Seth choked down his own fears. "We'll take care of it," he promised, then watched to make sure she made it safely down the snow-covered lane to the plowed main drive.

Travis and Brent holstered their weapons and headed for the door. "Come on," Brent said. "Let's go see what's going on. We'll follow you. I know where the coffee shop is."

Seth's thoughts spun the entire way to Emsworth. It wasn't lost on him how close the café was to Dead Man's Hollow, to Dixmont, and to Thirteen Bends Road. *Thane's stomping ground,* he thought. He turned the pieces of the case over in his mind incessantly: the hellhound, Thane/Cade Roberson, the missing amulet and anchor. Thane was way ahead of them, and if they didn't catch up fast, Brandon—and Evan—would pay the price.

His gut told him Evan's disappearance had something to do with

Thane. Before, he might have worried that Evan had run off, but now, that explanation didn't sit right. He and Evan had done a lot of talking, made a lot of progress toward building a real relationship, not just a sex-and-adrenaline-fueled connection doomed to fail. Evan seemed happy, and maybe a little too invested in the case.

I encouraged him to get out, to go to the coffee shop. I put him right in Thane's path. Seth blamed himself, but he knew that Evan couldn't stay locked up in the RV. And if a guy like Thane wanted in badly enough, even the wardings and protections Seth had placed on the trailer wouldn't keep a powerful warlock out forever. Evan had been right to want to stretch his wings. Seth had been reasonable in encouraging him to do so. Thane had just been closer than they expected.

None of that made Seth feel any better.

By the time they'd reached Emsworth, the heavy cloud cover made the late afternoon darker than usual for the time. Kona Café was still open, and the warm lighting from coffee shop cast the snow outside in a golden glow. It didn't look like the scene of a crime or the hangout of a serial killer, but Seth knew appearances were often deceiving.

He spotted the red Toyota immediately, off by itself a distance from the shop. Seth pulled in nearby, but not too close to disturb evidence. Travis wheeled the big sedan into the space beside him.

When Evan parked, mid-morning, the walk to the café would have been fine in daylight. Now, a partly burned-out overhead light barely lit that corner of the lot, leaving the edges in shadow.

"I'll go in and ask around at the café," Brent offered. "Alex and I stop by whenever we're in the area, so most of the baristas know me." He jogged off, leaving Seth with Travis.

"Come on," Seth said, leading the way toward the Toyota, with a knot in the pit of his stomach. "Let's see if we can figure out what happened."

Seth pulled his Glock, but he kept it down by his leg, out of sight. He knew Travis was carrying from the bulge at the back of his jacket, but Travis didn't draw his weapon. He looked distracted as if his mind were elsewhere, and Seth wondered what extra-sensory mojo the former priest might be tuning in to see or hear.

"See any visions? Any ghosts?" Seth asked.

Travis didn't say anything for a moment, and then seemed to come out of his thoughts and shook his head. "No. Not right now, anyhow. I'm sorry."

Seth tried to hide his fear and disappointment. He stopped several feet away from the Toyota and threw out an arm to keep Travis from going closer. "Hold up. I don't want to contaminate the scene." Seth ventured closer, and Travis hung back a step behind.

"Someone pulled in on either side," Seth said, standing a few feet behind the borrowed car. "It looks like there was a scuffle on the driver's side."

"Minivan, probably," Travis said. "Wheelbase would be right. And the footprints are mid-vehicle. Awkward to drag someone into the crew cab of a pickup. A commercial van would have the doors in the back. But a minivan with side doors..."

"Yeah," Seth said, replied, nodding. "Fuck." They edged closer to the Toyota. "The back window's broken."

Travis shook his head. "I'd lay my bets it's been shot out, not just shattered."

Seth felt his heart skip a beat, but he pushed the fear down, retreating into soldier-mode again, willing himself to be an impartial observer. Evan's life depended on his ability to put the puzzle pieces together.

"Two sets of footprints," he said as they got closer, looking at the trampled snow. "Definitely a scuffle—and one of those sets of prints is the right size for Evan. The other is a smaller shoe size."

Travis edged around to the other side of the car. "His satchel's in the front seat. Want to bet he came out to get in the car and whoever nabbed him was waiting in the van?"

Seth scanned the snow and the side of the car, desperate to know if Evan had been injured. He peered in the broken back window and saw where a bullet had lodged in the cushion of the seat. But to his relief, he didn't see any blood, on the ground or on the car.

Brent strode across the lot to join them. "One of the baristas pulled a double shift. She said she remembered Evan because he had been in several times and always left a nice tip," he added with a smirk. "She didn't notice when he left. Said the car alarm went off for a long time, but no one was around. She thought the battery finally died. And she remembered hearing a loud noise—like a firecracker—around the time Evan was here."

"The gunshot," Travis said, with a nod toward the Toyota.

"Shit," Brent said, frowning. He looked at the empty space next to the car, pulled out his phone, and took pictures of the tire prints. "Might not matter," he answered their questioning looks, "but sometimes, an uneven tread pattern can ID a car. Can't hurt."

Seth did a slow turn, taking in the lot. A line of tall bushes separated the street from the parking area, effectively blocking any traffic camera view from the intersection. A small camera angled toward the café door, but Seth couldn't see any surveillance of the lot itself. "I was hoping maybe there'd be a camera and I could hack into the feed—"

"Whoever took Evan knew what he was doing," Brent said, and Seth could imagine him in an FBI jacket. "He—or she—planned it so no one inside the café was likely to see."

"Evan wouldn't have gone easily," Seth said. "We've been training, sparring. He's good in a fight. And he's stubborn."

"The attacker had a gun," Travis noted, with a nod toward the Toyota. "And look at the footprints—they were practically on top of each other. That doesn't leave much room for maneuvering. Evan might have gone along with him, hoping he'd get a break later. Or he might have been injured, maybe unconscious."

Seth closed his eyes and swallowed hard, trying to get a grip. He looked up when Travis laid a hand on his shoulder. "We'll help you find Evan. And we can help with Robeson, too. This witch-disciple problem is the kind of thing Brent and I would have gone after if we'd have known. You don't have to do this alone."

Seth nodded, afraid he couldn't speak. "Thanks," he managed.

"Since this isn't something we can bring the cops in on, how about if you jump the battery on the Toyota, and I drive it to the campground and meet you back there?" Brent bent down and picked up the keys from where they had fallen beneath the car. "Lucky no one stole his bag," he added, reaching in and handing the satchel to Seth. "Don't know how you're going to tell that nice lady she's got a bullet in her back seat."

∼

THEY GOT THE TOYOTA STARTED, and then Seth followed Brent and the loaner car back to the RV park. Travis peeled off shortly before they got there, then pulled in behind them by the time Seth had finished explaining the damage to Mrs. Kelly and offering to help pay for a new window. Travis held two steaming pizza boxes, and Seth realized he hadn't eaten since breakfast. He wasn't hungry and didn't know if he could keep anything down from worry, but he figured passing out didn't do anyone any good.

Brent and Travis followed Seth into the RV. He offered drinks; Travis took a Coke while Brent and Seth opted for beer. While they ate, Seth filled them in on more of the details, as well as the importance of finding the anchor and amulet.

"I can go out to the murder swamp and see if the ghosts can tell me more than they were able to tell you," Travis said when Seth finished his story. "The way they communicate with me is different. It takes less energy for them to show themselves because I have a natural ability to see and hear them. Since they don't have to crank up the power just to be noticed, they can use it to talk to me—and I can understand them. Considering that you're not a medium, it's pretty impressive that you got what you did from ghosts that old. They usually fade too far to do much besides scare people."

"These ghosts were pissed," Seth said, forcing himself to swallow a bite of pizza. It smelled good, and from the way Brent and Travis dug in, it must have tasted great. But worry turned it into ash in his mouth.

"If Alex didn't send you everything he found before he took off with Brandon, I'll make sure either he or I get it to you in the morning," Brent promised.

"Thank you," Seth replied, sincerely grateful for the help. Yesterday, he would have refused assistance, wary of working with any more outsiders. Now, he considered their awkward meeting at Dead Man's Hollow to be a lucky break.

"I've got a number of...associates...with a variety of psychic gifts who help me out when they sense something," Travis said. "I won't share details—won't need to. If they have something for me, they'll already know. I can't guarantee anything, but we've found that by staying in touch and pooling our insights, we come out ahead."

"I might be able to get some dirt—or at least details—on Robeson and his previous persona, Bennington," Brent mused. "Let me do a little digging."

By the time the pizza was finished, they had covered everything Seth could think of to say about the witch-disciple that hadn't already been said. Brent and Travis promised to be back in touch first thing in the morning. Seth saw them out and watched the Crown Vic pull out of the driveway.

The RV was far too silent. Funny that Seth had lived for two years by himself and never minded. Now, he kept waiting to hear footsteps, the vibration of someone else moving through the parked fifth-wheeler, the sound of Evan's voice.

Evan's messenger bag sat on one of the leather chairs. Whoever had grabbed Evan hadn't wanted his computer or his wallet—or the car. That just proved that the attacker had been after Evan himself.

Seth went through the satchel but found no ransom note—not that he expected one. No hastily jotted warnings from Evan, no cryptic messages. And no phone. Evan wasn't answering, but the phone wasn't in the car or in the bag.

Shit. Had Thane realized that Evan was the missed victim of the Richmond disciple? Seth squeezed his eyes closed, but he couldn't stop picturing the tunnel in Richmond that Valac had turned into his ritual chamber, or the image of Evan, bound and bloody, awaiting the killing blow.

He rubbed his hand over his mouth. Seth felt too jittery to sit still, but he had nowhere to go. Every instinct screamed for him to go search for Evan, but without a clue to his location, it would just be meaning-less driving. Maybe whoever took Evan would try to contact Seth. Not asking for ransom, exactly, but gloating? Leaving a trail of clues to dare Seth to find Evan in time.

Or maybe I've been watching too much TV.

He forced himself to stop pacing, but TV or movies couldn't hold his attention, and he was far too antsy to read. Seth tried surfing the internet and realized he hadn't yet picked a Christmas present for Evan.

Please, let him be okay. Let him be alive and here with me for Christmas. Just let him be all right. Seth hadn't really prayed since Jesse and his parents died. He wasn't sure he believed in any cosmic power anymore. But if prayer would bring Evan back safely, Seth would light every candle in Pittsburgh.

Seth's phone pinged with a message, and he reached for it so quickly, he almost fumbled. He frowned to see a text message from Evan's phone number.

"I'm sorry—I can't do this. I was wrong to think you and I could make this work. I'm out. Don't look for me—I don't want to be found."

10

EVAN

EVAN WOKE UP WITH A POUNDING HEADACHE AND DOUBLE VISION. HE rolled to one side and retched. From the smell, he'd pissed himself as well.

Mike. Mike's back. Mike with a gun. Mike's gonna kill me.

Awareness and panic came back before the rest of Evan's body rid itself of enough of the drug to respond to his commands. He tried to move and found that he was bound, wrists and ankles, with zip ties.

Evan raised his head and saw that he was in a dark, windowless space. Dim light outlined a large door at one end, but it looked wrong to belong to a motel room or a house. A garage, maybe?

He managed to roll and wriggle away from the puddle of sick, inching his way across the floor. Evan reached a cement wall and maneuvered himself to sit. If Mike intended to come back and kill him, he'd make the bastard look him in the eyes when he did it.

Just that exertion made Evan's heart pound and his stomach threaten to rebel again. He had no idea what had been in that syringe, but it had put him down hard. Evan didn't know how long he'd been out, although he guessed it had been hours.

Shit. Seth. He knows by now that I'm missing. Did he find the car? Or does he think I've run away?

Evan took a couple of deep breaths, trying to calm himself. He remembered texting Seth right before he left Kona Café, sending him the video of the guy who might be Thane, letting Seth know he was on his way back.

Except that he'd never arrived home.

Mike took him away in a van. Evan remembered that much. So, unless Mike went back later to dispose of Mrs. Kelly's Toyota, then someone—the police or Seth—should have found it. There'd been a gunshot. Evan felt certain he remembered that. But he didn't get hit. At least, he didn't think so.

Fuck this shit. Think!

Evan focused on his body, moving down from head to toe, cataloging his injuries. His head throbbed, his mouth tasted like puke, and his throat was so dry, he could barely swallow. No gag. Maybe Mike had been afraid he'd choke, and that would ruin all of his plans.

Stay focused. Evan felt bruised, probably from being manhandled out of the van and into—wherever the hell he was. But no searing pain like he imagined he'd feel if he'd been shot. That was good. Not that he could do much, tied up, but at least he wasn't going to bleed out before Seth found him.

Seth. Evan felt tears threaten. Seth would have realized by now that something was wrong. He was a good hunter; he knew how to track people. And the two of them had been closer than ever over the last few weeks, so there should be no reason for Seth to think Evan had left on his own. Seth would come looking for him. Probably was already turning the city upside-down trying to find him.

Whether Seth would be in time to save him was another matter.

Evan's thoughts moved sluggishly as he fought off the last of the drug. He still felt floaty, as if he wasn't completely "in" his body, a weird feeling. He wondered what Mike had used to drug him and how long it would take to wear off. Even if he could get rid of the ties, he doubted he could crawl, let alone run, until the anesthetic was out of his system.

His mind raced, and his body could barely move. Where was Mike? And the driver—who was he? Were they watching? Evan looked around the darkened room for cameras but couldn't see much. Had

Mike left him here to starve? Gone to get Thane? Or worse, did Mike intend to come back and make good on his threat?

We're going to make up for lost time. Mike's threat made Evan shiver with fear. He'd been running from his abusive ex-boyfriend for years now, covering his tracks, lying low. How had Mike found him? Evan wracked his memory for when he might have slipped up and realized that it had to have been the apartment fire in Richmond. He'd had to sign his lease and his car loan with his legal name. That had to be it.

But then, how did Mike find him here in Pittsburgh? Evan couldn't come up with an answer to that. He hadn't exactly "disappeared" from Richmond—Liam and Izzy still heard from him. Not that Evan told them where he was or what he was doing.

Had Mike hacked his phone or computer? Possible, but not likely. Seth knew all about hacking—and how to prevent it as well as how to do it. He'd made modifications to Evan's phone to prevent unwanted tracking.

My boss says I can't kill you...

Evan felt himself go cold with terror. Mike wasn't working on his own. He had orders. And since Corson Valac was dead, then Noson Thane was the likely culprit.

This keeps getting worse.

Alone in the dark, Evan drifted. As the drug wore off, his bruised body hurt worse. He had no idea what time it was or how many days he had been gone. His stomach growled, and his head felt like he'd taken an ice pick to the eye. It had been late morning when he'd been grabbed, before lunch. So his last meal was...a long time ago.

The door opened with a rumble of hinged steel on tracks, deafening after the silence. Evan turned his head as the high beams of a vehicle flooded his cell with light.

"You're awake. Good. It would have been a shame if I'd gotten the dose wrong." Mike stood silhouetted against the glare. Evan had to keep his eyes averted or be completely blinded. The sudden change from dark to light made his head feel like it might explode.

"Bastard." That one word managed to convey all his loathing for his ex-boyfriend.

"Not very nice," Mike chided. "Considering that your life is in my hands." He walked closer, only partly blocking the brightness. He bent down in front of Evan and reached out to touch his cheek. Evan flinched away, but Mike ran his fingertips down Evan's jaw.

"You ran out on me. Left me. Broke your word." Mike shook his head.

"You tried to strangle me." The drugs hadn't fogged Evan's memory enough to forget that.

"You had a safe word." Mike shrugged.

Rough games had been Mike's kink, not Evan's. Maybe other couples both enjoyed that kind of thing, but Evan didn't—never had—and he'd always suspected in their case that Mike's "games" were just a cover for abuse. He knew for damn sure he couldn't have croaked out a safe word with Mike throttling him hard enough Evan nearly blacked out.

If Evan had anything left in his stomach, he would have thrown up. Anger, fear, and revulsion churned in Evan's gut. The light made his head hurt so badly, he almost hoped he'd black out. "Get your hand off me."

Mike moved fast, backhanding Evan across the face. "You don't get a say! You walked out. Ran away. Left me. That was a big mistake. Now, I'm gonna make you pay for it."

Heavy footsteps headed their way, and a dark shape grabbed Mike and pulled him back. "The boss said you can't hurt him. You get what's left when the boss is done. Not before." Mike jerked out of the man's grip, but his whole posture made it clear he was looking for a fight.

Evan squared his shoulders. His wrists were bound behind him, but he could at least muster enough defiance to let Mike know it wasn't over yet. "Seth will kill you."

Mike laughed, a harsh, loud sound that felt like another blow to Evan's pounding head. "Your trailer trash lover? He's not going to give a fuck about you. Not after the text I sent him from your phone."

Evan went still and cold. "What text?"

Mike's face was mostly lost in shadow, but what little Evan could see, squinting against the light, contorted into a leer. "The one telling him to fuck off and die. To get lost because you didn't need him anymore. The one that told him you didn't want to be found."

"He won't believe it." Evan hoped and prayed that was true.

Mike chuckled. "Oh, he'll believe. Especially when I send him this." He touched his phone and then turned the screen so Evan could see the video that was playing. Evan strained to make out the images, and his eyes widened. Two men, having sex...and one of the men was him.

"How did you get that? I never gave permission—"

"I didn't ask," Mike gloated. "I've jacked off to this so many times over the years, all the better because you didn't know I'd recorded us. That kept you...spontaneous."

Fury settled in Evan's belly. "You fucking bastard." He'd never have allowed Mike to video them, but as usual, Mike hadn't given him a say. Seeing himself on screen, younger and victimized, made him shake with anger.

"So hot. Think your boy will like it? He'll figure you've moved on without him. And once he's out of the picture, and my boss is done with you, it'll just be you and me—like it's supposed to be."

This isn't happening. It can't be real. I'm going to wake up in a cold sweat with Seth calling my name, safe in the RV. I can't...I won't...Not again.

Evan's chest felt like a steel band tightened around his ribs, cutting off his air. He clenched his fists and focused on not passing out.

"You always thought you were better than me. How're you feeling now, Evan? Did the 'ads' I sent your phone and email make you uncomfortable? Did you realize I was watching you? The witch helped me." He chuckled. "My boss is a powerful man. Money. Status. Rules don't apply to him. He's about to do a really big deal, and he's going to take me with him, give me a piece of the action." Beneath Mike's boast, Evan heard echoes of the greed and lust for power that he'd realized, too late, were core rot.

"It's really all up to you, how this goes. Show me how sorry you are, make it up to me, and I can put in a word with my boss. Maybe he'll let me keep you and take the others instead. I can save your life, Evan. But you're gonna have to beg for it. So pretty." Mike stroked his finger along Evan's jaw.

Evan remembered well enough how Mike used to bait him, seeking an excuse to lash out. Despite the sedative, he had enough presence of mind to stay quiet, although his heart pounded so hard he could feel it throb behind his eyes, and the zip ties rubbed his wrists bloody as he strained against them.

"Nothing to say? Ah, well. That'll change." Mike started back to his car. "I have food and water, but not until you ask nicely."

Evan stayed silent.

"You know, I won't let you starve. So if you're thinking about going on a hunger strike, it won't work. Just making it worse for yourself. But then, you were always good at that." He turned, and his gaze raked over Evan.

"You were always going to be mine, Evan Malone. The sooner you realize that, the better off you'll be."

Mike stalked out, and then the door closed in another metallic thunder crash. Evan was alone in the dark again.

I am so fucked.

Evan made himself go through the breathing exercises he'd learned. Mike thought he was stubborn? He didn't know the half of it. Mike had never seen Evan for who he really was. He'd seen what he wanted, needed, Evan to be for him—and for a while, Evan had been willing to play the role. But Mike's tastes had grown darker and his moods mercurial. After one too many trips to the emergency room, Evan ran, and kept running.

Just to end up here, at Mike's mercy all over again.

No. Never again.

The thought that Seth might give up on him made Evan's heart hurt. But he couldn't worry about that now, no matter how much the loss—if it happened—would devastate him. Right now, he needed to figure how to get away from Mike, or he was going to wish he'd died back in Richmond, with Valac.

Think! You fight monsters. Mike's just a man.

Monsters. Magic. Sigils.

For the first time since he'd awakened, Evan had a reason to smile.

His stomach clenched with fear and hunger, but Evan couldn't be bothered. He thought over the sigils he had learned. "Sense undead" wasn't going to help. But "fasten/release" and some of the others might come in handy...

He needed to be ready when Mike came back. No way in hell was he going wherever Mike's "boss" wanted him to go. Evan decided he'd rather take a bullet to the head. Once that decision was made, an icy calmness settled over him. Evan wondered if it was what Seth meant when he talked about being in "soldier mode." His fear, his worry about Seth, everything receded, and only clear, cold logic remained.

Evan intended to escape or die trying, but he was never going back to being Mike's plaything.

First, to draw a sigil and get out of his bonds. He didn't have a pen on him or his chalk. Evan had gotten a glimpse of his prison when Mike turned on the headlights. Not a cell...more like a storage unit, the kind inside an old warehouse that had been converted. That explained the cement floor and the rough brick walls.

Evan wriggled away from the wall and hoped to hell he was still as limber as he had been the last time he'd gone to yoga, back in Richmond. He'd always been able to clasp his hands behind his back and slide his body through the opening, ending with his hands in front. The zip ties around his wrists cost him precious inches compared to his laced fingers, but given the stakes, Evan didn't care if he had to dislocate his wrist to make it work.

Fortunately, it didn't quite come to that. Several minutes later, sweating and aching, Evan's bound hands were at least where he could see them. He leaned forward and traced a sigil in the dust. Then he poured all his fear and hope into his will and focused on sending it into the mark of power.

Release.

The sigil glowed, faintly at first and then brighter, and the zip ties sprang loose. Evan rubbed his wrists, and his hands came away slick with blood. He wiggled his feet, trying to get circulation going again. There was no telling when Mike would be back, and Evan needed to be gone.

Evan climbed to his feet, shaking out his tingling limbs. The storage unit was so dark he could barely make out a path toward the door, and he guessed that any outside light was fading fast.

Would there be people around the storage facility, if Evan could get out of the locked unit? He'd seen plenty of TV shows about murderers leaving bodies in abandoned units. He thought about yelling and decided against it, not knowing how far away Mike had gone. Counting on the mercy of strangers was dicey, and he didn't want to find out that everyone in hearing distance was committed to minding their own business.

Which meant that if he was going to get out alive, it was entirely up to him. He stumbled as the toe of his shoe kicked something solid. Evan bent down and picked up a broken piece of smooth stone about the size of his palm. It felt like a piece of broken countertop—perhaps someone had stored building supplies in the unit—just a little smaller than his slate. And that gave him an idea.

Evan dipped the index finger of his right hand into the bloody furrow on his left wrist. He drew the sigil for "light" and pushed his will into the marking. Once again, the rune lit up with power, but this time, the glow did not fade. Evan smiled a predator's grimace.

Game on.

Evan sidled up to the large front door. The glow-rock gave him enough light to make out the tracks for the garage door. That meant a padlock on the other side held two hasps together. He wasn't sure his sigil would work through the door, or how much more energy he had to draw on, but if the alternative meant waiting for Mike to come back and open it, Evan was willing to try until it drained him dry.

Once again, blood sufficed. Maybe that amplified the magic; he didn't know and didn't care, as long as it worked. Evan drew the mark over where he felt the bolt poke through the track and then focused once more. He struggled to keep hold as the power nearly slipped from his grasp. He was new to using rote magic and working it drained even a seasoned practitioner.

Evan drew in a deep breath. This time, instead of pulling from his fear, he thought about Seth. Not about the doubt or hurt or mistrust that damned text and video might cause, but what he felt for Seth— love, trust, and security. He held onto those feelings like an anchor and pulled with everything he had in him, then pushed it into the hasp and the lock.

The bolt shifted. Evan strained harder. A warm trickle of blood started from one nostril, and his head pounded hard enough to make him gasp out loud. Then he felt the resistance give, and a clank on the other side of the door told him the padlock had fallen away.

Evan dropped to his knees, lightheaded from the outlay of energy. He didn't have time to rest. He felt his way to the center of the door, shoved the light-stone into his pocket, and fit his fingers under the edge of the metal panel. Squats weren't his favorite gym move, but now he thanked Seth for all the hours spent training. Evan hunkered down, concentrated on using his leg muscles, and lifted.

The door creaked and rumbled, moving more sluggishly for him than it had for Mike. Evan wasn't sure he could push it all the way open. Then again, he didn't need to—just far enough to get out.

Moving carefully, mindful of just how heavy the door was despite being balanced on its runners, Evan shifted his stance, edging under the opening until he was finally on the outside. He eased the door down, unwilling to make noise and draw attention to his escape. He threw the bolt, picked up the lock, and slid it back in. Every second it took for them to figure out he was gone counted.

The storage unit faced a driveway. It was one of a long line of doorways stretching down the wall of a brick warehouse. From the dented and rusted appearance of the other doors, as well as the cracked asphalt of the drive, Evan suspected the facility had long been abandoned. Just as well he hadn't wasted his energy shouting for help.

He checked his pockets. His car keys were gone, along with his phone and the pepper spray canister he'd carried instead of his gun. Obviously, Mike had gone through his pockets. That meant he had nothing to defend himself with—and his crazy stalker ex had a gun.

Evan glanced around, desperate for a weapon. *Anything, everything, can be a weapon if you know how to fight*, Seth had told him.

It was time to remember that he wasn't the Evan Malone who had fled with the clothes on his back. He'd taken martial arts and self-defense classes. More than that, he'd sparred with Seth, practiced at the firing range, and knew magic. He'd killed fucking monsters, dammit. Real monsters with fangs and claws, so much worse than the twisted, sick bastard that was his ex.

He'd fought ghosts and ghouls and a goddamn Boo Hag, for fuck's sake. He could hold his own against Mike fuckin' Bradshaw.

He saw a chunk of concrete the size of an apple and stuffed it into his pocket. Near one of the abandoned units lay a broken broom handle. The splintered end wasn't nearly as sharp as his Ka-Bar, but it would do. Not much farther, and he found an empty beer bottle. He pushed the bottle into the pocket on his other side, gripped the broomstick in one hand and the light-rock in the other, and tried to figure out which way was out.

The glow from his sigil didn't illuminate much, but that meant it also wasn't likely to draw unwanted attention. Evan would have given a lot for a full moon or a working security light. He glanced down at the snow and saw the tire tracks that marked where the van had driven in. Now that he knew which direction to go to find the entrance, Evan headed toward the road, keeping to the shadows of the big, dark building.

He had no idea whether the facility had a fence around it, or how close he was to the city. From the age and condition of the warehouse, Evan guessed he might be in one of the towns along the river, where there'd been shipping, trains, or manufacturing. He needed to get away from the storage building and find somewhere to hide, or a public place he could go to call Seth.

Evan kept close to the side of the building, hoping the tire tracks led to the exit. The driveway led uphill, and as the road rose, Evan glimpsed the lights of traffic in the distance. He reached the edge of the old warehouse and sized up the gap between it and the side street that led to the facility. He'd need to make a break from cover, but Evan figured anything was better than staying where he was.

He reached the side street and paused to get his bearings. Far to the left, he could see the glow of lights reflected from one of Pittsburgh's three rivers. As he feared, the old warehouse was in a decrepit industrial district that looked largely abandoned. Here and there, a few security lights burned dimly, but darkness shrouded most of the area. To the right, in the distance, Evan saw a well-lit road and heard traffic.

Getting to it was the problem. Parking lots and darkened buildings filled the span between him and the road. He guessed it to be the length of at least two football fields, and there was no telling what kind of debris and dangers—human or inanimate—filled the crumbling lots. Since he didn't have a choice, Evan started across the side street, intent on reaching the main road.

Headlights came up from behind him, catching him in their glare. Evan ran.

A shot rang out.

11

SETH

Seth stared at his phone. His hand shook. What the hell had he just seen?

The text message had been bad. But the video of Evan with someone else...seeing that had frozen Seth's heart in his chest and made him gasp for breath.

Evan had just dumped him. And, apparently, lost no time finding someone else. They hadn't really discussed exclusivity, although they'd danced around the subject recently after a disastrous intelligence gathering foray to a bar that resulted in one of their first real arguments. The bartender had hit on Evan, who had used it to his advantage to get information. Seth had been an asshole about it, then apologized. With everything else going on, they hadn't circled back around to come straight out and discuss not being with anyone else.

But for Chrissake, they were living together. Seth had certainly meant that as a statement of his commitment, although he should know better than to assume. He and Evan had seemed closer than ever these last couple of weeks. There were plenty of conversations they needed to have, since fate and murder threw them together, and Seth felt like they were gradually working through those discussions, although hunting a century-old serial killer put a crimp in downtime.

Maybe he should have asked.

The asshole instinct that had roared to life in that bar paced at the edge of his thoughts, reminding him that Evan could do so much better than Seth. A guy like Evan—smart, gorgeous, witty—could have his pick of partners. He could find someone stable, someone who wasn't on a crazy suicidal quest, someone who would keep him safe and not drag him into danger.

But Seth could hear Evan's repeated assurances that he wasn't planning to leave, that he didn't want to be anywhere else, that he loved Seth and wanted to have his back, be a partner in every way.

Remembering those promises made Seth's heart break a little bit more. Had it all been a lie? Seth couldn't help thinking about how tender Evan had been the last time they'd made love, just last night. Evan had rocked his world, an enthusiastic and attentive lover. Seth closed his eyes, remembering Evan's scent, the touch of his skin, the gleam in his eyes, the silky feel of his hair as Seth tucked a strand behind his ear.

Wait a second. Time out.

He re-read the text message, then forced himself to watch the video clip and pushed himself into a soldier's mindset. He swallowed hard as Evan's thin body moved above his lover, who was out of the screen-shot. Evan bent forward, and his long hair fell across his face...

Evan's never had hair that long since I've known him. It wasn't that long this morning. And he's also not that skinny—he's gained muscle, just in the last month. That's an old clip, has to be years old.

Now that he knew what he was watching, Seth noticed that Evan never once looked at the camera, didn't act like he was putting on a show.

Fuck. He didn't know he was being recorded. And I'll lay my bets he'd never have agreed to it. Shit.

The text message didn't make sense. Evan had given Seth no reason to doubt his love or commitment. In fact, Evan had been the one looking forward to Christmas and casually mentioning a future that Seth wanted so badly, his whole body ached at the thought.

The Toyota had been abandoned, its alarm blaring, a window shot out. There'd been a struggle. Another vehicle—a van—had been parked next to Evan's car. The evidence screamed abduction, and Seth was terrified that Thane had decided to add Evan to his list of victims. The kidnapper had to know that, sooner or later, they would find the car and the bullet and realize what had happened. So why the text and the video?

Seth frowned. The messages didn't fit. If the kidnapper wanted Seth to really believe Evan had run off on his own, they'd have stolen the Toyota and ditched it in the river. They hadn't even stolen Evan's satchel. So the kidnapper not only didn't care if Seth knew he'd taken Evan, he was taunting Seth with the evidence.

The text message felt personal, like a competing script to explain what happened. The video definitely was meant to wound. Thane might want Seth to know he had taken Evan, might want to force Seth to choose between saving Brandon and rescuing Evan. It worked against his purpose for Seth to think Evan had left on his own. Thane would want Seth distracted, panicked.

No, Seth felt certain Evan hadn't sent the text or video, hadn't betrayed his trust or walked out on him. In the next heartbeat, terror shot through him as he realized who Evan's abductor had to be.

Evan's stalker ex-boyfriend, Mike Bradshaw. And the motherfucking bastard had not only kidnapped Evan, he'd tried to drive a wedge between him and Seth.

And for a few awful minutes, it had almost worked.

Seth got up, paced the RV's living room, and resisted the urge to punch the hell out of the couch, just to let off some of the toxic brew of emotions bubbling inside him. He wanted to scream, or better yet, pound the ever-living shit out of stalker-Mike.

Save Evan. Deal with Mike. And figure out how the hell to save Brandon, and stop a killer.

Seth knew how to channel fury for a purpose, and he'd kept himself alive for two awful years taking sustenance from vengeance. Evan had started to smooth out Seth's rough edges, to give him hope for a reason to live beyond meting out justice. But now, Seth knew he needed to use the energy of the storm inside him to rescue Evan. That meant shutting down every other emotion until he was what the Army had been trained him to be: an efficient combat operative and a ruthless killing machine.

He glanced at the time. Evan had been gone for about five hours. Maybe Seth was already too late. No, Seth thought he had a handle on Mike Bradshaw's type. If Mike was in control and not just Thane's tool, Mike might end up trying to kill Evan, but he'd want to get payback for Evan leaving him. That didn't bode well for Evan, but it gave Seth more precious time to plan a rescue.

First things, first. Seth dug Evan's laptop out of his messenger bag. Since Seth had given him the laptop to replace the one lost in the apartment fire in Richmond, Seth had set everything up on it, and Evan had told him to keep administrator privileges because Evan didn't want to deal with the technicalities. That meant Seth could log in without feeling like he was violating Evan's privacy. He wasn't sure what he was looking for, but he figured email was the place to start.

Seth read down through Evan's inbox, seeing absolutely nothing of note. Inquiries from Evan's graphic design website and discounts from online retailers made up the whole list. Frustrated, Seth saw that Evan hadn't emptied his email trash in a while and clicked to open the folder.

"Shit." At least a dozen emails since they'd arrived in Pittsburgh stood out, all with subject lines that seemed to know just a little too much about Evan's whereabouts. Seth understood data mining and knew how to use the techniques for military intelligence. And while retailers could profile customers with scary precision, Seth would bet money those emails had been hand-crafted to make Evan uncomfortable.

He mentioned the GPS thing. Was this what he wanted to show me, the day we went to the tunnel? Evan's panic attack had pushed that earlier conversation out of mind for both of them, so it hadn't come up again. Then again, the emails didn't actually threaten harm, and Seth could imagine Evan figuring there were more important things to focus on.

Seth chewed his lip as he thought. Then he grabbed his own laptop and logged into their shared cell phone account. Seth had set that up for Evan as well, trying to replace the equipment lost in the fire. He handled the online billing, and Evan repaid him for his share of the bill. That meant Seth had access to Evan's call history, something he would never access without a dire reason. Seth figured current circumstances counted.

He wasn't surprised that almost all of Evan's outgoing calls were to him. He spotted a couple to Toby and Milo and figured those were Evan reaching out for help with lore. He saw one to a phone number he recognized as belonging to Alex Wilson, and another call to an unfamiliar number right before that—God, had it only been this morning? That must have been Evan's call to the VFD to find Brandon, after discovering the barista had quit at Kona Café. Right after that, Evan had called Seth—the last time Seth had heard from him.

Seth opened the advanced settings. His hacker background made him wary about a phone's ability to give away a person's location, so he and Evan had turned those off as much as the carrier would allow. That made him wonder whether the stalker texts and emails had some help from magic. Bradshaw wouldn't have needed any ability of his own. He could have found a rote spell or paid an unscrupulous witch. Now, Seth toggled the services back on for Evan's phone and waited for the profile to update, holding his breath that it would reveal the user's current location.

"Currently out of service, turned off, or powered down."

"Fuck," Seth muttered, wiping a hand across his eyes as he fought down a surge of frustration. He tried a few more adjustments to the settings but received the same error message each time.

That probably meant Bradshaw had saved Evan's phone long enough to send the text and video, then either destroyed or disposed of the phone to prevent being tracked.

Mike Bradshaw was a sociopathic bastard, but he wasn't a master hacker. Seth set to work with the breadcrumbs of information he could glean from the stalker-coupon emails and the robocalls, forcing himself to be patient and methodical, when he ached to be able to assure Evan's safety right away. Seth lost track of time on the hunt as he followed the digital trail. With a few key pieces of data, Seth built a program to auto-scan the internet, looking for details regular search engines would never find.

While his program trolled the Deep Net, Seth fished search engines for public records and hacked into a few key databases. Put the results of all searches together, and he felt certain he would discover something that would lead him to Evan's stalker.

Bradshaw hadn't tried to keep a low profile. He also hadn't put much effort into staying out of trouble. Seth turned up an arrest for assaulting an officer, resisting arrest, and breaking parole. He also had more than one restraining order against him, and he'd been charged with violating those orders on multiple occasions.

"He's a fucking model citizen," Seth muttered as he read down through the arrest record. Bradshaw would never pass a background check, and the information confirmed to Seth that the other man was a serious threat.

The phone calls Evan received were a dead end—probably from a burner phone or an anonymizer app that hid the identity of the caller. So were most of the emails. Seth figured Bradshaw had been stalking people long enough to figure out how to use a Dark Net browser to hide his IP address. But on one email, Bradshaw slipped up and used an address Seth could track.

"Bingo." One mistake led to another, and Seth followed the clues like a bloodhound. A weakness in a mobile app made it easy for Seth to hack into Bradshaw's bank account. Once there, Seth found a credit card and started a trace.

His first search pinged with initial results. In the years since Evan had left his abusive boyfriend, Bradshaw's life had unraveled. Seth uncovered a rotten credit history, tax problems, and a checkered work history. The search also turned up a couple of drunk and disorderly charges Seth's first scan had missed. Unfortunately, nothing provided a trail to Pittsburgh.

Seth went back to the bank account. Most of the time, Bradshaw coasted by with a few hundred to a few thousand bucks to his name. He'd racked up lots of overdraft charges. But then, two weeks ago, a nine-thousand-dollar deposit showed up. Seth let out a low whistle, gathering everything he could about the source of the deposit. He fed that information into another program, with an awful suspicion of where the clues would lead.

Another ping told him he'd hit pay dirt with the credit card. Bradshaw didn't have the credit history to get a high-end card. The no-name bank online site proved easy for Seth to hack. He managed a humorless smile when he scanned the transactions. A recurring charge for an extended stay hotel in a rough part of town and payment for a couple of speeding tickets.

Seth noted the address of the hotel, then dug deeper on the tickets. All four had occurred off Route 28 along the Allegheny River, an older, industrial area. Seth pulled up a map and zoomed in close. The old buildings would be a perfect place to hide. Not too far from Bradshaw's hotel and in a neighborhood that wouldn't notice someone coming and going. He ran the addresses through a title scan and came up with a list of possibilities. Three of the buildings were still in use. Those dropped to the bottom of his list. One had been badly damaged in a fire. That went to the bottom, too.

Three other structures in that cluster remained likely. Two were warehouses whose owners had gone bankrupt, letting the buildings fall into ruin. The other had a brief rebirth as a storage facility, before running into tax problems that shut it down.

Seth dialed Travis's number. "I think I know where Evan is—and who took him."

"Give me the details."

"What about Lawson?" Seth asked.

"He couldn't get ahold of Alex and Brandon, so he drove up to check on them. The cabin's a couple hours away, so he probably hasn't gotten there yet. It's east of here, and they've got more snow out that way," Travis replied.

Travis listened as Seth laid out the results of his investigating. "Damn. That's good work. Don't tell Brent I said this, but he could probably pick up a trick or two from you."

"He'd be thrilled to hear you say that," Seth remarked. "Look, can you go check out the hotel, and then meet me over by the warehouses? I'm going to head straight there. I want to rule out the hotel, but the industrial district seems like a better place to hide someone."

"Okay. Just—be careful. We already know this guy has a gun."

"So do I. See you down there."

~

YESTERDAY, Seth kept wishing Brent Lawson would go away and mind his own business. Now, Seth wouldn't have minded backup. He drove through the darkness, catching the highways after the last of rush hour had passed. A slow, steady snowfall threatened to fill in the tracks of countless cars that had already passed this way. Icy patches meant that even with good tires, Seth couldn't go nearly fast enough.

He hadn't been kidding about going in strapped. His Glock was snug in his holster at the small of his back, and he had a shotgun loaded with buckshot, not salt. Mike Bradshaw had hunted Evan. Now, Seth intended to return the favor.

He turned off Route 28 and headed toward the stretch of buildings his online search had identified. Once he left the main road, lampposts and security lights were few, leaving the rundown industrial area unsettlingly dark.

Seth drove past the first two buildings on the list, but it was clear from the untouched snow around them that no one had been near either structure. He slowed when he came to the drive leading to the defunct storage building. Fresh tire tracks—very fresh—led in and out, and in the high beams of his truck's headlights, Seth could also make out footprints.

Nearby, a gunshot echoed in the quiet night.

12

EVAN

EVAN RAN FOR HIS LIFE. HIS BICEP HURT LIKE HELL WHERE THE BULLET HAD grazed it, and blood ran down his arm, but he didn't dare stop.

Mike's attack forced Evan away from the road, back into the brush-filled strip of land that separated the industrial park from the highway. It had become a dumping ground filled with trash and cast-offs, which left Evan grateful for his parkour training as he dodged a rusted washing machine and vaulted a tangle of bent shopping carts.

He heard Mike crashing through the bushes and saplings, closing on him. Evan wasn't sure how much farther he could run; he still felt the effects of being drugged. He lacked his usual coordination, stumbling more than running, and his legs felt wobbly, as if they might go out on him at any moment. Evan realized he couldn't keep up his pace much longer, and when he slowed, Mike would catch him.

Based on the shouted curses that carried on the wind, Evan wondered if Mike would beat him to death or just shoot him and be done with it.

He still had the bottle, broomstick, and rock he'd grabbed at the storage facility, and the glowing stone that he didn't dare use to light his way tucked deep in his pocket. Evan tripped, sprawling in the snow, and knew he had reached his limit.

Evan spotted a tangle of bushes that might serve as cover. He ran past it, leaving footprints that led toward the warehouses. Then he doubled back, using a fallen branch to smooth his path in the snow. He crouched down in the cluster of evergreens and drew two sigils in the snow: one for silence, and one for distraction. Calling on his waning energy, Evan found enough of himself to send a faint glow through the marks before they went dark. He stayed motionless, unsure the rote magic had worked.

Mike wouldn't give up until he found Evan. Not when he'd been so close to having Evan at his mercy. Which meant Evan couldn't hope to just out-wait his pursuer and sneak off. The only way Evan was going to get out alive was by taking Mike on in a fight. No one said it had to be fair.

Evan needed a distraction, something to capture Mike's attention long enough for Evan to ambush his ex-boyfriend and have a chance of getting in a strike that would stop Mike and let Evan get away. He drew one more sigil in the snow and laid his palm over it, investing the last of his focus and hoping the images in his mind conveyed his intention.

He'd banished ghosts before but rarely summoned them. Evan hadn't even been sure there would be ghosts nearby to heed his call. But as the wind picked up, carrying the top layer of snow with it, Evan felt a chill that he knew wasn't due to the weather.

Mike sounded like a bull stampeding through the scrub bushes and trash-filled high grass, so close that Evan expected to see him burst into view at any second. As Evan stared out of his warded hiding place, he saw pinpricks of light appear from nowhere, then larger orbs dancing in the dark air, just like he had seen out on Blue Mist Road. At the edge of his vision, Evan saw gray shapes dart in and out of the shadows.

Mike came barreling past, and Evan held his breath, holding still and hoping his thudding heart didn't give him away.

"What the fuck?" Mike roared, as the orbs and gray figures closed around him. Evan had sent a mental picture of Mike holding him at gunpoint and striking him, hoping the ghosts would help. Whatever the spirits had picked up from his thoughts, they had taken a dislike to

Mike, and the apparitions closed around him as the orbs zoomed and dove at his head.

Evan knew it was now or never. He wasn't sure how long the ghostly distraction would last, and when it ended, Mike would be all the more ruthless. Evan slipped from cover, moving as silently as he could, and came up behind Mike, then swung the beer bottle at his head, ready to block a punch with the broken broomstick.

"You little shit!" Mike staggered, but the bottle didn't drop him to his knees like on TV. He raised his gun, and Evan dove at him, shoving the gun hand to one side and taking them both to the ground.

The gun fired, but the bullet went off into the darkness. Evan lost the broomstick as he grappled to keep the gun hand down. Mike swung at him from the left, but Evan saw it coming and blocked the blow just like when he sparred with Seth. He put his weight into keeping Mike's right arm—and the gun—pinned. The bottle had gone flying, and as they grappled, the chunk of rock fell from Evan's pocket. Mike bucked beneath him, trying to fling Evan loose. If that happened, Evan knew he was a dead man.

Mike grabbed at Evan's face. Evan bit down, hard, on Mike's fingers. Evan grabbed the rock chunk with his free hand, ignoring how much it hurt to move his injured arm, and smashed it into Mike's temple. Blood spattered, and Mike's eyes rolled back in his head. His grip on Evan went slack. Evan scrambled to his feet and kicked the gun from Mike's right hand.

Evan pulled out his light-rock. Its glow had begun to fade, but it remained bright enough for him to get a look at his attacker. Blood matted the hair on one side of Mike's head, but he was still breathing, so Evan hadn't killed him. He wasn't sure how he felt about that, relieved not to have a death on his conscience, or conflicted that the threat wasn't over for good.

"Evan!"

Two voices, coming in from different directions, both shouting his name. He couldn't place one of the voices, but he knew the other. Seth. Seth had come for him.

"Over here!" Evan yelled in response, moving away from Mike's prone form toward where he had heard Seth's shout. He lifted the light-rock in one hand and waved it in the air.

Seth and a stranger converged seconds later, trampling down the underbrush and picking their way around the larger pieces of junk, the beams from their flashlights bobbing in the darkness.

"Seth! Watch out!" Evan grabbed for the broomstick, ready to charge in to protect his boyfriend from the newcomer.

Both men raised their hands in surrender, and Evan stopped, confused.

"This is Travis. He's a hunter—and a friend."

It took a moment for Seth's words to register, then Evan lowered the stick and nodded. The two men closed ranks around Evan, and Seth's eyes widened when he saw the rip in his parka tinged in blood.

"What—"

"He shot at me and missed. Mostly." Now that the adrenaline of the fight was fading, Evan felt woozy from the pain and exertion.

"Where is he?" Seth demanded.

"Over there." Evan raised an arm, pointing. Seth and Travis turned, and Evan followed the beams of their flashlights.

Mike was gone.

"Shit." Seth moved toward the bloodied snow where the depression made it clear a man had been lying minutes ago. Travis caught him by the arm and didn't let go even when Seth tried to jerk free.

"He's got a gun," Travis reminded him. "And it's dark. We don't know how well he knows this area. Getting yourself shot isn't going to help. He's gone for the moment. If he meant to shoot at us, he'd have done it. We need to get out of here."

Evan staggered, and Seth was beside him before he could hit the ground, slipping under one arm to keep him on his feet and sliding an arm around his waist. "Come on," Seth coaxed. "Let's get you home, and we'll take care of you."

"I'd like to come, too," Travis said. "Found some things at that hotel you'll want to hear about."

Seth gave a curt nod. Evan had held it together during the crisis, but now that he was safe, his body seemed to take it as permission to fall apart. *Grandma would have said I had the collywobbles*, Evan thought, and the memory seemed so out of context that he giggled.

"Evan?" Seth sounded worried as he supported—half carried—Evan toward the parking lot.

"Nothing," Evan managed. "Just...maybe having a little break-down. I'll be okay."

∼

EVAN FELT a surge of happiness when he spotted the RV as they pulled into the campground. Seth came around to open his door and help him down from the truck, then pulled Evan into his arms.

"God, I was so scared," Seth murmured, burying his face in Evan's hair. He angled his head for a desperate kiss, and Evan leaned into the embrace. Evan's eyes flew open as he remembered.

"The text message! And the video. Seth, I didn't—"

"Shh. I know. Figured it out for myself." Seth helped him up the steps to the trailer, and Evan turned to face him.

"I swear I wouldn't leave—"

Seth placed a finger over Evan's lips. "It's okay, baby. I get it. Let's just go inside and see about that arm, get you warmed up, huh?" His voice was rough, and Evan realized that Seth sounded ragged.

Seth helped Evan out of his coat and boots, along with the rest of his outdoor wear. He made sure Evan was comfortable on the couch before he went to start a fresh pot of coffee, and Evan felt certain that when Seth returned, his cup would have a shot or two of Jamison in it. He hoped so.

Evan felt cold to the bone, both from the temperature and from his brush with death. He shivered and drew one of the cozy throw blankets around him, burrowing in. *I'm safe. I'm home. Seth came. He didn't believe the text. The video didn't make him give up on me. I'm safe. I'm home.* His thoughts looped, and Evan found himself staring straight ahead, gripping the edges of the blanket he pulled close around him as if he were afraid someone might try to tear it out of his hands.

Everything hurt. His head throbbed. Evan had never tried to work that much rote magic at one time, sigil after sigil. Later, he would be

145

proud of himself for what he'd done, but right now, it took all he could do to think through the pain.

His left bicep felt like he'd been stuck by a hot poker. The rest of him ached from the fight, the awkward way he'd been manhandled and left tied up, and from the ungainly, headlong run that had him twisting and vaulting over obstacles in the trash-strewn dividing strip. *Probably should get a tetanus shot.*

The idea seemed so totally normal, after a night that definitely wasn't, that Evan found himself giggling again. This time, he couldn't stop. It started as a few chuckles bubbling up from inside and then continued until he was laughing hysterically, arms wrapped around his tight belly, heaving for breath, tears running down his face. The manic laughter continued without his permission and beyond his control until his breath came in shallow spasms and his eyes burned.

"Evan? Baby, what's wrong?" Seth ran from the kitchen and knelt in front of Evan, holding him by his shoulders as Evan wheezed and shook.

"I...can't...stop." Evan's face was locked in a grin so wide it hurt, his throat felt raw, and he thought maybe he had lost his mind.

"Shh. It's the let-down. It'll be okay." Seth wrapped his arms around Evan, adjusting his grip when Evan winced at the touch against his shoulder. Gradually, the involuntary laughter subsided, only to give way to wracking, uncontrollable sobs.

He didn't think he had any tears left, but his body managed. Evan cried and shook, each breath tearing from his lungs, so hard he thought he might throw up. Seth just rocked him, one hand on Evan's head, pressing him against his chest, the other around his waist. He had no idea what Seth said, but he knew that Seth's reassuring words and calm voice never wavered. Evan sniffled and swallowed as the panicked reaction finally subsided. It left him wrung out and completely spent.

Seth pressed a kiss to the top of his head. "I'm going to get that cup of coffee for you, and then we're going to patch up your arm. Travis should be here soon."

Evan found himself staring at the TV, which wasn't turned on. It seemed as good a focal point as any. Now that the terror had passed,

Evan guessed shock was setting in. It seemed unfair to escape death and then feel so disconnected.

"Drink this. You'll feel better," Seth said, giving Evan a warm mug. The potent vapors confirmed that it contained more than a dollop of whiskey.

"I'm sorry," Evan whispered, bending to sip from the cup. Seth stared at the bloody cuts on Evan's wrists, seeing them in the light for the first time, and his expression darkened.

He pushed the hair back from Evan's face. "Babe, you've got nothing to be sorry for. You were badass." He eased back the blanket and caught his breath when he saw the bloody sleeve.

"I'll be right back," Seth promised, heading for the medical kit they kept under the bed, since it was too big to fit in the tiny bathroom's almost non-existent storage space. He returned with the bag and led Evan over to the table, where the light was better.

"Okay, not as bad as it looked," Seth said, letting out the breath he had been holding. "It really is a graze. But we need to clean it carefully because the bullet went through the fabric, and if we don't get the fibers out, you'll end up with a nasty infection. You might want to take a few big swallows of that coffee. This is gonna hurt."

Evan did as Seth suggested, but even after they waited for the whiskey to hit his system, cleaning the wound still hurt like fuck, despite how careful Seth tried to be.

"Sorry," Seth said, wincing as Evan flinched. "On the bright side, it doesn't need stitches. And you'll probably have a scar. Chicks dig scars."

Evan narrowed his eyes in a glare. "Did you forget the part where I'm gay?"

Seth grinned. "Nope. Just wanted to see if you were paying attention." He shook a few pills into his palm. "Take this," Seth said, offering the capsules to Evan. "Antibiotic. I'll ask Travis if he knows somewhere you can get a tetanus shot tomorrow that won't ask questions about a gunshot wound or your wrists."

"Brandon's an EMT," Evan mumbled.

Seth nodded. "I thought of that—but Brandon's hiding in a cabin somewhere. So, that's not going to help. I looked up the St. Dismas

Community Center Travis runs. It's got a clinic. Maybe he can get a favor from the doc."

Evan held out his wrists so Seth could clean the wounds, then apply antibiotic ointment and wrap them with gauze. He checked Evan's ankles as well, but the ties had gone over his socks, so the bonds had bruised and chafed, but not actually cut into his skin.

"Any body blows?" Seth asked, gently sliding his hands over Evan's body, checking for injuries. "Do your ribs hurt? Did you hit your head?"

"Ribs are okay. And I didn't hit my head. I think…he was saving the rough stuff…for when his boss was through with me." The words were out before he had time to process.

"His—" Seth's jaw clamped with anger, and his eyes blazed. This time it took visible effort to calm himself. "Fuck. I can't even—"

Evan slipped his hand over Seth's wrist. "It didn't get that far. Don't make it worse thinking about what might have happened." Because Evan sure as hell couldn't. He was pretty certain his overwhelmed brain was just going to shut down any moment.

"Finish the coffee," Seth instructed. "I'll give you some pain pills before we go to bed. But I figured you'd want to be awake when Travis got here." He looked down. "I'm sorry to ask, but if you can tell your story, it would help a lot. Just once—when everyone's here."

"Anything if it helps catch that bastard," Evan replied. He looked up and met Seth's gaze. "You need to know—he said 'his boss' told him he couldn't kill me. I think he's working with Thane."

Seth passed a hand over his eyes. "Shit. I was afraid of that."

A knock at the door had Seth jerking to his feet. His gun was in his hand before he straightened. He checked through the window and opened the door to let Travis into the RV. The gust of cold air swept a sprinkling of snow in with him and made Evan reach for his blanket again.

Travis looked to them with a grim expression. "Brent called. Someone got to the cabin before he did. Alex is injured—and Brandon's gone."

13

SETH

"How the fuck did that happen?" All of Seth's pent-up frustration and anger over Evan's injuries seemed to explode into a single comment. He caught himself and drew in a deep breath. "Sorry. Sorry—it's been a long night."

Travis stripped off his jacket and toed out of his boots, shoving his hat, scarf, and gloves into his sleeve. "I get it." He looked at Evan. "How are you holding up?"

Evan managed a wan smiled. "Been better."

"The bullet grazed him, the zip ties cut the hell out of his wrists, and he needs a tetanus shot—"

"Matthew runs the clinic at St. Dismas. He'll take care of that—no questions asked."

Seth nodded. "Good. That's what I hoped. Now—what's going on with Brandon?"

Travis went to the kitchen and made himself a cup of coffee. "You know what I know. Brent is bringing Alex here. Safety in numbers."

Normally, Seth would have balked at having the RV offered as the gathering point, but he didn't have a good alternative. If someone got to Brandon and Alex in a location Brent had thought was secure, then the RV was vulnerable, no matter how good the wardings and security precautions. They might as well make it their secret hideout, for all the good it would do.

Travis settled into one of the leather recliners at the end of the room while Seth and Evan headed back to the larger couch. Evan pulled the blanket over them and curled up next to Seth, resting his head on Seth's shoulder. Seth slipped an arm around him, drawing him close.

"Didn't get a chance to tell you about Bradshaw's hotel room," Travis said and paused to taste his coffee. "I went back after we left the storage facility. It was like something out of one of those serial killer TV shows." He stared at the mug in his hand, frowning. "I don't know if Bradshaw was always unhinged, or if something's made him more so. But the hotel room had printouts, photos, and clippings all over the walls. Some of them were years old. He's obviously been stalking Evan for quite some time," he added, looking at the man huddled beside Seth.

"Years," Evan said quietly.

"Since I was already breaking and entering, I did a sweep of the place," Travis continued. "No computer or tablet—must have them on him. I grabbed everything that connected him to Evan and brought it with me. Didn't want anything left behind if the cops go looking, or the hotel manager evicts him."

"Thanks," Seth said. He had one hand on Evan's good arm, lightly running up and down in a soothing gesture. Which of them might find it more comforting was up for debate.

"Brent found some more photos of Robeson, and even one of him when he was Bennington," Travis said. He walked over and held out his phone, showing them the pictures. Two of the shots were blurry and caught only the lower portion of the man's face, his eyes hidden by large sunglasses. Those photographs were just his head and shoulders and looked like a reporter had snapped them holding his camera above the crowd. The third and four pictures were three-quarters views, revealing a forty-ish man with a round face, compact body, and expensive taste in suits.

"Wait," Evan said. He moved forward, peering intently at the pictures, then used his fingers to enlarge the image. "There." He looked from Seth to Travis. "That's his amulet. His wristwatch." He grinned. "Like the ghosts told us. *Watch*."

Seth remembered the warning the ghosts at Blue Mist Road had given them. "You're sure?"

Evan nodded. "It was something I noticed in the pictures of Thaddeus Ramey and Adolph Brunrichter. They were all wearing the same watch. Now this? Can't be a coincidence."

Evan retreated into the safety of Seth's embrace, and Travis went back to his seat. "No, I'm sure it's not a coincidence," Travis replied. "What do we have to do with the amulet?"

A few days ago, Seth would have bristled at the assumption that Travis and Brent would be part of the effort to take down Thane. Now, he welcomed their help. He knew that despite his injuries and the likelihood that Bradshaw would be wherever Thane was, Evan would insist on going, and Seth knew better than to try to talk him out of it. This fight belonged to both of them now equally, for different reasons, and the fact that Evan was alive and here with him tonight was proof that he could hold his own.

He was so fucking proud of his boy.

Travis's gaze gave Evan the once-over. "No telling when Brent and Alex will get in, and I'm thinking that sleep and some pain meds would do Evan a world of good. How about if you tell us what happened, and Seth and I will fill Brent in later."

Evan looked like he intended to argue, then yawned and blinked. "Yeah. Okay. Probably a good idea. I'm kinda done for, and pain pills sound frickin' awesome."

Seth and Travis listened in silence as Evan recounted everything that happened, from the kidnapping at Kona Café to waking up in the storage facility and afterward. Seth stiffened in suppressed fury as Evan told them about Mike's threats. When Evan described matter-of-factly how he had used the sigil to loosen his bonds, Travis's eyebrows shot up, but he didn't interrupt.

Hearing Evan talk about how he'd eluded Bradshaw made Seth grateful for all the training they had done, and all the lore they had studied. He silently cheered Evan's strategy in the wooded median strip, making more use of his sigils. That Evan had the determination and grit to hold his own against Bradshaw, injured and terrified but still so damn stubborn, made Seth flush with pride.

"And that's when you showed up," Evan finished. He leaned back against Seth as if telling the tale had drained the last of his energy. Seth kissed his temple and cuddled him close for a moment, eyes closed, realizing how close a call it had been.

I could have lost him. Almost did. Fuck.

Travis leaned forward. "How did you learn magic?"

Seth couldn't tell whether Travis disapproved or was merely curious. "I figure it's kinda like prayer, only not addressed to a particular listener," he replied.

Travis seemed to pick up on the edge in Seth's voice. "No, you're misunderstanding me. I'm not against it. Just…interested."

"I guess the Vatican wasn't much for magic?"

Travis grimaced. "You'd be surprised. They just found ways to use the power and deny the source. I wasn't just a priest—I was part of a secret organization that fought dark powers. I didn't like the way they did things. One reason why I'm not part of that anymore." Seth would have loved to learn more, but he knew that conversation—if it ever happened—would have to wait for another time.

"My mentors taught me what they'd learned, things they'd picked up over the years," Seth answered. "They've been hunting for a couple of decades, seen a lot of shit go down. And they have a couple of friends who are light witches. Simon Kincaide filled in a few of the other blanks."

Travis nodded. "Simon knows a little bit of everything. He's like a walking Wikipedia of the weird."

"You're not against magic?" Seth couldn't help the hint of challenge in his voice. He didn't expect Travis's bark of a laugh.

"No. If you only knew… No, I'm the last person to tell you not to use what works. I have a habit of co-opting the other side's assets and using them as a weapon. Got me into all kinds of trouble with my superiors. And from what you've said, I doubt there's anything

demonic involved with your spells. Simon would have warned you."
He raised an eyebrow. "If he ever does—"

"I'll be sure to listen," Seth replied. He shifted a little beneath
Evan's weight. Evan was drowsy, and Seth needed to get him somewhere comfortable. "Let me take him in the other room, and I'll
be back."

Evan was a warm tangle of limbs, too exhausted to manage to
stand on his own. He protested groggily as Seth scooped him up into a
bridal carry and headed for the bedroom.

"Argue all you want, but you'd like it less if I slung you over my
shoulder, and you can't walk," Seth told him. Evan wasn't arguing
very vehemently, and Seth figured it was mostly his pride talking.

"Just figured if we ever did this, there'd be fucking at the end of it,"
Evan mumbled. "I feel cheated."

Seth smiled. If Evan was thinking about sex, the odds of a full
recovery looked promising. "First, pain pills. Trust me when I say
they're the opposite of Viagra. We'll talk about your little swept-off-
your-feet fantasy when you wake up."

Evan barely stayed awake long enough to swallow the medication
with a glass of water. Seth tucked him into bed and kissed him gently.
"I'm so fuckin' proud of you," Seth said, unashamed of how his voice
caught. "You saved yourself—like a frickin' ninja."

"You were the cavalry, coming in over the hill," Evan replied in a
sleepy murmur. "Knew you'd come."

"I'll always come for you," Seth replied, kissing Evan again, a
brush of lips. He let his palm linger on Evan's cheek, and Evan pressed
his face against him.

"Love you," Evan whispered.

"Love you, too," Seth answered, wondering if Evan could hear the
unshed tears in his voice. "I won't be far. And I'll check in on you. But
I'm probably not going to get much sleep tonight, or at least, not for
a while."

"Thasss okay," Evan slurred as the pills took effect. "Be right here."

Seth knew when the medicine kicked in because Evan's body relaxed,
and the hand he had placed on Seth's arm dropped to the mattress. Seth

tried to arrange the pillows to make sure Evan's injured arm was comfortable, then he left a light on in the bathroom and headed back to the living room, leaving the door ajar so he could hear if Evan needed him.

He stopped in the kitchen before rejoining Travis and poured himself a couple of fingers of whiskey, neat. When he walked back to the living room, he held up the glass, offering the same to Travis. The ex-priest shook his head.

"Save it for Brent and Alex. They're going to need it."

Seth sat down on the sofa and pulled the throw blanket into his lap, taking comfort from its warmth. "Did you catch the part where Bradshaw said his 'boss' said he couldn't kill Evan?" He knew his voice conveyed all his pent-up fury.

"Yeah. You figure Thane somehow got Bradshaw working for him?"

Seth nodded. "Gotta be. Bradshaw would have signed on to have a chance at Evan, and if he bragged about his boss being a 'big man' and having a 'big score' coming up, then he's gone full Renfield," he added.

"I was thinking Igor, but there's not much difference," Travis said, nursing his cup of coffee. "Bradshaw's sold his soul, or at least thrown in his lot with Thane, up to and including, murder. So, by my former employer's rules, he has forfeited his innocence and becomes a 'righteous kill.'"

"Shit. Those ninja priests play hardball."

"You have no idea. And I hope you never do."

Seth thought before he spoke, a question that had weighed on his mind since he had found out who Travis and Brent really were. "This Vatican black ops group—how come they don't get involved in something like tracking down the witch-disciples? I mean, it's not exactly the apocalypse, but over a century, with twelve witch-disciples, the death toll has to be in the hundreds."

Travis sighed and looked away. He was quiet long enough that Seth didn't think he was going to answer. "Because it's in the hundreds, not the thousands or the hundreds of thousands," he replied. "The same is true for the government's supernatural special ops organizations. While they themselves want to stay in the shadows, they need to be able to take credit—at least internally, to their minders—for averting the end of the world to keep their funding and their shiny high-tech toys. With something like this, there aren't enough casualties to make the news cycle, and we're too far out in the boondocks for anyone to care."

"I promise you, plenty of people care." Seth's voice was icy.

"Of course they do. But not the *right* people," Travis replied, his voice bitter and heavy with sarcasm. "Did you think I was kidding when I said I quit?"

Seth swore under his breath. "So...no help from that direction."

Travis shook his head. "I reached out to my contact—against my better judgment—on a big situation not long ago. Which *was* closer to the apocalypse—at least locally—than I want to think about, and they turned me down, for exactly the reasons I just told you. Brent did the same with the government group that comes sniffing at his heels. Even with a chance to get their hooks into us, they wouldn't come to the rescue."

"What happened?"

Travis's eyes had gone cold. "We handled it."

Seth made a mental note to ask Toby and Milo what they knew about that mysterious near-end of the world and debated whether he wanted to find out.

The familiar rumble of a pickup truck made both men look toward the windows. "That'll be Brent," Travis said. Still, both of them drew their guns. Travis remained out of sight of the door when a sharp rap summoned their attention, while Seth checked before admitting the two stragglers.

"Shit," Seth said, taking in Alex's appearance. One eye was swollen nearly shut, he had a split lip and a bloodied nose. Those were the visible injuries.

"You got a med kit? He needs some attention," Brent said in a brusque tone as he half pulled, half dragged Alex into the RV. Seth stuck his head out and looked around to make sure there was no one behind them.

"We weren't followed. I checked," Brent replied in a curt tone. He helped Alex to the table, where the med kit was still out. From the way

Alex held himself, Seth suspected bruised, if not broken, ribs. Seth went to get a warm washcloth and a towel, which Brent accepted gratefully.

"There're antibiotics and pain meds in there, and everything you need short of real surgery," Seth said.

"Thanks. I don't think there's anything beyond a few stitches," Brent replied. Seth and Travis sat quietly while Brent ran through triage.

"I'm fine," Alex snapped. "We need to be looking for Brandon. They took him. He could be anywhere. He could be—" His voice cracked, and he squeezed his eyes shut.

"You're not fine, and we have every intention of going after Brandon," Brent replied, continuing his field medic routine without a pause. "But if you aren't suitably patched up, you won't be going with us."

"The fuck I won't."

Brent raised an eyebrow. "Not if you're off your game. You get yourself killed because you won't do this the right way, and Brandon will have my ass. Then Travis will summon your whiny ghost, and we'll all have to listen to you lament not having listened to me before it was too late."

Travis's eyebrows shot up, and Seth stifled a snicker, despite the situation.

"How did they get in?" Brent asked as he cleaned Alex's wounds. His voice was measured and patient, more like an older brother than a boss. Seth figured that might sum up the two men's relationship since he guessed Brent probably had at least five years on Alex.

"All the lights went out. The whole cabin shook—hard enough to rattle the plates—and I heard wind outside, but when I looked out, none of the trees were moving. We had all the doors and shutters locked—and all of a sudden, they blew open," Alex recounted, his words slurring a bit from his fat lip.

"Magic." Seth, Brent, and Travis spoke almost in unison.

Alex gave them an incredulous look. "Seriously? This isn't a TV show."

"No, and they get it wrong on TV all the fuckin' time," Brent replied, carefully stitching a gash on the side of Alex's head.

"Maybe I really did hit my head too hard," Alex said, "because I thought you all blamed magic."

"Nothing's wrong with your head—or your hearing," Seth replied. "Evan and I came to Pittsburgh to save Brandon's life. We weren't stalking him—we were trying to protect him. That's why Evan was at the coffee shop. He was keeping an eye on Brandon—and a lookout for the guy who wants to kill him."

"Kill Brandon?" Alex's eyes widened, and he paled. "Why does someone want to kill him? He never told me that he owed anyone money—"

Seth gave a short version of the story, starting with the hanging of Rhyfel Gremory. He managed to recount what happened the night Jesse died in a flat tone, although it made his chest tighten and his gut churn, like always. Then he told Alex how he'd trained to become a hunter, spending two years honing skills and gathering information, in order to head to Richmond and save Evan, the next descendant of those long-ago deputies, from becoming another victim.

"Which is how Evan and I got together," Seth finished. "That was a little over a month ago. Technically, Noson Thane—the real name of the dark warlock who's after Brandon—wouldn't need to kill him until October, on the anniversary of Gremory's hanging. He gets a power boost out of it, and it renews his immortality. But there's nothing stopping him from leveling up early. We thought going after him sooner would stop him before he could target Brandon. But Thane does things differently."

Alex looked to Brent. "You believe this stuff?"

Brent gave him a world-weary look. "Where do you think I am, all those times I ask you to cover for me? Or what did you think I was doing when I drag in beat to shit?"

Alex grimaced. "I figured you had a drinking problem. Or owed money to the Mob. I mean, private investigator and all."

Brent just looked at him incredulously. "Do you have a booze problem we need to discuss? Or a bookie you owe money to? Because you're a PI, too, doofus."

Alex glared. "No. I just have anger management problems with perps who hit kids." He let Brent check his ribs and belly, wincing at the touch. Even from where Seth sat, he could see bruising in the shape of a boot.

"Anyhow, all of a sudden, there were these guys who looked like Mob muscle swarming the cabin." Alex continued his story. "Brandon and I tried to run, but they came in front and back. We fought, but they were big—and they had guns. Two of them grabbed Brandon. I used every dirty trick in the book, but they put me down like a chump." Seth could hear the self-blame in Alex's tone.

"You did everything you could," Seth said. "You're lucky they didn't just shoot you—or take you with them, as an extra sacrifice."

"Sacrifice?" Alex echoed. "You're serious? Like something out of *Temple of Doom*?"

"Close enough," Seth replied.

"How do we stop them?" Alex's blue eyes had turned cold. "Because they can't have Brandon. I won't let him die."

"Then let's clean up the table, I'll go get the bottle of Jack, and we'll plan our own private war," Seth said.

Seth returned to the table with the whiskey, three more glasses, and his computer. He poured for everyone and refilled his own. Then he looked to Travis. "Did you ever have a chance to go out to the murder swamp and talk to the ghosts?"

The ex-priest nodded. "Yeah. It's been so busy, I didn't get a chance to tell you. Thane's been dumping bodies out there all along. He's just gotten better at picking spots where they won't be found and people who won't be missed. The ghosts described him and then identified him from the images I showed them. The most recent spirit I could contact was only a few months dead."

"Shit," Brent replied. "He's been under our noses all this time."

Travis shrugged. "We had a few other things going on," he said, with a meaningful look at Brent, and Seth figured that referred to the near-apocalypse they had averted.

"Travis explained why there won't be any ninja reinforcements," Seth added. Brent looked surprised at that but said nothing. "So I guess we're it. We need to find Thane's anchor and amulet—they help him store power, and he's weaker without them. He might still be too strong for us even if we destroy them, but if he's got them, we're screwed."

Seth brought up a map on his screen. "The amulet is something he'll have on him all the time. For Valac, in Richmond, it was a pendant he wore. Evan thinks Thane's is a wristwatch—and I'm pretty sure he's right."

"What about the anchor?" Brent asked.

"I don't know exactly *what* it is, but I'm pretty sure I know *where* it is," Seth replied. "The 1907 railroad tunnel at Livermore—could be either end, but my bet is the closer side. It's gated, but that wouldn't be hard to break into. Evan and I went out there, but something came up, and we had to head back before we could explore the tunnel." Close enough. He wasn't about to share the details of Evan's panic attack with the others.

"Alex and I can go look for the anchor tomorrow, as soon as it's light," Brent offered. His casual acceptance that Alex would be back on his feet seemed to cheer the other man, who managed a wan smile despite his split lip. "Just tell us what we're looking for."

"The witch-disciples aren't really immortal. Their lifespan is prolonged by a spell, which has to be renewed every twelve years with a blood sacrifice—one of the descendants of the deputies that hanged their master. So, to sustain a powerful spell over a long period—like a century—the witch needs to ground his power to an energy focus," Seth explained.

"The anchor is a spelled container with something very personal to the witch, like a lock of hair or nail clippings. When he does the ritual, he'll soak the amulet in the blood of the sacrifice, but the container with the element would be hidden someplace safe."

"Brandon," Alex said, his expression a mix of fear and determination. "Brandon's blood."

Seth nodded. "Yes. By the time I found Evan, Valac had begun the ritual. From what I saw, some part of Gremory survived in spirit form, locked away, and the ritual allows him to open a door from where he is long enough to give some of his power to the disciple."

"Another damn genius loci," Brent muttered. Travis rolled his eyes. Seth had no idea what they were talking about.

"How did you stop Valac?" Travis asked.

"I shot Valac's assistant and used a spell to get Evan out of the handcuffs. Evan snatched the amulet and got across the warding. Gremory's ghost was pissed he didn't get a sacrifice and sucked Valac through the door instead. Ate him, I guess," Seth answered. He realized all three men were staring at him.

"I didn't think anything would surprise badass ninjas like the two of you," Seth snarked.

Brent scratched the back of his neck. Alex looked a bit poleaxed like he was still struggling with "magic is real." Travis let out a patient sigh, then looked speculatively at Seth.

"You were military?"

"Army. Special Ops."

Travis glanced at Brent, who nodded. "Figured," Brent replied. "So was I. Then FBI, then Pittsburgh PD."

"The only thing that surprises me is that you and Evan survived without highly unusual training or experience," Travis said. He held up a hand. "That's not meant as an insult. Brent had several run-ins with demons before we tackled something similar, and I had years of very specialized preparation from my...organization. So I'm impressed. You did a helluva job. Surviving once is admirable. Deciding to make it a personal crusade—"

"Is completely wackadoodle," Seth answered. "And yet, here we are."

"So this anchor could be anything—as long as it is a container that could keep the elements safe," Brent mused. "Probably not a wooden box if it's stored outside."

"Valac's was a metal vial, and he hid it in a mausoleum," Seth said.

Brent nodded. "That would work. Some kind of weather-proof box —like a time capsule. Which I guess it is, in a weird sort of way. What do we do with it once we find it?"

"Destroy it. I bombed the mausoleum, but I have a tendency for overkill."

"Fuck. You don't do things halfway." Alex sounded torn between admiration and being appalled.

"Not when I've got to get it right the first time."

"Okay, so we'll need bolt cutters to get through the lock on the gate, and explosives," Brent said like he was putting together a mental shopping list. "Anything else? Lamb's blood? Eye of newt, toe of frog?"

"Personally, I'm partial to a little 'hair of dog,' but only when I drank too much the night before," Seth said with a smirk.

"Apologies to Macbeth," Travis said with an amused expression, recognizing the quote they had completely slaughtered.

"How can you joke about this?" Alex looked angry and mortified. "Brandon's out there, a prisoner of some weird psycho warlock who's going to kill him, and you're cracking jokes?"

Brent rested a hand on Alex's shoulder. "Do you remember the kind of humor cops use, cleaning up a bad accident? Among ourselves, when no one else can hear? It's inappropriate as fuck, but it's how we cope. Same thing happens in the military. The more awful it is, the darker the humor. It's what we do when we can't scream or shoot something."

"Or beat the shit out of an appropriate target," Seth added.

"So while we go get the anchor, what are the rest of you going to do?" Alex challenged.

"We're going in after Brandon, and we're going to make sure Thane never goes after anyone again," Travis replied. He gave Seth a look as if expecting a challenge.

"You, me—and Evan," Seth said warily. Travis nodded.

"Where?" Brent's tone was sharp.

"I think he'll do the ritual in Dead Man's Hollow," Seth said. "Thane had strong ties to that area, and until just recently, it was out of the way, so he didn't need to worry about being discovered. I imagine he'll come up with a ruse to keep people away—not that there's likely to be a lot of folks out in this weather." The glimpse he'd gotten outside the RV when Brent and Alex arrived told him that several new inches of snow had fallen since he'd returned from rescuing Evan.

"I think you're right," Travis replied. "In fact, that's probably one reason why the hellhounds were there. Civilians would report a 'wild animal attack,' word would get around, and they'd stay clear."

"There's been a lot of blood shed on that land," Seth said. "Factory accidents. Quarry deaths. It's more remote than some of the other sites he might have used in the past, like out on Blue Mist Road. And more sheltered, with the ruins that are still standing."

"Supernatural practitioners value sentimental attachment to a site," Travis replied. "It has to do with energy. The choice is rational—up to a point. But why he would pick one place over another that seems equally likely? Something about its energy calls to him." He glanced at his phone to check the time. "When we finish up, I'm going to spend some time meditating and see how far I can reach for ghosts. They can probably validate whether Thane's been around."

"Think they might give us a lead on the anchor?" Brent asked.

Travis shook his head. "Doubtful. I don't imagine Thane visits the anchor often. And Livermore wasn't a tragedy, despite what the urban legends say. So the ghosts don't have any reason to hang around. Dead Man's Hollow, on the other hand…"

"Just please, bring him back alive," Alex begged. Seth could see the worry in the other man's face and remembered far too well what it felt like when Evan was in the grip of a madman. "I bought a ring for him for Christmas," he said, his voice hushed. "I was going to propose on Christmas Eve. Please—"

Brent laid a comforting hand on Alex's forearm. "We're going to do everything in our power to get him back safely."

"How will we know when Thane's going to do the ritual?" Alex asked. "Oh, God. Maybe he did it tonight already—"

"What's the date?" Travis asked, then checked his phone again. "Fuck." He looked up. "Tomorrow is December 21. The Winter Solstice. It's one of the most powerful nights of the year for magic."

"Halloween falls on Samhain, another powerful night," Seth agreed. "If Thane is in a hurry to recharge his batteries, he'll do the ritual tomorrow, or he'll have to wait until the Equinox in the spring, or all the way to June, for the Summer Solstice. Shit. I should have figured that."

Travis shrugged. "What would it have changed? You were where you needed to be."

"And I fucked everything up," Alex said. He had a desolate look in his eyes. "I got spooked when I saw Evan in the coffee shop, after all the weird swamp murder stuff you had me looking into. I panicked. If I hadn't talked Brandon into running away—"

"Thane would have found you, regardless," Seth said. "He knew Brandon was at Kona Café. I, um, hacked their security feed. Thane was a regular. Keeping an eye on his ace in the hole."

"Shit," Brent muttered.

"Want to bet Thane sent Bradshaw after Evan as a distraction?" Travis mused. "He didn't count on Evan being able to hold his own. Because if Bradshaw had taken Evan and you hadn't been quick to figure it out, we'd have been going crazy trying to find him, and it would have taken us longer to realize they'd snatched Brandon."

"Which means Thane double-crossed Bradshaw, too," Seth said. "Because he'll need to kill several people before the main event in order to ramp up his mojo. And he has to realize that Evan was supposed to be one of the other disciple's offerings, so he—and I— would be prime blood."

"You?" Brent asked.

Seth looked away. "The disciples are supposed to take the first-born. But that night, they took Jesse by mistake. It should have been me."

It was after one in the morning before Seth slipped into bed beside Evan, after all of the battle plans had been laid. He thought he would be exhausted, between the whiskey and the events of the day, but his mind raced.

Seth lay staring at the ceiling in the dark, listening to Evan breathe. His emotions were a total clusterfuck, careening between rage at Mike Bradshaw for all the ways he had hurt Evan, now and before, and fear for Evan's safety.

A part of Seth truly hoped Bradshaw gave him an excuse to put a bullet in his brain. Another part hoped Bradshaw got what was coming to him from Thane himself and lived long enough to realize the double-cross. In the next heartbeat, Seth found himself worrying about how much Bradshaw's attack had set Evan back with his PTSD and anxiety. And an instant later, Seth took himself to task for his—however fleeting —jealousy and mistrust when he'd first seen that awful sex tape.

The tape wasn't Evan's fault. He didn't know. He thought he could trust his lover, and Bradshaw used that trust against him. I'm going to kill that fucker.

Evan snuffled in his sleep, and Seth looked at him, instantly on alert. He always left a dim light burning in the bathroom, a concession to his own troubled dreams. Waking in total darkness guaranteed that a nightmare would turn into a full-blown incident. Now, the faint light let him see Evan's features. The medication put him into a deep sleep, but even so, Seth saw a tightness at the corners of his mouth and eyes that made him wonder whether that sleep was dreamless.

After all the years Evan spent looking over his shoulder, running from that bastard, to have him finally show up? And then to threaten— Just thinking of Mike's physical and sexual threats made Seth's blood run cold. *If it frightens me, how much worse was it for Evan? Does it help that he got away—and fought off Bradshaw—on his own?*

Seth felt guilty that Brandon wasn't his top focus. After all, they'd come to Pittsburgh to save him. And Seth *did* care. But he wasn't going to apologize to anyone for caring more about the man sleeping next to him. Nights like this, when his heart felt shredded and his emotions were raw, Seth couldn't imagine how he had ever managed without Evan, how he had not realized he had an Evan-shaped hole in his life. He hadn't known it was possible to love someone so much, aside from his parents and brother. Now that he knew, he vowed to protect Evan with everything he had.

He sighed. *I'm sure Alex feels the same about Brandon, and he's sleeping on the couch, not knowing whether his boyfriend is dead or alive. Valac only had Evan for a few hours, less than a day. If Travis is right, and Thane's chasing the Solstice energy, it'll be more like a day and a half for Alex, bracing for the worst. I hope to hell we get there in time.*

Beside him, Evan shifted slightly, and Seth reached over to pull the blanket up over his lover's shoulders. *Evan's been doing so well, learning to trust. How far will this set him back? How will it affect us? Getting snatched would be traumatizing under any circumstances, but with all that history, it's likely to make his anxiety worse. Shit, we're both a hot mess. I wonder if Travis knows a good shrink who works with hunters? Couples' counseling—his and his PTSD. Matched set.*

Seth slipped his hand over to brush fingers with Evan. Just that simple touch grounded him. Tomorrow, they were headed into battle. Together.

14

SETH

Despite their late night, everyone except Alex and Evan woke a little after sunrise. Given that it was mid-winter, the sun rose late, but not late enough for Seth, who was too antsy to sleep despite not having rested well.

Thank fuck he hadn't had one of his flashbacks. It was a small mercy, but much appreciated. To his relief, Evan had slept soundly through the night. When the first pale rays of sunlight outlined the dark curtains, Seth slipped out of bed and tiptoed into the bathroom to get changed. He figured that since Travis and the others had signed on to his damn fool quest, he at least owed them coffee.

Alex lay sprawled on the long couch. Travis and Brent had found the two leather recliners and were talking quietly. Seth got the coffee going, rummaged in the cupboard to see what he could offer for breakfast and came up with cold cereal and muffins.

"Coffee'll be ready soon," he said quietly, heading into the living room and sitting down at the table. "There's stuff for breakfast in the kitchen. You're welcome to use the shower. The campground bathhouse has central heat, but you'll freeze your balls off walking there and back."

"How's Evan?" Travis asked.

"He slept," Seth said with a shrug. "Alex?"

"Once I convinced him to take a damn pain pill, he slept just fine," Brent grumbled.

Seth looked to Travis. "Any luck with the ghosts?"

Travis's black hair was long enough that the static electricity had strands poking out everywhere. "Not as much as I'd like—but distance is probably a factor. I got enough to know Thane didn't try to do the ritual at dawn. Ghosts make great spies. If they're strong enough and willing, they should be able to tell me a lot about his set-up."

Brent ambled out to get coffee and came back with mugs for himself and Travis, who accepted the cup gratefully. "We need to talk timing," Brent said. He glanced toward Alex. "The guy is going to be a wreck today. Can't say I blame him."

"Give him credit," Seth said. "He'll do what he needs to do. He's got a lot riding on this."

"I'm going to head over to Dead Man's Hollow, see what I can get from the ghosts when I'm closer to them," Travis said. "I'm afraid that even if Thane had intended to do the ritual later, he'll move it up to noon now that he knows Evan got away from Bradshaw, and he probably realizes that he's being hunted. I don't think he'll wait."

"Valac knew I was after him. He didn't care. Didn't think I could hurt him," Seth replied.

"You had surprise on your side," Brent observed. "Who knows whether the witch-disciples talk to each other, but maybe word gets around. The first guy disregarded you, and he's dead. The second guy might be more cautious."

"Or, Thane figures Valac made a mistake and that he won't be as easy to catch," Seth pointed out.

Travis went out to the kitchen, grabbed a muffin, and refilled his coffee. "We'll also want to time destroying the anchor so that Thane doesn't panic. We don't want to force his hand."

"How do we know Thane doesn't have magical traps set to keep intruders—or us—out?" Seth asked.

"We don't. Not yet. That's one of the things I'm going to try to sense for when I'm closer. If there are traps, either I'll find a way to disable them, or we'll get the ghosts to lead us around them," Travis replied, sounding more confident than Seth felt.

"What I'm really hoping is that once we're in position, doing an exorcism will slow down Thane's ritual—and Gremory's appearance—long enough for us to stop him," Travis added. "Brent and I had some luck using the rite with another kind of dark entity, but this sort of thing isn't exactly what they teach in seminary, or in my 'extra' training."

Seth knew that they needed to strike after Thane began the ritual to trap him inside the warded circle and keep him from using magic against them, but before he could complete the ritual. And if they moved in too soon and Thane realized it, they risked having him bolt —and take Brandon with him. Thane might prefer to do his ritual at Dead Man's Hollow, but Seth felt certain the warlock could work his magic elsewhere if need be.

Travis disappeared into the RV's bathroom and returned before his coffee was cold. "I'm heading over to get the ghosts primed," Travis said, finishing off the last of his drink. "You know the plan. I need to be line of sight for the exorcism when Thane opens the rift and Gremory's spirit appears."

"I'd like to stop him before that happens," Seth replied.

"So would I. And maybe we can. But if not, we've got a backup plan. A big piece of this depends on you and Evan taking out the guards when the ghosts draw them off," Travis reminded him. "And we still don't know if Bradshaw is a loose cannon out there some-where, or back with his master."

Too many unknowns, as usual, despite their late-night strategy session. Just like every military maneuver in Seth's career. Somehow, they'd make it work. They had to.

"As soon as we've pulled some the guards away, I'll cue Brent to detonate the anchor," Travis added as he shouldered into his coat.

"Assuming he can find it."

"He'll find it. He's like a rat terrier on a scent—and I mean that in the nicest possible way," he added with a grin aimed at his partner. The ex-priest laced up his boots, then grabbed his hat, gloves, and scarf. "I'm going to head over. I'll call when I'm in position."

Brent raised an eyebrow. "How are you going to hide that gunboat of yours?"

Travis grinned. "Leave it to the ninja priest." He went out into the cold, and moments later, they heard the rumble of the Crown Vic.

Brent grabbed a muffin and ate it in two bites. When he was finished, he woke Alex, who frowned, groggy.

"Morning?" he asked. Seth saw him look around at the unfamiliar trailer, and his eyes widened. "Oh my God. Brandon. We've got to go rescue Brandon!"

"We will," Brent said, placing a hand on Alex's shoulder. "But first, you and I need to find the anchor."

"But—"

"Travis went to stake out Dead Man's Hollow," Brent assured him. "Seth and Evan will head over as soon as Evan's up and moving. So go eat some breakfast while I shower, and then as soon as you're cleaned up, we'll go."

Alex looked as if he meant to argue, then saw Brent's determined expression and caved. "Okay," he said. "But make it quick."

Brent chuckled. "We can't destroy the anchor until closer to the ritual. But don't worry—we should have plenty of time to find it and rig the explosives. Army training—the gift that keeps on giving."

Alex made his way stiffly into the kitchen. Seth handed him a cup of coffee and a muffin, and Alex mumbled his thanks. In daylight, Alex looked worse than he had the night before. An ice pack overnight had taken down some of the swelling around his eye, but the bruises made it clear that he'd been punched. He moved like everything hurt, and from the careful way he held himself, that included tender ribs. Seth was glad that having Alex go with Brent to neutralize the anchor would keep him out of the fight. He feared Evan might be in similarly bad shape, but he also knew his partner would never agree to stay behind.

Brent was in and out of the shower in minutes. "You know, for a guy who was Army, that was more like a Navy shower," Seth joked. Brent flipped him off and pulled on his coat and boots. "I'll call you when we're at the tunnel," he said over his shoulder. "Send Alex out."

By the time Alex finished his shower, he looked a little more awake.

Seth wasn't surprised when the other man turned down any pain medication besides ibuprofen. "Brent went out to clean off the truck," Seth explained when Alex looked around the trailer, puzzled. "We got a good bit of snow last night."

Alex glugged down another cup of coffee. "I don't know how you held it together when that warlock took Evan. Because honestly, I'm a mess." His hand shook, sending ripples across the surface of the liquid in his cup.

"So was I," Seth admitted. "I was terrified. And to make it worse, Valac had planted evidence that made Evan think I was the bad guy. By the time he figured it out, it was too late." Seth let out a long breath. Just remembering how it had gone down made his heart pound.

"But you did it. You destroyed the anchor, stopped the ritual, and saved him." Alex gripped the cup tightly enough Seth feared it might crack. "I thought I was a tough guy. I'm not. Brandon depended on me, and I let him down."

"You got the shit kicked out of you when you were outgunned and outnumbered," Seth pointed out. "And if you hadn't gone down, they would have shot you. So...you lived to fight another day. And make no mistake—we are going to fight today."

"But I won't be there, in the thick of it."

"If you bring the anchor close to where the ritual is, you risk having Thane somehow take it from you—and then we're screwed six ways to Sunday," Seth said. "This way, you've got Brent's back, and it keeps you from being used as a hostage."

Alex looked down. "That's how they got Brandon to go with them. They threatened to kill me. He...he said he'd do whatever they wanted him to do if they let me live."

"And that's what they're still holding over him," Seth replied. "But once he knows you're safe, it's going to change everything. You can get there in time for the cleanup."

"Thanks," Alex said. "I'm sorry I freaked out over Evan."

Seth shrugged. "You made a logical assumption. And there's no way to say that all this wouldn't have still happened, even if the two of you hadn't gone to the cabin. So don't worry about it." He jerked his head toward the driveway, where he could hear the growl of Brent's truck.

"Go. Brent's waiting. Make sure you text when you find the anchor, and we'll tell you when to blow it up."

"Will do," Alex promised. Seth watched him head out, then locked the door behind him and went to wake Evan.

He found Evan already stirring and sat down on the edge of the bed, reaching out to smooth a strand of dark hair out of his lover's face. "Hey," he said quietly. "You awake?"

Evan groaned, definitely more from discomfort than arousal. "Yeah. I'm getting there."

"How do you feel?"

"Like I got hit by a truck," Evan said. "But I imagine Alex is worse." He was stiff enough that he accepted Seth's hand to get to his feet. Seth pulled him close, wrapping his arms around Evan and snuggling him gently against his chest. Evan leaned into him, holding on tight.

"I was so scared yesterday," Seth admitted, laying his cheek against the top of Evan's head.

"So was I. But then I got really angry. I just wanted to make it back home—to you."

Seth felt his heart leap at the casual way Evan linked home with the RV and him. "You were amazing," he murmured. "I heard the shot, and I thought…"

"I wasn't sure you'd come," Evan confided. "Mike bragged about the text and the video he sent you, and I was afraid that you would believe it."

After their fight a month ago, Seth thought they had talked the whole jealousy thing through, but apparently, Evan wasn't completely sure the matter was settled.

"It shook me when I first saw it. I couldn't help thinking maybe you'd met someone. We never really talked about commitment—"

"For the record, I'm committed. All in."

"So am I." He bent down to kiss Evan. "I will always look for you. Always find you. Always come and get you. No matter what."

"I know you will," Evan said, and kissed him back, a gentle, lingering affirmation. "And back atcha. Because we're partners. We save each other."

"Yes, we do," Seth replied, meaning more than just physical backup. "Partners." That word had taken on much more meaning now that it applied to their relationship. Although it was still far too soon, Seth found himself hoping the partnership would be permanent. He'd never found endearments comfortable to give or receive, before Evan. With Evan, sharing what he felt seemed to come naturally, and the walls he had built around himself got lower every day.

Evan shifted his stance and winced at stiff muscles. "Fuck. I'm going to go shower and hope it loosens me up. I feel like I'm eighty years old." He drew back reluctantly, and Seth watched him hobble toward the restroom.

"Take ibuprofen!" Seth yelled after him before the door shut.

He went back out to the kitchen, made a fresh pot of coffee, and sat down by the window while it brewed, watching the snow. By the time Evan finished his shower and joined him with coffee and the last muffin, Seth's phone rang.

"I'm in position," Travis reported. "And even better—so are the ghosts. I'm actually a mile or so away from the site, but close enough that the ghosts responded when I called. So they're our eyes, and they say no one's around."

"What about the hellhound?" Seth asked. "We really don't need a repeat performance."

"They haven't seen any hellhounds since we fought that one the night you were there." Travis chuckled. "Apparently, the ghosts were impressed that we managed to survive."

"Thanks to reinforcements," Seth said drily. "Still, if those creatures come back again—"

"We'll handle it," Travis said matter-of-factly. "Gotta go. I'll see you when you get here."

"So we're heading over?" Evan asked, playing with the rim of his coffee mug.

"Yep. We've got some tricks up our sleeves that we came up with after you went to sleep. I'll fill you in on the way over."

Evan stared at his coffee like it was a crystal ball. "How was Alex?"

"About like you'd expect." Seth ran a hand back through his hair. "Worried as fuck, blaming himself, scared we'll get there too late. I...understand."

Evan reached out and took Seth's other hand in his. "Let the past go," he said quietly. "That was something I realized when I was tied up in that warehouse. I'd spent years being afraid of exactly what happened, and in the end, the fear didn't change anything. Didn't prevent it. But Christ, all that time I spent being afraid, and I won't get those hours back. How much I held back, things I didn't do because I was scared to go out, how I kept everyone at a distance. I ghosted myself," he added with a bitter laugh. "I let him win."

Seth tightened his grip on Evan's fingers. "You did what you had to do to survive. And one way or another, we're going to make sure Mike won't hurt you or anyone else, ever again."

"I know that," Evan said with a determined smile. "Because I won't let him." He headed over and started to pull on his coat and boots. "Let's go." Evan looked scared and determined, an expression Seth remembered well from the faces of the men in his Army unit. Seth turned to face Evan.

"You sure?"

Evan's expression hardened. "Yeah. As sure as I'm ever gonna be." He looked braced for an argument.

"Okay then. Let's go." Seth got dressed, then opened the door and waited for Evan to go out. Evan stared at him.

"Just...like that?"

Seth stepped up to him. "You say you're all right, then that's what we go with. Doesn't mean I won't be right behind you."

"Better be," Evan replied, and the rigid set of his shoulders eased. "And I'll have your back, too." He brushed a kiss against Seth's mouth. "For luck."

Brent and Alex's call came in when they were almost to the parking lot where they agreed to meet Travis.

"We're here. Livermore. Godforsaken place, isn't it?" Brent observed. Seth could hear the wind wailing in the background.

"I'd like to come back and see it in the summer," Alex put in. "When we aren't stopping a crazy man."

"I couldn't get through to drive on the old bridge," Brent said. "Too much snow and they obviously aren't keeping that route clear since it doesn't go anywhere. So we're hiking in. It's going to take a bit to get there, but on the plus side, there's no sign that anyone else has been out here since the snowfall."

"Let us know when you get to the tunnel," Seth said. "Travis has his ghost sentries in place, and we're about to hike in. We'll be ready to move when Thane gets here."

"You sure we can't just blow up the damn anchor when we find it? I hate waiting around."

Evan shook his head. "Thane will know," he argued. "Valac collapsed while he was making his preparations. I didn't know why at the time; now I realize it was when Seth destroyed his anchor. It weakened him, but he also realized something had gone wrong, and so he started to rush so no one could stop him."

"Got it," Brent replied, although he didn't sound happy. "I'll let you know when we get into the tunnel."

Both Seth and Evan were on edge by the time they pulled into the Dead Man's Hollow parking lot beside Travis's Crown Vic. Travis got out to meet them. "Hope you wore good boots. We've got about a mile hike in to the old pipe factory from here. We'll have to take one trail and then switch back on another, but the cars will be hidden, and we can come in from the back." Travis's smile was predatory. "And the ghosts will keep them distracted."

"You sure he won't see the cars here?" Evan asked, looking around the otherwise deserted lot.

Travis shook his head. "It's not the closest parking lot to the ruins, which is why I picked it. Thane's not going to want to drag a struggling sacrifice farther than he has to."

Seth grabbed one gear bag, and Evan took the other. Both men carried their Glocks, with Ka-Bars in sheaths on their belts. Their bags held a variety of other knives, sawed-offs, ammunition, and salt, plus extras they had added, just in case. One of the most important, and tricky, parts of the plan rested on the tranquilizer guns both men carried. Seth had bought them after Milo suggested it, as a way to handle demon-possessed humans and animals without lethal force. They hadn't had a chance to use the new gear for more than practice shooting, and Seth hoped to hell it worked in the field.

Seth had spent the sleepless night before rehearsing his rote spells. Evan carried chalk and his slate, but the snow around them offered an even easier way to make his sigils.

"Stop."

Seth turned to see Evan standing by the truck. He looked scared and determined, beautiful in a wild, desperate way. Evan closed the few steps between them. "I love you. I just wanted to stay that." He kissed Seth, a brush of lips more potent for what it held back.

"I love you, too," Seth murmured. "So we're going to do everything in our power to be back here, alive and well, when it's over."

They trekked for a while in silence. The ghosts kept watch, ready to alert them to Thane or his guards.

"So Thane's not here yet?" Seth asked as they kept a brisk pace.

"No. But it's just after nine. I don't expect him to get here until close to noon—that's when energy will be strongest before it peaks again at midnight," Travis said.

"He's probably doing the first part of the ritual somewhere else, like Valac did at the old house," Evan replied. Seth swallowed hard at the memory of following Evan's trail, only to find an abandoned house awash in fresh blood and the corpses of several vagrants the witch-disciple had used to prime his power.

"I wish we knew whether Bradshaw was with him," Seth muttered.

"The ghosts are watching for any newcomers," Travis replied, leading the way. "They'll let me know when anyone shows up. My bet is that Bradshaw ran when he fucked up his boss's plan."

"I wish I thought he'd give up that easily," Seth replied.

"He won't," Evan stated, his expression grim and determined. "One way or the other, he'll be back."

Travis led the way, Evan followed, and Seth brought up the rear. Knowing that they didn't have to fight off vengeful ghosts lifted one worry, but even with Travis's help, they were going to have a fight on their hands once Thane arrived.

Seth couldn't see ghosts like Travis did, but some primal sense made the hair on the back of his neck stand up, and he slipped into battle mode. Evan looked equally twitchy, scanning the bare brush around them for threat, armed with a gun in one hand and a Ka-bar in the other. Even the forest seemed to be on high alert. The woods were eerily silent. No birds fluttered through the branches overhead, and there was no rustle of small animals in the underbrush.

He remembered the apprehension before the start of a battle. His whole body thrummed with pent-up energy, waiting for the signal to fight for his life. He glanced to Evan, assessing. Evan didn't have Seth's combat experience, but his survival instincts had been honed by years running from a stalker. Evan's tension and the coiled readiness of his stance told Seth his partner's mood mirrored his own.

Seth had filled Evan in on the details he missed the night before. Seth, Evan, and Travis each would hold down hiding places just out of sight of the old sewer pipe factory ruin, to avoid discovery when Thane and his helpers showed up. Then, they each had a part to play to disrupt—and stop—the ritual. The plan was utterly insane, but it was the best one they'd been able to come up with, and they'd run out of time.

The ruins of the old sewer pipe company came into view.

"Be careful," Seth murmured to Evan when they reached the split-off. "Come back in one piece."

"You, too," Evan replied, and this time, Seth moved for the kiss. Turning and walking away was hard, but Seth knew he didn't dare look back when they turned and went separate ways, as planned. Forcing himself into soldier mode was harder than it used to be, with Evan's life on the line, and so many more reasons to live.

He trusted Evan. His partner had proven his grit and skill, and the plan was as good a one as they were going to get. Splitting up made sense. Travis and Evan had argued for the plan, and Seth had to grudgingly agree. He still didn't like it, but he'd followed plenty of orders he didn't like in the Army.

When this was over, there'd be one fewer monster in the world, and the men of Brandon's family would no longer be hunted, generation after generation. Alex would have his lover back, and the many, many victims of the witch-disciple would have their revenge and long-overdue justice.

He didn't doubt that their work was essential. But adding Evan to the calculus of vengeance changed the way Seth looked at his quest. Knowing that it had become personal now for Evan saddened him as much as it assured their paths were intertwined. He hadn't factored in the loss of innocence that came with learning to kill, though he'd seen it in himself and in all the starry-eyed new recruits in his military years. The last month had changed Evan in an irrevocable way, and while Seth knew it increased his partner's safety, a part of him mourned its passing.

Seth found a hiding place not far beyond the sight line from the factory ruins, behind a tumble of broken stone and brick. His position was over a rise about a half of a football field's length from the old factory building where they were sure Thane planned to do his ritual. He hid behind the crumbling cement remains of a broken wall. The ruins provided shelter from the wind and kept him hidden from the trails leading up from the empty shell of the main building.

He hoped Evan had found suitable cover. A large chunk of stone made an adequate seat, and Seth settled in to wait for Travis's alert. He activated one of the hot packs in his pocket to keep his hands warm. He was used to being on watch in the Army or staking out a location waiting for one of the creatures he hunted. Although his military career had been in the desert, it had still gotten cold at night. *But there hadn't been all this damn snow to make everything damp*, he thought, huddling in his parka.

Seth had studied the park map and had paid close attention when he had visited the ruins before the snow. All that remained of the Union Sewer Pipe factory was a right angle of cement walls, open to the sky. He had initially dismissed the graffiti spray painted onto the walls as the work of vandals, but now he wondered if Thane had marked some sigils of his own that went unnoticed among the gang tags.

Seth took a video call from Brent, sending the audio through his earbuds. "We got the damn gate open. Didn't just have to cut off the lock—the thing was rusted closed. Took a hell of a lot of work to get it open."

"You're in?" Seth asked.

"Yeah. You see it?" Brent asked.

Seth peered at the image on the phone. Brent had brought heavy-duty mobile lights, which lit up the inside of the tunnel like daylight. "Yeah. Are those ice stalagmites?" Seth asked, looking at the odd, otherworldly columns that stuck up from the tunnel floor.

"Uh huh. Stalactites, too. Means we have to keep ducking or bring down a shit ton of ice on our heads." The video feed clicked off.

"So if the gate was rusted shut, it's a good bet Thane hasn't moved the anchor recently—if it's there," Seth said.

"It had better be here," Alex muttered.

"No one's been in here in a long time," Brent replied. "It doesn't go back real far. Concrete wall, just like you said."

"Be careful about blowing the tunnel to destroy the anchor," Seth cautioned. "That wall isn't just to keep people out. There's probably a lot of groundwater inside, even though the other end of the tunnel isn't under the reservoir."

"Lovely," Brent muttered. In the background, Seth heard a sound like glass shattering. "Hey! Quit kicking those!" Brent yelled to Alex.

"I'm not going to walk around the fucking things. They're all over the place," Alex returned.

"You see anything that might be the anchor?" Seth asked.

"Not yet. Think Thane buried it?"

"Maybe," Seth replied. "If he put it there soon after the tunnel was sealed, he might have wanted to make sure no one would find it if they checked on the wall."

"We brought shovels," Brent said, sounding unhappy about the idea of digging. "Of course, the ground is frozen because it's friggin' December."

"What about the walls?" Seth asked. "Brick or concrete?"

"Brick and stone around the front, and then concrete farther in."

"Before you try to dig, look for loose stones," Seth instructed. "I dug up a grave in Richmond thinking he'd buried the damn thing, and then realized he'd want to be able to get to it if he needed it without a whole lot of fuss. Turns out he hid it inside an urn in the mausoleum."

"With the ashes?" Brent sounded curious, despite himself.

"Fortunately not. Decorative vase. Did you completely miss the point of what I was saying?"

"Bring the light over here," Alex called. They heard the shuffle of feet and Brent swearing.

"Find something?" Evan asked.

"Maybe," Alex replied. "I think a lot of the bricks might be loose— if they weren't frozen."

"Move," Brent muttered. More shuffling sounded through the phone. "These lights put off a lot of heat. I moved it up close. That should melt anything that's going to come loose."

Footsteps crunched in the background. "There's not as much loose over here," Alex said. "I think it'll be over there. God, I hope so. I can't feel my fingers."

Seth heard the edge in Alex's voice as he tried to keep his worry for Brandon at bay and do his job.

"Give us a bit to thaw this out, and we'll call back when we've got something," Brent said. "And hope it's in the wall because the ground is solid as a rock. We won't be able to dig into it until spring."

At ten thirty, Travis's call made Seth's phone vibrate.

"Showtime. Tell Evan. The ghosts say that some of Thane's hired muscle showed up to get things ready. No sign of Thane, Brandon, or Mike Bradshaw, but that means he's going to do the ritual at noon, so we need to get our asses in gear."

"Got it," Seth replied. "I'll let Evan and Brent know."

"Did he find the anchor?"

"Not the last time I talked—" Just then, Seth's phone showed an incoming call. "That's Brent."

"Hold off on the explosions until my signal, like we planned," Travis said. "Tell him to stand by." Travis dropped off the call, and Brent's voice came through.

"Found it! Had to thaw out half of the damn rock in the front arch to get to it, but it's a small, locked steel box." He sent a photograph of a metal rectangle roughly the size of a man's hand and a few inches thick.

"You're sure it wasn't in the cornerstone, right? It really isn't a time capsule?" Seth probed, whispering. "And for God's sake, don't open it."

"Yeah. There's no date carved in the stone or any kind of plaque. And I did a 'sense magic' rote spell on it. Came up reeking of it. Not my first rodeo," Brent added.

"Travis said to hang tight. Thane's goons showed up at Dead Man's Hollow to get the place ready."

"Has he seen Brandon? Is he alive? Is he hurt?" Alex's voice came through loudly enough Seth wondered if he'd snatched the phone out of Brent's hand.

"Travis hasn't seen anything himself. He's using the area ghosts as spies," Seth replied. "Thane and Brandon—and Bradshaw—haven't shown up yet, but if the goons are here, we figure odds are good Thane's gonna try the ritual at noon, even if he was going to wait before." He paused. "And I'm sure Brandon's still alive. Thane needs him alive for the ritual."

"Shit," Alex sounded desolate.

"So do we nuke the box?" Brent asked.

"Hold off for now," Seth instructed. "We don't want to spook Thane."

"We could—" Alex objected.

"No, we couldn't," Brent said firmly. "Even if we don't set off the blast in the tunnel, it's going to be a lot easier to get away with blowing shit up out here than anywhere else. I've managed to stay out of prison this long—think I want to make it a habit."

He returned his attention to Seth. "I'm actually still thinking the tunnel *is* the best place. If there's any groundwater in it now, it's frozen like those damn stalagmites. And if I do it right, I'll bring down enough of the ceiling and walls to seal it up real good."

"You're the guy with the explosives," Seth replied. "Just make sure it destroys the box and doesn't just bury it."

Brent snickered. "Don't worry. The box'll be vaporized."

"Good." Seth juggled the phone. "Stay where you've got a good signal, and be ready to blow that shit sky high when you hear from Travis or me."

"You've got it," Brent replied and ended the call. Seth texted Evan with the recap, then settled in to wait.

Just after eleven, Seth's phone vibrated. "Thane's here. He's got three more guards—that makes a total of five—and a prisoner."

"Brandon," Seth whispered. "Is he still alive?"

"Yeah. No sign of Bradshaw yet."

Through the phone, Seth could hear Thane's guards making plenty of racket crunching through the snow. "They've got Brandon," Travis said in a whisper. "Not sure whether he's been drugged or magicked. They're building an altar."

A photo hit Seth's phone and he opened it to see several big men in parkas with high caliber handguns around a stone slap with black pillar candles ringing it, and Brandon's slumped form between them.

Seth spotted Thane. Unlike in the photographs of real estate mogul Cole Roberson, in his custom-made suits or investment banker-hermit Conrad Bennington in sleek Armani, Thane had cast aside his invented identities and gone back to his roots, wearing a dark, hooded robe. It might have been mistaken for a laughably low-budget movie if Seth hadn't known how high and real the stakes were.

"We're outgunned and outnumbered," Seth murmured.

"Ghosts say five guards coming in from the other parking lot," Travis reported. "No sign of Mike Bradshaw. They're setting up where we figured, in the corner of the main ruins, where the dark energy is strongest."

"I'll tell Evan. Watch your back."

With the guards coming, their communication would be limited to texts. Seth updated Evan. Then he checked in again with Brent.

Waiting was always the hardest part. No matter what the weather, long stretches when nothing was happening made it difficult to stay hyper-alert. Seth had far too much time to rehash the plan, thinking of all the things that could go wrong.

None of them had real magic, so going head-to-head against a warlock would be suicidal. If they attacked before Thane was committed to the ritual, he could use his magic to destroy them before they ever posed a threat. That meant they had to wait until Thane started the ritual and was both protected and trapped within the warded circle and unable to halt the spellcasting. But it also meant they were cutting it fine. Any error with timing and it would not only cost Brandon his life but their own as well.

"Go, *Seth!*" The text came from Travis. A second later, their group text showed Evan's message as well. Seth summoned his will, drew in a deep breath, and spoke the simple spell to summon ghosts.

Seth didn't pretend to understand how Travis's gift as a medium worked, or how he could arrange a deal with the sentient ghosts of Dead Man's Hollow to serve, on cue, as a distraction. Now, as he felt the rush of power flow through him and swayed with the life energy the spell cost, Seth just hoped the ghosts remembered their role and who the bad guys were.

The ghosts manifested in the flat area just beyond Seth's hiding place. He cued a recording from the player and speaker he had placed in the center of the clearing, a cacophony of glass breaking, metal banging, and stone falling on stone that echoed through the stillness of the woods, alarmingly loud. Seconds later, a similar ruckus sounded from near Evan's position.

Running footsteps followed. Seth got in position and took aim with the tranq gun. Evan and the others had balked at just shooting the goons dead on principle, although Seth knew the guards would have no such hesitation if they spotted him. He and Brent had objected because the gunshots would alert Thane to their presence. They figured the goons had already thrown in their lot with the enemy. The glares that Evan and Alex had leveled at them reminded Seth how different a civilian and military perspective could be.

Two guards burst into the clearing, big men in bulky parkas with guns already drawn. Seth cursed silently. Those parkas were going to make it hard to hit the targets with darts. That's where the ghosts came in.

On cue, the spirits sent a spray of snow into the air, stopping the guards in their tracks. Before the men could get their bearings, the ghosts began to pelt them with chunks of ice, harrying them from every direction, with no solid target for the men to shoot.

Seth aimed for the buttocks of the guard nearest him, figuring that if the dart could penetrate the thick skin of a cow, it should go through a pair of Levi's. In seconds, the big man swayed, then stumbled. He called out a slurred warning and fell flat on his face in the snow.

His companion looked around, wide-eyed, scanning for threats. Seth dropped back behind his cover. The ghosts seemed to enjoy their game because he heard the sound of pebbles pelting the ruin walls, and he eased back into position as the remaining guard turned toward the noise, presenting his ass as a target. The guard jerked when the dart hit him, reaching back to pull it free, but by then, the drug was already in his system. He gave an incoherent shout and stumbled back the way he came, but only made it a few steps before he fell to his knees, then collapsed and lay still.

Seth hesitated, in case the guard's shout brought reinforcements, then ran from cover. The dose had been calculated to keep its victims out for several hours, and Seth suspected they would feel mighty sick for a while after. He checked to make sure they were both truly unconscious, then whispered a "thank you" to the ghosts and moved with stealth and silence back toward the old ruins where Thane prepared his ritual.

He breathed a sigh of relief when Evan texted that he was also in position. That meant he had taken out the guards sent to check on his side of the ruins.

Seth moved into a line of sight position, down by the main pipe factory ruins. One guard remained, standing over Brandon, who knelt, slumped with defeat. The goon held a gun against Brandon's neck, but the weapon didn't seem necessary since Brandon's hands were bound in front of him, and all the fight seemed to have gone out of him.

Is he sacrificing himself for Alex, to keep Thane from harming his lover? Seth could imagine that threat having powerful leverage. He knew what he had been willing to risk to protect Evan back in Richmond when their relationship had barely gotten started. Seth didn't know how long Alex and Brandon had been a couple, but he understood completely why Brandon would offer himself without a fight to spare his partner. He didn't want to imagine how Alex was holding up, out in Livermore with Brent, waiting to learn Brandon's fate.

The next step in the plan was the truly dicey part, one that Seth had agreed to only grudgingly, and because he couldn't come up with a better alternative. Common sense would beg them not to allow Thane to drag Brandon inside the warded circle and begin the ritual. But without strong magic of their own, they couldn't beat a century-old warlock in a head-on fight. The rote spells and sigils that Seth and Evan could do, and even the litanies Travis knew from his time with the "ninja priests," weren't the same as the power of a true warlock. As Travis had explained, it was the difference between a Howitzer and a BB gun.

Once inside the warding, and with his energy directed to the ritual, Thane would be unable to stop the working or leave the spelled circle. He would be vulnerable, even to magic less powerful than his own, unable to strike outside the warding. Seth reminded himself that under the right circumstances, a BB gun could kill.

They were just cutting it awfully fine, with no margin for error.

Thane should have looked like a TV villain in his dark, hooded robe, but the predatory vibe he gave off was strong enough that it made Seth shiver. Thane walked counterclockwise around the cement altar, chanting as he went, and the sense of malice, of evil, hit Seth on a primal level. Thane wasn't a guy in a Halloween costume. He was a full dark warlock, a witch-disciple, and scary as fuck.

Thane finished his circuit around the altar. Nothing visible had changed, yet Seth felt the tension in the air like static electricity. Thane nodded to the guard, who jerked Brandon to his feet and shoved him toward the warlock as if even he did not want to get too close to his master. Brandon stumbled, then lifted his head and squared his shoulders, like a man going with dignity to his execution.

Thane reached out and yanked Brandon inside the circle.

A green-yellow shimmering curtain of light rose from nowhere to cut off the witch and his sacrifice from the others.

Seth aimed his dart gun, sending a shot toward the guard's ass. And missed.

The simultaneous pop of another gun, followed by the guard's sudden wobble and collapse, told him that Evan's shot held true. The goon went down and did not get back up.

Travis's text to Brent came across Seth's phone, copying Evan as well. *"Now."* A moment later, Brent sent back two photos, showing the explosion and the tunnel's collapse.

Thane staggered and screamed, a cry of rage and pain. Brandon, sensing that something vital had shifted, tried to throw himself out of the circle, but the sickly green light curtain held him as if it were made of steel. Thane regained his balance, and even from a distance, Seth could see the fury in every line of the man's stance. With a gesture, he pinned Brandon back against the altar and began to chant, calling to the ghost of Rhyfel Gremory to appear to him and grant him renewed power to extend his unholy existence.

Travis raised his voice in the ancient Rite of Exorcism, and the Latin words rang out clear and strong on the cold wind. *"Exorcizamos te, omnus immundus spiritus..."* The wind picked up, sending Travis's black hair flying around his face, but determination—perhaps obsession—fired in his green eyes and concentration made his body rigid.

Seth moved closer to the warded circle, and moments later, Evan joined him. Seth could see the terror in Brandon's eyes as Thane gripped the knife and raised it for the killing blow.

Seth and Evan exchanged a glance. In unison, Seth spoke the "unfasten" spell, focused on Brandon's bonds, as Evan touched the sigil he had drawn to do the same thing, concentrating on making an opening in the warding for Brandon to escape.

Brandon's ropes fell to the ground, and he kicked with both feet, hurling Thane backward as the air inside the warding seemed to shimmer and take on a blood-red taint.

"Tear off his watch and run!" Evan screamed.

Brandon seized his chance, ripping at the timepiece on Thane's arm, and bolting off the altar. He nearly made it across the glowing circle before Thane grabbed his arm as he continued his chant. Brandon tore loose, dove across the curtain of light, and fell to his knees on the other side, slamming the watch-amulet against a rock and shattering the timepiece that focused Thane's magic.

Travis's exorcism and Thane's chant dueled, a clash of cosmic powers. The exorcism might be slowing Thane, draining his power, but he had enough remaining energy that his words split open the air above the altar, a bright red pinpoint in the fabric of the world.

Something crashed through the trees behind them with a screech of fear and fury. Mike Bradshaw, still wearing the bloody clothes from the night at the warehouse, ran from the forest with the singlemindedness of a berserker. His eyes were wide and wild, his face unnaturally pale. He gripped a knife with a wicked blade in his right hand, and to Seth's horror, he launched himself straight at Evan.

Evan reached for his gun, seconds too late. Bradshaw collided with him, and the two went down, wrestling for the knife, rolling back and forth in the snow just feet from the edge of the warded circle.

Seth drew his own gun, but he dared not shoot for fear of hitting Evan. Bradshaw's eyes were fever-bright with madness, but sheer fury lit Evan's expression, and his training proved a match for his attacker, as the knife inched closer, then pressed away, a desperate struggle for survival.

Thane thrust one arm out of the warding and locked his hand around Brandon's ankle.

A shot rang out, striking Thane just below the elbow, and the warlock howled in pain as Brandon scrambled free. Alex stood just on the other side of Travis, heaving for breath, his face flushed as if he had run all the way from the parking lot, gun gripped tightly in one hand. Seth wondered where the hell Brent was and wondered if Alex had abandoned him at Livermore to come to Brandon's rescue.

Travis's liturgy never faltered, resolute despite the chaos around him. Inside the warded circle, the glowing red point of light began to expand.

Thane shouted his litany, and his hands began to weave a complex pattern in the air. Seth felt his gut tighten, fearing the worst. From the woods behind them came a deep, feral growl, and seconds later, two of the black dog hellhounds, bigger than the one that challenged Seth before, burst from the tree line. Each of the infernal beasts stood as tall as a bear, thick-set and broad across the shoulders, with demonic red eyes. Alex, looking utterly shell-shocked, pivoted in unison with Seth, pumping round after round at the hellhounds, bullets that hit but seemed to have no effect.

Bradshaw screamed, locked in battle with Evan, and the knife dipped so close to Evan's throat that Seth stopped breathing. Evan brought his knee up between their bodies, flipping them, and in that motion, Seth lost sight of the knife. Both men suddenly stiffened, and Seth's heart pounded, fearing the worst. Then Evan crawled backward, and Bradshaw lay on the ground, the knife deep in his belly, blood beginning to stain the snow crimson beneath him.

Bradshaw's grimace became a madman's grin. With his waning strength, he rolled toward the circle, and Thane, desperate for a sacrifice to offer to his master, reached out to pull him in.

Travis's voice shook, but he never took his eyes off Thane and the fiery hole in the fabric of reality. The tension between the power of the ex-priest and that of the dark warlock was palpable, an electricity in the air that made Seth's hair raise.

"Cover me!" Seth shouted to Evan and Alex, as a desperate plot took shape in his mind. Seth spoke three spells in quick succession, pushing himself to draw hard on his own energy. *Break warding. Summon ghosts. Fire.*

With Thane's focus on forcing back Travis's competing liturgy to enable Gremory to manifest, he had nothing to spare to close up the breech Seth's spell made in the warding. The angry spirits of Dead Man's Hollow streamed through, attacking Thane with all the fury they could muster, tearing at his skin and stripping away his flesh with their teeth. Fire streamed from Seth's outstretched palm, striking Bradshaw squarely between the shoulders as he dragged himself toward the circle, intending to seal Thane's ritual with his own blood.

Bradshaw's shirt caught fire, engulfing him in flames. He screamed and flailed, lurching closer to the warding, and threw himself into the hole Seth's spell had torn. Thane snatched at his blistered arm with his undamaged hand, drawing him toward the altar to present as Gremory's blood offering.

Seth shut out the sound of Travis's liturgy and Thane's manic incantation, Bradshaw's screams, the growls of the hellhounds and the fusillade of gunfire. Seconds remained until the hole in the warding would snap shut and Gremory would break through the Veil to impart new power that would make Thane immortal for another lifetime.

He brought his Glock up in one smooth movement, aimed, and pulled the trigger.

His bullet pierced through the break in the warding and caught Thane right between the eyes.

Between one heartbeat and the next, everything changed.

The hellhounds vanished, and so did the green glow of the warding. Thane stumbled backward toward the rift, already dead, his hand still locked around Bradshaw's wrist, dragging the other man with him. In the split second before the red rift in the sky snapped shut, Thane and Bradshaw careened into it and vanished. The shift in energy sent Seth's head spinning.

Travis still chanted, his voice hoarse but determined as he shouted the last, defiant words of the exorcism, banishing Gremory and all the infernal powers Thane had invoked. When he fell silent, no one spoke, as if they each found themselves suddenly, unexpectedly and inexplicably alive.

"Brandon!" Alex broke the silence and rushed forward, dropping to his knees beside his lover and pulling the man into his arms.

Seth reached out to Evan, gripping his arm in wordless affirmation. They were still alive, together and whole.

Pounding footsteps coming from behind them tore Seth and the others from their haze. Brent ran into view, looking utterly frantic. Soot smudged his face and parka from the explosion, and despite the December chill, sweat ran down his face from his sprint. He had his gun in hand, ready for a fight, and his eyes widened as he slowly took in the scene in front of him.

"Holy Mary, Mother of God, Christ, and all the angels...what the everlasting fuck happened here?"

15

EVAN

"Where are we going?" Evan felt like he should know the answer, but after the fight at Dead Man's Hollow, his brain was fuzzy, and he felt out of it.

"St. Dismas. The outreach center Travis runs," Seth replied, in a worried voice that confirmed he'd answered the question before.

"Sorry."

"It's shock. Or the adrenaline crash. Goes with the territory. The other hunts we've been on haven't been quite so...cinematic," Seth added with a wry smile. "Not quite as hard a fall afterward."

"Can't we just go home?" Evan's tone sounded plaintive, even to his own ears.

"You're covered in blood, dude. Someone might notice."

Evan realized that his coat was stained with Mike's blood, and he fought the urge to throw up. "I can take off the coat."

"We're all meeting up there. Travis has a medic who can check us over, and he promised hot showers plus a second-hand clothing selection so you can leave without looking like an extra from a horror movie. Food, too. I think we need to decompress, debrief." Seth went quiet, looking like there was more he wanted to say but wasn't quite sure how.

"It's nice to have backup," Evan said. "I think we did okay back there."

"Okay?" Seth echoed. "That was seriously badass. I need to learn how to do that exorcism thing. That could come in handy."

"Do you have to be celibate? Because we'll find another way." The aftereffects of the fight didn't exactly leave Evan horny as much as desperate for connection, a primal need to remind himself that he was alive. *There's a reason people talk about fighting and fucking.*

Seth chuckled. "Travis isn't a priest anymore. So I don't think that's it. But nice to know sex is on your mind."

"It usually is—when I'm not scared I'm about to die," Evan replied. Despite his off-hand tone, the comment rang true enough that he had to look away.

"You were amazing back there," Seth said, as if he guessed the turn Evan's thoughts had taken. "I just about had a heart attack when Mike came out of nowhere at you with that knife, but you handled him."

"It wasn't Mike anymore," Evan said quietly. "I mean, it was Mike Bradshaw. But he wasn't the person I used to care about. That man is long gone, if he was ever real in the first place. That made fighting him a little easier, like it was a stranger wearing Mike's face."

Mentioning Mike reminded Evan about the video. Seth had done his best the night of the fight at the storage units to reassure Evan, but now that the threat was really over, would Seth change his mind?

"I deleted it." Seth didn't look at Evan, but once again, he seemed to know what his boyfriend was thinking. "Neither of us needed to see it again. Old news. We both have a past and we've moved on...and while I'm not aware of any videos out there, it's no secret I *wasn't* celibate. It was shitty of Mike to betray your trust. I would never do that. Just so you know."

A small smile flickered at the corners of Evan's mouth. "I didn't think you would. But now that I look back, I'm not surprised Mike did it. I didn't realize how manipulative he was, at the time. He probably got off on doing it, but it wouldn't be out of character if he also thought the tape would make good blackmail, if he ever needed some."

"I'm really glad he's dead," Seth said, matter-of-factly. "Because if he wasn't, I'd need to fix that, and you might think poorly of me for it. But he needed to go."

Evan wasn't sure exactly what it said about either of them that Seth meant every word, or that Evan might have accepted the offer. The whole shitshow with Mike had dredged up a lot of stuff Evan hadn't wanted to think about.

"I guess I never really dealt with the whole abuse thing," Evan said, staring out the window because it was easier than looking at Seth. "I mean, it's hard for women to tell someone. But a gay man? Men aren't supposed to have things like that happen to them, and I was afraid that if I did tell someone, they'd think I had it coming because of the gay part."

Seth didn't say anything, but Evan could feel his partner's attention. "I, uh, guess I just pushed everything down and buried it. There were a couple of years there where I was so busy running, I didn't let myself think about much. Maybe..." He paused, working up his courage. "Maybe I should. Talk about it. Because it's not just me now. It's us."

Seth's hand slipped over and gripped Evan's thigh. "I love you. And whatever you choose, I'll support you. If you do want to talk to someone, do it most of all for yourself, because you need to heal."

"It affects us. My crazy rubs off," Evan said with a bitter laugh. "I don't want what happened back then to hurt what we're building. I guess what I'm saying is, I want what we've got enough to be brave about dealing with what happened before. All of it." If Seth figured that there was more Evan hadn't told him about, he didn't ask.

"Maybe Travis can connect you with someone you can trust, maybe even someone who knows about hunting," Seth suggested. "The less you have to lie, the better it'll work." He shifted uncomfortably as Evan turned to look at him.

"I, uh, probably have some shit to deal with, too. I mean, I know I do. The thing with Jesse, this whole vengeance quest—" Seth swallowed hard. "After they put me in that psych ward when Jesse died, I kinda got a bad taste for shrinks. But I think if it was someone like Travis, someone who understood about magic and monsters, maybe it would be different. Not gonna lie; it's hard for me to trust a stranger."

"We've both got scars," Evan said, placing his hand on Seth's. "But this 'quest'—stopping Thane and his buddies? I get it now. When you told me about Jesse, I thought I understood. When I was the target, I was too busy trying not to die to really think about the big picture. Now, seeing what almost happened to Brandon, and how it affected Alex—I understand. Stopping the witch-disciples matters because if we don't, who will? No one else has stepped up in a century. So I'm all in."

Seth pulled into a lot in a seedy section of Pittsburgh. Evan glanced around as he got out of the truck, wrapped in a blanket to hide the blood. "Are you sure about this?"

Seth chuckled. "You might not have heard Travis say that he's put wardings and protections on the lot. Cars and people with good intentions are safe."

"I'm going to seriously need to recalibrate my definition of 'priest.'"

"Ex-priest," Seth corrected. "I don't know the story, but he's touchy about it. Kinda like Brent doesn't talk much about the military or the FBI. There's a story there, but I don't know that we'll ever hear it."

"I just want to go home and wrap myself around you and never let go," Evan confided when Seth slung an arm around his shoulder.

"Sounds like a plan to me," Seth replied. "Debrief first; hot monkey sex later."

"Tired sloth sex," Evan said. "Without needing to lean on my left arm. Still hurts like hell."

"Sloth sex...whatever that means...you're on."

"Slow and hot like the jungle," Evan whispered as they neared the door. "So very slow but with stamina." He chuckled when Seth adjusted himself.

"Damn. Could you not talk dirty right before we go inside a churchy place?" Seth glared, but the heat behind the gaze was lust, not anger. He knocked on the back door, and it opened right away.

"Come on in," Travis said. "Everyone else is already here." Travis wore a Henley over jeans, and his hair was wet. "We've got showers and clean clothes. Jon—my second-in-command here at St. Dismas—is going to see what's left over from dinner, and Matthew—our medic—is on hand to check you over. He's with Alex right now."

"Nice place," Evan said. "Did it used to be a hotel or something?"

Travis nodded. "Yeah. The building is getting a second chance, just like the people. We are a community resource center—food bank, soup kitchen, halfway house, addiction counseling, mental health clinic, free clinic, clothing program...there are probably half a dozen things I've forgotten."

"Part of the Church?" Seth asked with a raised eyebrow.

Travis's face darkened. "We receive funds from a lot of sources, including the Diocese, but we're non-denominational and largely secular."

Travis led the way into a small break room, and the smell of hot coffee made Evan's heart sing. Brent and Brandon sat at the worn kitchen table, with mugs in front of them. Both men looked freshly showered.

Evan's heart hurt for Brandon. His sunny smile from the coffee shop was gone, and he had a haunted, hunted look that Evan understood too well. He guessed the clean clothes came from Travis's stash, but they were a bit big on Brandon despite his muscular build, and the yellow plaid shirt clashed with Brandon's red hair and pale skin, making him look unwell.

Brent sat beside Brandon, and he seemed to be extending the big brother routine to include Alex's boyfriend as well as Alex. It struck Evan that Travis and Brent were probably close to ten years older than he was. Time to have been around the block a few times, and the weight of those years showed in the eyes of both older men.

Evan couldn't hear the conversation between Brent and Brandon, but from the body language, Brent was reassuring the younger man, and Brandon seemed to be investing all his energy, unsuccessfully, in not flinching at every sound. Brent looked up, and when he met Evan's gaze, Evan could practically see the wheels turning in the other man's mind.

Evan took that as an invitation and sat down across from Brandon. All the life had gone out of the barista, and he looked like he wished he could hide. "Hey. I didn't mean to freak you out, coming to the coffee shop. I'm sorry about not being completely honest, but if I'd told you—"

"That there was a batshit crazy warlock who wanted to slit my throat as an offering? Would have made me freak out more." Brandon managed a weak smile. "I get it. And thanks."

Evan felt his face color. "I let you down. I'm sorry. Kinda got kidnapped myself, while I was trying to keep you from getting grabbed." He swallowed hard, psyching himself up, and Brent took that as his cue to leave.

"How about if I get you both more coffee and check on dinner?" Brent hurried away so quickly even Brandon chuckled.

"He's trying really hard, and I appreciate it, but he's not Dr. Phil," Brandon said.

"And I'm not Oprah," Evan replied. "But…you and I do belong to a very exclusive club of People Who Survived the Batshit Crazy Warlocks. Small fraternity, hazing is insane."

"Do we get t-shirts?" A hint of Brandon's smile ghosted across his features.

"Maybe." Evan took a deep breath. "Look…I'm still dealing with everything that happened to me a month ago back in Richmond. But it's not the kind of thing just everyone can identify with. You, me, people who escaped serial killers…except they don't get the magic part."

"Yeah, that's a lot to wrap my head around," Brandon admitted. "I know the warlock and your ex got sucked into that hole in the sky. So they're dead, right?"

Evan knew he couldn't lie. "With the whole magic thing, I don't know if he's dead, but we don't think he can come back from that. There was a pretty big hole in the warlock's head and Mike…well, he sure wasn't in good shape."

"But there are other witch-disciples, right? And that's what you and Seth and Brent and Travis really do? Hunt down warlocks and monsters? Like on TV?"

Evan rubbed the back of his neck. "There are other witch-disciples; we aren't sure how many. And yeah, that's what we do. But the people on TV heal faster than in real life. And they get background music."

"Alex and I want to help," Brandon said. He still looked scared, but a new defiance and determination came into his features. "Alex wants to help Brent with his *other* cases. Back him up. And now that I know how much guys like you get thrown around, I'm thinking you could use an EMT who knows the real score."

Evan smiled. "I think that's a great idea. What did Brent say?"

Brandon rolled his eyes. "Brent's a little overprotective, and he takes the big brother thing a bit far, but he means well. So…he'll come around. He's just worried."

"I think you'll be great additions to the team," Evan said. "We can use some more good hunters."

He glanced up to see Seth and Travis in deep conversation, and Evan guessed his boyfriend was picking Travis's brain about exorcisms, or maybe asking for a referral to a good shrink who specialized in supernatural PTSD.

"Food!" A man Evan didn't recognize came in with a large server's tray. On it was a pan of lasagna, a basket of bread, and a big bowl of salad. "Plates are in the cabinet, silverware's in the drawer, cups on the shelf over the sink. Serve yourselves, and just put the dishes in the dishwasher." He set the tray down in the middle of the table.

"This is Jon. He keeps St. Dismas running while I'm out shooting things," Travis said, and his grin made his affection for his friend clear. Jon was five-ten and forty-something, built like a fireplug, with close-cropped dark hair, wary eyes, and skin the color of espresso.

"Don't let him fool you. Travis pulls his weight around here," Jon countered. He glanced at Travis. "I've gotta go. We have a full night with the men's shelter overflow, and I'm still pulling things together for the Christmas dinner."

Travis nodded. "Go. I'll catch up later, once we've gotten everyone here patched up and fed."

"Start without me," Seth said. "I'm going to take a quick shower, and then it's your turn," he said with a look at Evan. "In fact, why don't you go first, get out of those bloody clothes before you eat."

"I can throw his parka in the wash," Travis volunteered. "And if that doesn't work, we've probably got something he can use."

Evan followed Travis's directions to find the shower and let the hot water sluice over his hair and body, washing away sweat and fear. He finished in record time and found that Seth had left him fresh clothing to change into. Seth was waiting outside the bathroom and greeted him with a quick kiss.

"Better?"

Evan nodded. "Yeah. I'll meet you back in the kitchen. I'm hungry."

Seth chuckled, then ducked into the bathroom, carrying a change of clothing. A moment later, Evan heard the water start. He paused, picturing a wet, naked Seth, then turned away with a sigh, knowing this wasn't the time or place to do anything about it—and that he was honestly too tired to live up to his sexy thoughts.

Evan had barely filled his plate and sat down when Seth was back, taking the seat next to him. Alex had returned from the clinic and was seated next to Brandon with their chairs scooted together so they were touching from shoulder to knee. Matthew, the medic, let Evan know he wanted a look at the gunshot graze once dinner was over.

The six men around the table ate and joked, and Evan felt himself relax for the first time in weeks. He and Seth had been on their own since Richmond, with phone calls from friends like Mark, Simon, Toby, and Milo, but no real live interaction. This felt…nice. Safe. And honest in a way social occasions rarely were. He didn't have to worry about slipping up and mentioning something he shouldn't say, or not being believed. Even if he triggered on something, these men would understand. Evan reached over under the table and took Seth's hand, giving it a squeeze, and his heart raced, in a good way, when Seth squeezed back.

"This lasagna is amazing," Alex said, helping himself to seconds. Evan noticed that even Brandon ate, though not with much gusto.

"We have an awesome kitchen staff and volunteers," Travis said. "I'll let them know you liked it." He leaned back, nursing a cup of coffee. "In a way, what we do here at St. Dismas is a lot like hunting. The people we serve do battle with their very own monsters. Sometimes, by the time they come to us, they've lost more than a few of those fights, got a lot of scars. We give them a safe place to heal, a community that understand their experiences, and the resources and skills to live to fight another day."

"There's a lot of overlap," Brent said. "Hunting changes a person. We see stuff most people will never know exists. It's a lot like going to war. Civilians don't understand, unless they've loved a soldier, or been in a war zone. It's not something you walk away from. It's always on your mind, and no matter what anyone tries to tell you, it's personal."

"Which is why it's good to have a partner," Travis replied, with a look to Alex and Brandon, and then Seth and Evan. "It took me a while to realize that myself," he added with a chagrined glance at Brent.

"Yeah, well. Me, too," Brent admitted. "But now, I get it. Definitely better when someone has your back."

"Partners who are friends start to share a bond through the magic. Travis and I have gotten really in sync, just in the time we've been hunting together," Brent said. "Sometimes, it's almost like mindreading—and I don't have any of his woo-woo abilities."

"And you might even find that for partners that are also couples, the magic takes on a different dynamic," Travis added. Evan and the others looked up, intrigued. "There are a lot of old manuscripts that say that a 'carnal partnership' strengthens the magic."

"Then what's with priests being celibate?" Brent asked.

"There's a trade-off," Travis replied. "Stronger magic, but a growing energy bond between the two practitioners that can be a distraction—and a vulnerability. I suspect that the Fathers didn't want to deal with the fall-out—among other hang-ups."

Evan managed not to shoot Seth a look, but Seth bumped his knee under the table.

"Maybe being together on multiple levels, like you guys are, will give you an edge to stop the witch-disciples and their cycle. If anyone else ever tried, maybe they didn't have that going for them," Brent suggested.

"I know your hunt for the witch-disciples takes you from place to place," Travis said. "But if we can ever offer assistance—knowledge, resources, connections—just let us know. And you're always welcome here, when you come to Pittsburgh."

Evan felt the meal and the adrenaline crash, along with the hot shower, finally take a toll. From the looks of the rest of them, every-one's energy was flagging. "Thank you," he said, and Seth echoed his appreciation. "But right now, I think it's going to take all the energy I've got left to crawl in to bed. The rest of the monsters are just going to have to wait."

～

"WHAT'S ALL THIS?" Evan asked, as Seth came into the trailer a couple days later, carrying a four-foot-tall pine tree and a bag from Walmart. "I thought you just ran out for milk?"

"It's a Christmas tree," Seth replied as if Evan were dense. "And a few decorations and lights. Christmas is almost here, not much time to decorate."

Evan stood, open-mouthed, watching as Seth trundled the tree into the RV's living room and set it up in a stand. He glanced back at Evan and looked suddenly vulnerable and unsure. "Is it okay?"

Evan shook off his surprise and closed the distance between them, wrapping his arms around Seth and stretching up to kiss him. "It's more than okay. It's perfect. I just…wasn't thinking." He shrugged. "I didn't bother with a tree when I was on my own, except what was at work. I didn't feel very festive."

Seth stole another kiss and folded Evan against him. "I haven't really thought about Christmas since Jesse died. I mean, Milo and Toby celebrated, and they included me, but I couldn't get past what was missing to enjoy it. But I'd like to change that," he said. "After all, it's our first Christmas together."

Evan found himself grinning like a fool. "I like the sound of that," he murmured, letting his hands roam under Seth's cable-knit sweater, up the t-shirt underneath, and then sliding across bare skin. "You know what I'd like even better? Making love next to the tree with just the Christmas lights on."

Seth angled his head to kiss him, and Evan groaned in pleasure, opening to Seth's tongue, bucking his hips against Seth's and sliding a hand down to grip his lover's ass, just in case he hadn't made himself clear.

"I want everything you're offering," Seth growled, with his lips close enough to Evan's ear that his breath sent a shiver down Evan's spine. "But I've got dinner reservations at a nice place for a surprise, and once we're naked, I'm not going to want to stop until morning."

Seth stepped back, and Evan felt a surge of disappointment. Then Seth worked open Evan's belt and zipper and pushed his hand inside the briefs that barely contained Evan's hard and leaking cock. He let go of Evan with his left hand just long enough to free himself, then wrapped long fingers around both of them and slid an arm around Evan's back, gripping his ass.

He pumped them slowly, a delicious slide of velvety skin-on-skin, as his mouth worked up and down Evan's neck and jaw, licking, sucking, and biting until Evan trembled and his knees felt wobbly.

"God, please Seth—" Evan begged, barely recognizing his own voice.

Seth's hand moved faster, slicking his palm with their mingled precome, brushing his fingers across the knobs, stroking the sensitive slits. "Fuck my hand," he commanded, bucking with his hips as if to demonstrate.

Evan's arms were wrapped around Seth's shoulders, fingers digging into his back to keep himself standing. His breath came in shallow pants, and he felt a flush rise as his release began to build.

"Tonight, I'm going to open you up, nice and slow," Seth murmured against his ear. "Then I'm going to fuck you so hard and long you'll feel me tomorrow. Own you, make you know you're mine. And then," he added as Evan bit back a moan, "next round, I want you to do the same for me. Want to feel you—have you inside me. Own me. Need that."

Evan came with a gasp, cock jerking as his spend flowed over Seth's long fingers. Seth followed seconds later, roaring against Evan's neck with a low rumble that Evan thought was the sexiest thing he'd ever heard. They clung to each other afterward, breathing hard, damp with sweat. Seth smelled like pine and flannel, soap and sex. Evan let his head fall against Seth's chest, and Seth nudged him to kiss his temple.

"Consider this an appetizer," Seth murmured, taking Evan's weight as Evan felt his legs tremble.

"I might not survive the main course," Evan said, still breathless.

Seth stepped away to grab some tissues and cleaned them up, wiping off his hand before tucking Evan away, then doing the same for himself.

"Go get changed," Seth said, his voice warm and indulgent. "I realized we haven't been on a date, except for that first night, and it didn't exactly go as planned." The sex had been fantastic, but having armed men break into Evan's apartment and then set the place on fire meant the night had been memorable for the wrong reasons.

"What's the dress code?"

"Slacks and a sweater," Seth said, and his eyes told Evan that Seth was indulging his own fantasy with the instructions. "I want to spend dinner thinking about stripping them off you."

Jesus. Evan's cock was doing its best to rise to the occasion, and the jizz from the last time was barely dry. "Where are we going?" Their usual fare tended to be diners and fast casual, nothing fancy.

"Somewhere nice. Brent gave me some suggestions."

Evan raised an eyebrow, clearly questioning Brent's expertise in fine dining, but just grinned. "Okay. I'd better go get cleaned up. Someone made a mess of me." He raised his head in a silent challenge for Seth to do it again and saw a hunger in his lover's eyes that had nothing to do with food. He could feel Seth's gaze on him as he sauntered to the shower, and if the RV's bathroom wasn't so tiny, he felt certain they'd have been sharing.

Seth ducked into the shower as soon as Evan finished, and by the time he came out with a towel wrapped around his hips, Evan was already dressed in a crisp white button-up, black sweater, and gray pants that set off his dark hair and played up his hazel eyes. Seth's glance swept over him appreciatively, and if Evan had any doubts about whether Seth liked his outfit, the obvious tent to the towel left nothing to the imagination.

Seth sighed and turned away. "Go wait in the living room, or I'll never get dressed, and I really want to take you out." Evan snickered but complied, although he couldn't resist giving Seth's toned ass a slap as he passed.

Seth came out dressed in striped shirt with a chocolate brown sweater that accentuated his brown eyes, blond hair, and broad shoulders. Evan swallowed, and Seth smiled, recognizing the unspoken compliment.

"Ready to go?" Seth held Evan's coat for him, a pleasant luxury, and Evan grinned.

"A guy could get used to this kind of thing," he teased as Seth held the door for him before locking up the RV and following him into the cold. A light snow had fallen, and Evan helped to brush off the truck as it warmed up. It didn't take long before they were headed into the city.

"So, where are we going?" Evan asked, watching Seth in the glow of the dashboard, appreciating his profile.

"Paulo's Trattoria," Seth replied. "On Mount Washington."

"There's a mountain?" Evan searched his memory of what he'd learned about Pittsburgh and came up blank.

Seth chuckled. "Sort of. You'll see."

Evan appreciated the city lights as they took the Parkway, then crossed the Monongahela River at the Smithfield Street Bridge. Seth pulled into a lot across the street from what looked like a small single railroad car on a very steep track.

"Our chariot awaits," Seth said with a grin and an exaggerated sweep of his arm.

"What is that?" Evan craned his neck to see the top of the slope.

"The Mon Incline," Seth said. "Come on." They bought a ticket and settled into their seats, looking out of the back of the car toward the city. Three rivers came together at The Point, and the city spread back from that triangle sparkling with lights. A tree made from draped, sparkling Christmas bulbs commanded the center of what was, in the summer, a large fountain.

"Pretty nice view, huh?" Seth said, slipping his arm around Evan and pulling him close.

"Yeah...it's gorgeous," Evan said, taken in by the panorama.

"Even better at the top," Seth promised. When the incline car reached its stopping point, Seth and Evan got out, and Seth walked him to an overlook. From there, the whole city spread out beneath them, the dark rivers of the Allegheny, Monongahela, and Ohio, Heinz Stadium, PNC Park, and the skyscrapers of the business district. Brightly painted bridges crossed the rivers like industrial jewelry, and far below, Evan could make out the shapes of barges and tugboats making their way along the swift, icy waters.

"Wow." Despite the bitter wind that mussed his hair and burned his cheeks and nose, Evan thought the view was one of the most breathtaking he'd seen.

"Let's get out of the cold," Seth said, guiding Evan back toward the sidewalk. Paulo's wasn't far, a wooden building cantilevered off the edge of Mount Washington, with one wall all windows to take in the view.

They checked their heavy parkas, and Seth spoke to the maître d'. Evan didn't miss the bill that changed hands or the host's deferent nod. "Right this way," the man said, gesturing for them to follow him to a table against the window, overlooking the brightly lit city in all its glory. Seth held Evan's chair for him and slid it in before going to his own seat.

Candlelight lit the darkened dining room, setting off the magnificent view. The restaurant had an intimate feel with its dark wooden walls and carpet the color of billiard table felt.

"Seth, this has got to be expensive—"

Seth put a hand over Evan's. "I want to spoil you tonight. Let me, please?"

Evan felt his chest tighten at the words. He smiled and realized he might be blushing. "I'd like that."

Seth ordered a bottle of wine for them, but Evan knew most of it would end up in his glass since Seth had to drive. Evan had just glanced at the wine list, but he knew whatever Seth ordered was pricier than the grocery store bottles they stocked at the RV.

"What looks good?" Seth asked as they read over the menu.

"Everything," Evan replied and sighed as his stomach growled. Good Italian food was his favorite, and while he and Seth made decent pasta dishes on their own, he saw several items on the menu that went beyond his kitchen skills.

"Get what you want," Seth said. "And don't worry; I just got a nice check from a client. We're fine. Pick something you really like."

The server returned to pour their wine and bring a basket of bread. Evan felt his shoulders relax. This felt so...normal. Just him and his boyfriend, out for a romantic date. Evan's heart did a little flip, watching Seth trying to decide on his meal. How did he get so lucky, he wondered, to end up with a guy like Seth?

Seth looked up, as if he felt Evan's gaze, and smiled that warm, vulnerable smile that only Evan got to see. Evan smiled back, utterly smitten.

They ordered the appetizer sampler with fried calamari, bruschetta, baked mozzarella wedges, and an antipasto assortment. Seth chose chicken marsala, while Evan's mouth watered for eggplant parmesan.

Evan glanced out the window, watching the incline train make its way back down the track. When he turned back, he found Seth staring at him. "What?" He wondered if he had something stuck in his teeth.

"You're so beautiful," Seth said quietly. "Just admiring the view."

Evan met his gaze. "I like what I see, too."

The appetizer could have fed a small army, but it was all so good—and Evan was hungry—that he had to finally push his plate away or there wouldn't be room for the main course, let alone dessert.

"They'll let us take leftovers home, right?" he asked. "Because if I finish that, I won't be hungry for anything else." It wasn't the first time he'd caught himself referring to the RV as home, and he saw Seth's eyes darken at the mention. It wasn't the RV. Home was with Seth, Evan realized.

"Oh, you'll be hungry," Seth promised with a wicked gleam in his eyes. But he moved his plate to the side as well. "And yes, we can take the extras with us. So make sure you save room for dessert."

By unspoken agreement, the conversation stayed away from hunting. Seth told funny stories about the trouble he and Jesse had gotten into when they were kids, and Evan found that he could recount some tales from before he left home that didn't hurt to remember. They debated movies and video games, argued over which of the Avengers was the sexiest, and tried to decide what to binge watch next on Netflix.

The food came out steaming hot, piled high, and smelling amazing. Evan ate slowly, savoring every bite, and he was certain that more than once, he caught Seth watching his lips close around a forkful of pasta or the way his throat worked as he swallowed. "Like what you see?"

"Always," Seth replied, licking his lips with a look in his eye that made Evan have to adjust himself. Seth chuckled, a low throaty sound that just added to Evan's delicious discomfort.

An older man with an accordion made the rounds, playing requests as he moved among the tables.

"That's Matteo. He's the owner's brother," Seth said. "Been playing here for thirty years. According to the website, there's a legend that if he plays a request for you and a special someone on your first date here, your love will last forever."

Just then, Evan looked up to see Matteo and his accordion heading right for them. If the man cared that they were two men holding hands, he didn't show it. Evan saw a look pass between Seth and Matteo, who nodded. "I understand there's been a request," he said, and a smile twitched at the corners of his mouth. With that, he began to play a haunting, sensuous melody Evan knew and realized it was *Can't Help Falling in Love.*

He met Seth's gaze, and the heat in his gaze made Evan wondered how he had ever questioned his lover's commitment. "I say, stick to the classics," Seth said, as Matteo played and the whole restaurant seemed to be looking at them. When the song finished, both men clapped and thanked Matteo, who grinned broadly.

"You boys have a nice night, huh? I hope the legend works for you," he added with a wink as he moved on to the next table.

Despite the heavy meal, the wine seemed to have gone right to Evan's head. He figured he probably wore a dopey grin and didn't care. Seth's smile was just as open, full of warmth and love. They ordered a tiramisu to share, and the server poured the last of the wine into Evan's glass. He wasn't drunk, just pleasantly buzzed, but it gave everything a warm glow.

"Did you like the food?" Seth asked, and Evan saw how much it mattered to him.

"I loved everything," Evan assured him. "This night is wonderful." After all the blood, fire, fear, and pain that they had endured over the last few months, it almost seemed too much to believe that they were here, safe and together, on something as normal as a real date.

The server brought the tiramisu, and the heavenly smell of cocoa, coffee, and cognac made Evan's mouth water. He caught Seth looking at him and dipped a finger into the filling, then licked it clean with his most wicked smile.

"Don't forget about that rain check," Evan said, in a low, husky voice filled with need.

Seth's expression froze, his eyes widened, and he looked suddenly uncertain. "I was going to wait for Christmas, but I decided to show you now." Seth reached for his phone, pulled up a screen, and slid the device wordlessly across the table.

Evan felt his heart speed up, unsure what caused the sudden shift in Seth's mood, afraid of what he would see. Seth looked away, but Evan knew his lover was still watching for his reaction from the corner of his eye.

He took the phone and stared at the photo for a moment, uncomprehending. A picture, of a piece of paper. He frowned and enlarged the image. Test results. Was Seth sick? A slew of dreaded diagnoses came, unbidden, to mind. Then Evan forced himself to focus on what the paper in the image actually said.

Oh.

"I was pretty sure it would come out like that, but I needed to be certain. I hadn't been with anyone in a long time, and I always used protection. So...like I told you on our first date, I'm negative. And I just thought, if you wanted to—"

Evan felt giddy with relief and reached for his own phone. "Apparently, we were thinking alike." He passed the phone over to Seth, with a photo of his own results. "I double checked, although I'd just had a test in Richmond before we got together, like I'd mentioned. I'm negative, too. So yes, I want to."

The thought of being together, with nothing between them, actually feeling Seth inside him skin-to-skin made Evan achingly hard. "Let's go decorate that Christmas tree," Evan said, reaching out to take Seth's hand.

The sexual tension between them was so thick, Evan could barely breathe as they drove back to the RV. He almost suggested just getting a room at a hotel downtown, then remembered that they had Christmas lights waiting for them.

When they got back to the campground, they tried to saunter from the truck to the trailer, but Evan felt certain that if it wasn't December and below freezing, Seth would have started peeling off clothing before they ever got the door open.

They were barely inside when Seth pinned Evan against the wall, fumbling with his coat and sliding it off his shoulders. "Want you so bad," he murmured, and Evan straddled Seth's thigh, rubbing against him, showing him just how badly Evan wanted him in return.

Seth shucked off his own coat, letting it fall to the ground, and moved back in for a kiss. His tongue slid along Evan's lips, and Evan opened to him, letting Seth plunder his mouth, tasting the tiramisu and wine. Sweaters went next, in a pile next to the coats, along with shoes. The buttons on their shirts reminded Evan why he liked t-shirts, as they fumbled to get each other naked as quickly as possible.

Evan arched against Seth, loving the rough of his body hair, longing to feel the burn of his stubble. Seth licked a stripe down Evan's neck, pausing to suck and nip at the juncture of his neck and shoulder, marking him.

"Lights," Evan managed to gasp.

"I think we can feel our way in the dark," Seth replied, ducking his head to flick his tongue across one of Evan's nipples, one hand between Evan's shoulders and the other firmly on his ass.

"The tree." Evan didn't know why it seemed so important to follow through on his romantic notion of making love beneath the lit tree, but he was surprised at how much he wanted it.

"Then we'd better get the tree decorated," Seth replied, moving one of Evan's hands down to feel the bulge in his slacks. "Because I don't want to wait."

Evan tugged him across the room, holding tight to Seth's wrist. He unwrapped two light strings and plugged them in, sending a multicolored glow through the RV's living room, tossing them haphazardly over the small tree that had already filled the RV with the scent of balsam. "Just thought we should make sure they work," he said, with a grin that was pure invitation.

"They don't really have to be on the tree the first time, do they?" Seth sank to his knees and nuzzled Evan's crotch through his slacks.

Evan's already-hard cock strained against the cloth, and he moaned as Seth tightened his grip, fingers holding his hips.

"No," Evan gasped. "They don't."

Seth worked open Evan's belt, then his zipper, and pulled both slacks and briefs off with one move. The feel of his breath on the sensitive skin of Evan's cock threatened to undo him, even before Seth's hot mouth touched him. "Tell me what you want," Seth murmured.

"I want it the way we said we were going to do it," Evan panted. "Want you in me. Want me in you. Bare."

Seth shivered at his words, and Evan smiled, realizing that his lover wanted him just as much.

"There's lube in the drawer," Seth reminded him, moving away long enough to grab the container. They had stashed lube in key locations throughout the RV, as well as condoms that were no longer needed.

Evan's heart raced at bit at that thought. Going bare was a commitment, a statement of trust, a physical way of stepping up to the next level. A month ago, he would have been uneasy about being so vulnerable. But now, he didn't fear vulnerability with Seth. He trusted him—with his heart and his body, and he found himself believing in the bond between them more than he ever imagined.

"Too many clothes," Evan said, watching the way the lights played across Seth's body and reflected in his eyes. Seth undid the last of his buttons and tossed his shirt away, then made quick work of his slacks, briefs, and socks, until they were both naked and bathed in the glow of the colored lights.

Seth moved first, taking Evan into his arms for a long, lingering kiss. Evan let his hands slide up and down Seth's muscled back, then to the dimples at the small of his back, and finally to cup those two perfect globes. He shifted, rubbing their pricks together, earning a low moan from Seth that sent a jolt right to Evan's balls.

They never let go as they knelt, still kissing, still wrapped in each other's arms. Evan was torn between keeping his eyes shut to focus on the intensity of sensation and opening them to see how beautiful Seth looked in the lights.

"I want you to fuck me," Evan said, stretching up to whisper in

Seth's ear. The difference in weight between them seemed like more when they were sparring or fucking, when Evan admitted that he found it arousing as all hell that Seth could pin him if he wanted to but wouldn't without permission. That control was a heady feeling, like chugging champagne, and it made Evan's dick throb.

Seth laid him back beneath the lights draped over the tree, never losing eye contact, breathing in unison without even trying. He knelt over Evan on all fours, drinking in the sight of Evan splayed and longing beneath him. Evan let his legs fall open, inviting Seth between them, offering himself, and Seth pressed forward into a claiming, bruising kiss that left them both breathless.

"I want to devour you," Seth said, and his dark eyes had a feral gleam, and his words made Evan's belly tighten with desire and his balls draw up. Evan's painfully hard cock dripped pre-come against his skin, aching for release.

"Do it," Evan urged, "make me beg."

Seth dropped to his forearms, kissing and licking his way down Evan's body, lavishing attention on the hard buds of his nipples until Evan trembled beneath him, tracing the tip of his tongue down the trail of dark hair that led to his groin. Seth lapped up the pre-come and raised his head, meeting Evan's gaze, and then licked his lips like the liquid had been the best treat. Evan reached down to squeeze the base of his cock to keep from coming, and Seth batted his hand away.

"Mine," he growled. He diverted his path, letting his tongue run up the groove where Evan's leg met his groin on one side, then the other, as Evan bucked up, all but shoving his desperate cock in Seth's face.

Seth chuckled and looked Evan right in the eye, then swallowed him down to the root.

"Son of a bitch," Evan swore, throwing his head back and arching up, afraid he might come before they ever really got started. After a few bobs, Seth pulled off, then moved backward to give himself full access as he pushed Evan's legs up. Evan sucked in a breath as Seth sucked one of his balls and then the other into his mouth, rolling them on his tongue, gently tugging. Seth let his tongue stroke down the sensitive taint, then rimmed Evan's pucker with just the tip until he was pleading for release.

Instead, Seth set to work like a man with a mission, feasting on his ass, alternating kitten flicks that brought Evan to the brink with thrusts to breach his hole.

"Fuck me already," Evan could barely form the words. "Don't make me wait."

Seth's response was to thrust two fingers in Evan's mouth to get them spit slick, then press first one digit, then both inside as Seth resumed sucking him off.

"Not gonna last," Evan warned. Seth turned his fingers just so, brushing against his sweet spot, and Evan came with a shout, crying out Seth's name.

Seth pulled his fingers out, slicked up his cock, and pushed inside. Both men gasped at the sensation of skin against skin, with nothing between them.

"You feel...amazing," Evan gasped, overwhelmed with sensation. Seth moved slowly, filling him until he was fully seated, and Evan could feel Seth's balls against his ass.

"Move," Evan ordered, bucking his hips for emphasis.

Seth pulled back, almost out, and then thrust in again, and Evan wrapped his legs around Seth's waist, digging his heels into his lover's ass to urge him on. He built up a rhythm, hard and fast, trapping Evan's cock between them with enough friction that Evan thought might drive him mad.

"Come for me," Evan whispered, pulling Seth close. "I want to feel you fill me up."

That did it. Seth cried out, slammed in once, twice...and then on the third thrust, sent a warm pulse deep inside Evan that made him gasp as he came seconds later. Seth looked utterly wrecked, dark eyes blown wide with desire, blond hair askew, face flushed. Evan felt a thrill of pride. *I did that to him.*

Seth let himself down without pulling out and eased them to the side, hugging Evan to him in a sweaty tangle of limbs.

"I love you," Seth murmured, wrapping Evan tightly in his arms. "So much."

Evan pulled him into a kiss. "Love you, too," he replied, drunk on endorphins, fucked into bliss. The Christmas lights set the room in a warm glow, and Evan felt his throat tighten with an onslaught of emotions. A tear leaked from one eye and down his cheek.

"Hey," Seth said, and kissed Evan, wiping away the tear. "What's wrong?"

"I'm just—" Evan couldn't find the words, didn't even quite know what he wanted to say. He felt utterly overwhelmed by the intensity of his feelings. Love? That was certain, but Evan had never felt anything quite this strongly. Desire? Absolutely, but never before had Evan wanted to possess and be possessed like a fire in his blood. A surge of protectiveness welled up inside so strong Evan couldn't draw breath for a moment.

"Yeah," Seth murmured, nuzzling Evan's neck. "Me, too."

They stayed like that until Seth's softening dick slipped free, and Evan felt the loss. "I want to fuck you back," Evan murmured sleepily. "I really do...only, maybe in the morning? Because I think you fucked me out."

Seth sighed happily, tightening his arm around Evan and drawing him close. "I'm fine with that—something to look forward to—but can we move to the bed? Because as pretty as it is under the tree, this floor is going to be hell on my back."

EPILOGUE

SETH

THEY HAD AGREED TO STAY AT THE CAMPGROUND UNTIL AFTER NEW Year's, taking time to rest, heal, and enjoy the holiday. That meant Seth had an address to use for ordering gifts, which he had delivered to the campground office. For the first time since Jesse's death, Seth found himself actually looking forward to Christmas, instead of dreading the emptiness.

Evan was still in a t-shirt and sweatpants, nursing a cup of coffee as he studied the screen of his laptop. "What are you working on? New project?" Seth asked. Evan's graphic design business had gotten off to a good start, and he usually had new contracts coming in every week.

"The next witch disciple," Evan replied without looking up.

"He's down in North Carolina, if the intel I got from Toby and Milo is right. Out in the boonies."

"Boone, not boonies," Evan corrected, still focused on his screen. "It's in the mountains. Looks like it would be a nice place, if it weren't for a murderous warlock."

"I think that line is 'if weren't for all the damn vampires,' but it's been a while since I saw that movie," Seth replied, managing a slight smile.

213

Evan had made good on his promise of hot morning sex, and Seth knew he was going to feel the way Evan had plundered his ass all day. The thought made him smile, as did realizing that Evan had left finger-prints on his hips that were likely to bruise. He loved fucking Evan, loved thrusting into his lover's tight channel and making him cry out in pleasure. But he thrilled just as much when Evan owned him, filling him with his spend.

Evan was watching him with a dirty grin, as if he knew exactly what Seth was thinking about, and that only made him hotter.

Their little Christmas tree took up one corner of the living room, decked out in plastic ornaments from Walmart and enough lights per square inch that Seth felt certain airplanes could use the trailer as a beacon. *God help us—if we ever settle down and get a house, Evan will deco-rate like the Griswolds.*

They had agreed to spend the days leading up to Christmas on "vacation," curled up on the couch with popcorn watching animated holiday specials both men remembered from their childhoods or bingeing all the movies they'd missed over the last couple of months. Evan had built a playlist of the best-ever holiday songs, and Seth now had some decidedly adult associations with several songs. He'd never think of "Jingle Bells" quite the same way after Evan's enthusiastic blow job with that song as the soundtrack. His "bells" had been utterly and completely jingled, that was for certain. *Ho, ho, ho.*

As Christmas drew nearer, Seth careened between excitement at the presents he had tucked away for Evan and worry that perhaps he hadn't chosen anything special enough. He kept reminding himself that they had only been together for less than two months, but they'd packed so many life-or-death experiences into that time that it seemed like much longer.

Evan had gotten cagey about a few packages, too, and Seth wondered what surprises his boyfriend was planning. Although he would treasure anything Evan got for him, Seth found that just the idea of spending Christmas with someone he loved made all the difference.

Christmas Eve was spent with a fire in the RV's electric fireplace, listening to Bing Crosby croon carols, making love under the tree again, which had, in its short life, witnessed enough steamy sex to wilt its needles. Seth lost track of how many rounds they went, but by the time they staggered back to the bedroom, his legs felt wobbly, and he wasn't sure he'd be able to get it up again from sheer fatigue.

Christmas morning proved him blissfully wrong.

A dull thumping noise woke Seth from sleep. Evan was draped across him, naked and snoring, his dark hair covering his eyes. It took Seth several minutes to realize that the pounding was actually his phone, vibrating on the nightstand.

He glanced at the ID and smiled. Milo and Toby.

"Merry Christmas," Seth said in a sleepy voice.

"Told you it was too early, and he'd still be fucked out," Milo yelled to Toby.

"You're just jealous, old man," Toby called back, affection clear in his voice.

"Who you callin' old? I'm a 'silver fox,'" Milo defended himself.

"Um, hello? You called me?" Seth stretched, and Evan stirred, waking slowly to the sound of conversation.

Toby must have seized the phone because his voice replaced Milo's. "Never mind my crude husband. We just called to wish you Merry Christmas. And remind you that you're welcome here any time, especially if you want to introduce the man you love to the two men who took you in and taught you everything you know." He cleared his throat dramatically.

Seth couldn't help laughing. "Of course I want you to meet Evan. We'll figure out a good time to road trip your way—after the holidays."

"Fair enough," Toby said. "You guys doing okay?"

Seth had put the call on speaker so Evan could listen, although his lover seemed barely awake enough to notice. "Yeah. We're doing better than okay," Seth said, and smiled, realizing that was true. He'd updated Milo and Toby after they'd won the fight against Thane and told them about the information they'd gathered on the witch-disciple in North Carolina.

"How about you?" Seth asked. "Taking care of yourselves?"

"Taking care of each other," Toby said. "We're all right. I have a nice ham for dinner, and Milo's going to make his killer scalloped potatoes. When it's all said and done, we'll have a feast that could feed an army, and a fridge and freezer full of enough leftovers for us to eat for weeks."

"We're taking it easy for a little while, until after the New Year," Seth confided. "I think we've earned a little time off."

"Good," Toby replied as if he'd been worried. Seth felt a surge of warmth at the older man's protectiveness. "I won't keep you. Just wanted to wish you a Merry Christmas and tell you that you're welcome here whenever the road leads you this way."

Seth's throat grew tight, and he blinked back tears. "Thanks, Toby. You guys have a good day, you hear?"

"Loud and clear," Toby said, acknowledging all the things Seth couldn't put into words. The call ended, and Seth laid back against his pillow, putting the phone back on the nightstand.

"Merry Christmas," Evan murmured, still mostly asleep.

"Merry Christmas," Seth replied, kissing the top of his head.

AFTER AN INVIGORATING ROUND of early morning sex, Seth and Evan padded out to their tree and the small pile of gifts awaiting them.

"How about we take turns?" Evan asked, flicking on the stereo and the fireplace. Holiday music filled the RV, and the fake flames of the electric hearth roared to life.

"Anything you want," Seth replied.

Evan raised an eyebrow. "Anything?"

Seth sighed. "Within reason. I still need to be able to walk."

They sat down cross-legged in front of the tree, and Evan handed out the presents. They each had four small boxes, and Seth felt as excited as a kid, wondering what Evan had gotten for him.

"Let's go together, one box at a time," Seth suggested.

With that, they each selected a gift and tore through the wrapping paper. Evan held up filters for his camera. "Wow! Thank you. This will help me add some nice effects and cut down on the glare. Awesome!"

Seth grinned, glad to see Evan so happy about such a simple gift. He held up a gift card for his favorite video game platform. "You know I needed this," he said. "Now I can go on that campaign I've been wanting to do."

Evan gave an exaggerated eye roll. "Just remember—loot first, then pillage and burn." He reached for the next present. Inside was a gift card for his e-reader.

"This is great! There are a bunch of new books coming out over the holidays. Thanks!"

Seth's next present was a new pair of leather gloves for riding his Hayabusa. He turned the soft hide over in his hands, appreciating the luxury. What mattered most was that Evan had thought to buy them, even though he and the motorcycle still seemed to have a love/hate relationship. "Go on," he urged.

Evan unwrapped his next gift and found a silver medal of St. George on a chain.

"I know you're not Catholic," Seth said. "Neither am I. But he's the patron saint of monster hunters. It's a protective talisman. To keep you safe."

Evan dropped the necklace over his head and stroked his fingers over the amulet. "Thank you," he said, and his gaze told Seth that he appreciated the protectiveness behind the gesture as much as he did the amulet itself.

Seth opened his third present, a silver and onyx bracelet on a braided leather cord and realized that he wasn't alone in wanting to give a protective talisman as a gift. "It's beautiful," he said, admiring the workmanship and slipping it onto his left wrist.

Evan looked a little uncomfortable. "It's, uh, also been blessed. So you can wear it all the time."

"Thank you," Seth said, meaning every word. "Last one —open up!"

Evan reached for the fourth box. He tore away the paper and found another silver medal—this one of St. Michael, with "*to Evan, from Seth with love*" engraved on the back.

"I couldn't make up my mind, and the lore didn't help much," Seth said in answer to Evan's questioning look. "St. Michael slew the dragon...which was a stand-in for the powers of darkness. So, you know, it's also a protective charm. Which you should wear, all the time. Because it can't hurt." He was babbling a little, but he wanted to protect Evan with every fiber of his being, and two silver charms didn't seem like much, but he knew how much power a simple amulet could carry.

He couldn't read Evan's smile, and then he opened his last gift to find the same silver St. Michael's medallion—engraved on the back with *'Love always, Evan.'"*

"I guess we both had the same good idea," Seth said with a chuckle, dropping the necklace over his head.

Evan leaned forward and kissed him. Seth kissed right back. "Thank you," Evan said. "This is the best Christmas I've had in a long, long time."

Seth grinned. "Me, too. And thank you."

The timer on the oven beeped, reminding them that the breakfast casserole was done. "Let's eat!" Evan said, standing and then reaching down to grab Seth's hand and help him up. They headed for the kitchen, and Evan inhaled the scent of fresh coffee, bacon, and cinnamon rolls.

"Everything smells delicious," he said, as Seth removed the two trays from the oven.

"Easy—but satisfying," Seth replied. "Eat up—we're due at St. Dismas in about an hour and a half, just enough time to get showers and look presentable."

"I'VE NEVER SEEN this much stuffing in my life," Evan said, looking at the serving line at St. Dismas. The community center offered a free Christmas dinner with all the fixings—ham, turkey, mashed potatoes, stuffing, green bean casserole, cranberry sauce, candied sweet potatoes, and an assortment of pie.

"I've never seen so much pie," Alex replied, a glint of hunger in his eyes. "And it all looks really good."

Seth, Evan, Brent, Alex, and Brandon had all volunteered to help Travis, Jon, and the other St. Dismas staff serve the annual Christmas brunch and dinner. Brandon blushed as he showed off the silver ring Alex had given him and invited them to the New Year's Day, Justice of the Peace wedding, since they had decided life was too uncertain to wait.

Evan found it sobering how many people turned out for the meal and wondered how rare it was for their guests to feel full and happy. For many of them, he guessed, it was a once-a-year level of contentment, which made him appreciate his comfortable—if unconventional —circumstances all the more.

Travis was on duty all day so that many of his staff could have the time at home with their families. Unwilling to leave him alone on Christmas, Seth, Evan, and the others had all agreed to pitch in, and then stay to celebrate the holiday. Brent brought movies, which they would watch later.

The next hours passed in a blur. Seth had the mashed potato station on the food line, and he lost count of how many scoops he served. He did his best to meet the eyes of each person he served and wish them a heartfelt "Merry Christmas." By the time the event was over, they were scraping the bottom of the warming trays.

"Thank you," Travis said, looking harried. "We really couldn't have done it without you." A couple of volunteers had last-minute emergencies, leaving the center short staffed.

Brent shrugged. "That's what friends are for."

Jon poked his head out of the kitchen. "Go eat," he ordered. "I saved you back portions—it's all set up for you in the break room. We'll take it from here," he said with a nod toward the dirty warming trays.

Seth followed Brent and Travis to the small gathering room where he had been before. He hung back, watching the easy camaraderie between the others. Alex and Brandon had grown more outgoing, although Brandon still was more reserved than before his run-in with Thane. Brent and Travis teased them like older brothers and extended that same barbed familiarity to Seth and Evan. Travis just looked tired, and Seth didn't envy the ex-priest his responsibilities.

"To a happy, healthy, and monster-free new year," Seth said, raising a toast of sparkling cider, since alcohol was off limits at the halfway house.

"Hear, hear!" Travis agreed.

Brent grinned. "Now where would be the fun in that?"

They ate their meals, then went to the common room up on the same floor as Travis's apartment, and settled in to watch action movies. Some of the residents wandered in and out over the course of the evening, pausing to watch the movies for a while before moving on. Jon and Michael joined them, once the clean-up was done, and Evan took it as his mission in life to replenish the microwave popcorn any time the bowls went empty.

By the time the final *Die Hard* movie was finished, Seth could have sworn he'd eaten his weight in popcorn. He slung an arm over Evan's shoulder, and his boyfriend curled into him, resting his head.

He looked around the room at his companions, and his heart clenched at the sight. A year ago—hell, six months ago—Seth had felt utterly alone, wrapped up in a quest for vengeance that he expected would kill him even if he won. Now, he was surrounded by friends and allies, and even more amazingly, had somehow won the affections of the man he loved. Seth blinked hard, unwilling to show just how much the change of fortune meant to him.

"I saw that," Evan whispered. "And I love you, too."

They took their leave not long afterward, promising to be back for New Year's Eve, and for the wedding the day after. The drive back to the campground was quiet, as both men watched the falling snow, still full from dinner, and relaxed from an evening among friends.

"I think this has been the best Christmas I've ever had," Evan said, staring out at the night.

"I was thinking the same thing," Seth agreed, reaching out to lay his hand on Evan's thigh. "And that's all because of you."

Evan grinned. "It's nice having friends, too. But…yeah. Having you here makes all the difference," he admitted.

They got back to the trailer around eight and put a frozen pizza in the oven for supper. Seth took a carton of eggnog out of the fridge and reached down a bottle of rum from the cabinet.

"Merry Christmas," he proclaimed, handing a glass to Evan after spiking both drinks with a substantial amount of alcohol. They clinked glasses.

"Merry Christmas," Evan echoed. He leveled a suggestive look at Seth. "Now finish your eggnog so we can eat and go to bed."

ACKNOWLEDGMENTS

Every book is a group effort, and it always takes a village to bring one to life. Thanks first and foremost to my hubby and first editor Larry N. Martin, who handles all the important behind-the-scenes stuff, without which the books would never come to life. Thanks to my editor, Melissa McArthur, and my cover artist, Lou Harper, for making the book so beautiful, and to my agent, Ethan Ellenberg.

Thank you also to Mindy Mymudes for all her help with my street teams, the Shadow Alliance and The Worlds of Morgan Brice. And many thanks to my wonderful beta readers and launch team: Amy, Andrea, Anne, Barbara, Cheryl, Chris, Darrell, Donald, Joscelyn, Laurie, Lynne, and Vikki, who help the book be the best it can be and helped get the word out. Thanks also to all the bloggers who gave a shout-out to my books, and to the folks at LesCourt Author Services, Gay Book Promotions, and Vibrant Promotions for helping boost the signal.

Thank you, most of all, to my readers for all your wonderful comments on social media and reviews at online booksellers, for choosing to spend your precious free time reading my books, and for your support and friendship when we meet in person and online. Because you read, I write.

ABOUT THE AUTHOR

Morgan Brice is the romance pen name of bestselling author Gail Z. Martin. Morgan writes urban fantasy male/male paranormal romance, with plenty of action, adventure, and supernatural thrills to go with the happily ever after. Gail writes epic fantasy and urban fantasy, and together with co-author hubby Larry N. Martin, steampunk and comedic horror, all of which have less romance, and more explosions.

On the rare occasions Morgan isn't writing, she's either reading, cooking, or spoiling two very pampered dogs.

Watch for additional new series from Morgan Brice, and more books in the Witchbane and Badlands universes coming soon!

Where to find me, and how to stay in touch

On the web at https://morganbrice.com. Sign up for my newsletter and never miss a new release! http://eepurl.com/dy_8oL.

Facebook Group—The place for news about upcoming books, convention appearances, special fun like contests and giveaways, plus location photos, fantasy casting, and more! Look for The Worlds of Morgan Brice. You can also find Morgan on Twitter: @MorganBrice-Book and Pinterest (for Morgan and Gail): pinterest.com/Gzmartin.

Support Indie Authors

When you support independent authors, you help influence what kind of books you'll see more of and what types of stories will be available, because the authors themselves decide which books to write, not a big publishing conglomerate. Independent authors are local creators, supporting their families with the books they produce. Thank you for supporting independent authors and small press fiction!

ALSO BY MORGAN BRICE

Witchbane Series

Witchbane

Burn, A Witchbane Novella

Dark Rivers

Badlands Series

Badlands

Lucky Town, A Badlands Novella - *Coming Soon*

The Rising - *Coming Soon*